The Loser Fandango

AND OTHER TALES OF AMERICANA

J. M. UNRUE

Contents

One

The Loser Fandango

Here's the thing about losers. There are those who know they are losers and those who do not.

Those who know are endowed with mean grace, relegated to a tenuous peace, resigned to deficient seeds of blanched fortune. They are, however, able to accrue wisdom, advance despite themselves and ill-footing, are endowed with a salient forthrightness, and withstand the wounds that injure but not kill.

Grief may be a familiar companion, and no measure of grit will much alter the course, yet some faint benign well-being endures. Though they may be foolishly inured to misfortune, they are seldom fools, and are ably gratified by effort and reckless hope.

They possess a philanthropy of actions, tend to take the roundabout way home, spend an inordinate amount of time backstroking through Jello, and invariably come to realize that the more one knows, the unhappier one is.

Losers who don't know may live less encumbered, happy patriots of ilk and kin, euphoric in unpurchased ambition, unremembered fools. They are irascibly oblivious, brash and imperceptive, rattling their chains like a Dickensian ghost, certain they, too, know the future.

Their suffering great, their responses to bound indignity shrill and untoward, as they are untoward in most every motion and deed with unrelenting penury of wit and skill and tact—though they persist unacquainted with inefficacy.

They are howlers, buffoons, rife with clamor and alibi, zealots to their own causes and void of contemplation except those misappropriated considerations that elevate them beyond authenticity.

Whatever else may come, grudging the luminosity of others yet immune to every misstep, they forever remain voyagers upon an empty sea, stargazers upon clouded night, pedestrians upon a treadmill of ruin wrought by their own hands.

Yet they may live grossly liberated.

Regardless, both are likely to remain much as they are because loserhood is as finely actuated in predisposition as argot, posture, and pride in one's emanations—or not.

I learned about whimsy early on, the peculiarities and potency of paradox and how this hoary old world may turn upon a spit while the critter thereupon remains diffident. I also became a hobbyist in pursuit of raw esoterica (octothorpe is the word for a hash tag).

Later I would discover abundant ironies and related theorems that mark our environments, especially in America.

A queerly gilt example would be our political systems, and specifically, the variances in philosophies, such as they are, those thin cracks cum crevices insufficiently addressed; rifts that rupture petulantly when threatened. How easily we feel threatened depends upon a multiplicity of stimuli and this itself could fill volumes, but essentially, any failure to be aware of one's own foibles creates a fetid glom inherent in all *losers who don't know* that such subjects rely on the sheer proliferation of constituent kinspeople to thrive.

Yikes!

The nurse blunders into my reverie and checks my IV. She does this from rote habit without a word or eye contact—a Roomba in Nine-B Nikes. I am untroubled. I'm twenty minutes into a three-hour infusion and she's an hour away from her recliner and Dr. Phil. Doubtless her instrument of repose is far more comfortable than mine. Billions in research and I'm tethered to a seat repurposed from Bud's Budget Airways.

Well, I shouldn't be unkind. I have my earbuds deep and my phone cradled. *Wah-Wah* from George Harrison accentuates the drip-drip-drip *mezzo marcato.* I've always felt for the guy. George, I mean, stymied by the only two people on earth who could get away with it and still succeed. The privation of a two-star general in a three-star war.

I was born in 1953, the same year as the Corvette and the word *frenemy.* Naturally, I am not a Corvette, more a Corvair, which, according to Ralph Nader, was the most unsafe automobile ever conceived by American ingenuity. And, like the word *frenemy*, I took a great many years to catch on.

Incidentally, DNA was discovered in 1953, though we're seven decades in and the most ennobling aspects of said discovery are the means to discover long-lost cousin Fred, him of missing incisors, MAGA cap, and disability check from the same government he detests even though he acquired such benevolence by being a chain-smoking fat prick—and also to put miscreants in the pokey, safely presumed as *losers who don't know*. Pray God long-lost cousin Fred may soon dwell among them, and before the next election.

Admittedly, *Loser* is a grossly unkind word, rife with peevish intent, a neo-savage description of character and essence. Even those prone to forbearance tend to make meager rationalizations as defense rather than overt endorsement.

"Someone has to lose. There can only be one winner. Even a person who finishes second in a marathon run by five thousand is technically a loser."

No, the person who finishes second after running over twenty-six miles is a moron like the rest of the five thousand, though *technically* a silver medalist. Pro golfer Briny Baird earned over thirteen million dollars—an average of over six hundred thousand dollars a year for twenty years—without ever winning a PGA Tour event. Would that the world grant such *defeat* to us all.

Nonetheless, I am a loser, and without subjecting anyone to such vainglorious justifications, there exists a story to be told, as there is a life endured, and divine breath to be insufflated.

I am of the sort who knows he's a loser. I had some inkling relatively early on, of course, as I was a dreamy little twerp who liked to sing to himself, but did not become fully enlightened until I was a middle-aged man. But I get ahead of myself.

We of the LsWK subspecies are often saddled with angst and sharp edges. Human beings were not designed to have sharp edges. Sure, we have elbows, knees, chins, and ways to stiffen our toes and fingers, but we are not designed as blades or bludgeons, but round and soft and inviting, like breasts, cheeks, lips, or a big ol' badonkadonk (resembling two marmots mating in a gunny sack).

The reason for this is simple. *Life* is thus delineated. Soft lines overwhelm every perspective—and not just bosoms. Only the environments we create in the inscrutable passage of time so boogers up the works.

On the other hand, genes are tricky buggers, and doubtlessly edge beyond hair and eye color. This is why there are more ugly people in the world than pretty people. Two ugly people can produce a perfectly lovely offspring, but the odds are as long as an undisputed election in Georgia. Take a lovely woman with undeniably defect-free features, say, Jane Fonda, and a comely gent with an Adonian aspect, say Robert Redford. Both are fair-complexioned, fair-haired, and eyes the colors of the Caribbean Sea. However, Jane has a full mouth, a broad chin, and wide-set eyes. Robert has a sharp nose, elongated ears, and deep jawline. In some illusory state one would envision a hale and winsome offspring such as Chris Hemsworth, when the unpredictability of the twenty-thousand or so coding genes conspire to create Jay Leno.

Additionally, ugly people have more of the genes that created such forlorn aspects in the first place with the certainty of unseemliness as a prevailing trait astronomically pervasive. Pretty people creating a majority of pretty people with the odd ogre finding its way clear of the vaginal lips, and ugly people creating pretty people in far fewer numbers, as well as the virtual certainty that most progeny will carry too many unprepossessing genes to countermand, sapient life is designed to replicate ignoble features in perpetuity.

Face it. Most of us are raging barkers deigned to create the same. Also, most crime is committed by ugly people. There are more of them, of course, but maybe they're just pissed, or else feel short-changed.

Big-headed wonks wax in dull verbosity how things such as sexual identity, athletic acumen—or lack thereof—and even how well one might smell urine is *inspired,* if not dictated, by itty-bitty dots of progeniture. These relate to certain inclinations and not physical appearance, of course, but we are the way we are because the people who created us were the way they were.

Naturally, there is denial from both big- and small-heads, expounding on the *fait accompli,* the intractable authority of choice, espousing that human intellect is not dependent upon such criteria as much as what one chooses to read while taking a dump (or not reading at all). Obviously, one can choose to abstain, refrain, and otherwise constrain from certain urges, but only by artificial means can one alter hair and eye color, general bearing, and even sinistromanual-ness, which sounds godawful, and has historically been viewed as such, though merely means left-handed. Incidentally, gauche is the French word for left, so southpaws have had it hard for a long time. Had Moses been left-handed the Red Sea would have swole back and drowned them all.

There are advantages to being a LWK, many of these ignored by the blatantly self-assured of our species. I know that I will never die in a plane crash because God would not kill so many innocents just to get at me. I do, however, scrutinize my fellow passengers to make sure we are not all of such class and kith. This also leads to the Darwinesque suspicion about the people of Pompeii.

There are also certain rules of life that seem obvious to us but are still ignored by our more erudite counterparts, perhaps due to the *fait accompli de perdants*—a brief sample...never drive with a phone in one hand and a half-caf skinny amaretto latte in the other, never zip up in a rush, and never change a diaper while the baby's still pooping.

1953 was also the year of the not-so-classic movie *It Came From Outer Space,* about aliens who crash-landed on Earth and masqueraded as humans until time to leave this world. So there's that.

Despite practical wisdom and like regalia, LsWK are not de facto pessimists. There really are no such things as pessimists. There are fearful optimists reluctant to believe that good awaits them because they have been too often disappointed. However, *losers who know* are ever and soundly reminded of their inclusion in not-so-subtle ways. My presence in this facility is a case in point.

In 2014 I discovered a knot on my neck. I prayed it was just a swollen node.

(Is all hope condemned or merely sentenced to life in prison?)

Cancer. Miracles don't happen for people like us. Repercussions—even when not the result of poor decisions—are always disproportionally punitive. We are the '73 Pintos of auto accidents, the '62 Mets of baseball. The capital punishment of Murphy's Law.

When I was informed that the grape-sized lump had not spread I gratefully exhaled. When I was told I only had to undergo three rounds of chemo I was likewise relieved. Instead, I was to have radiation therapy. Once a day, five days a week, for seven weeks. (For the mathematically challenged that's thirty-five doses). Admittedly, I found it somewhat ignominious that I was expected to adhere to the schedule as if my very existence depended upon it yet the technicians weren't available on weekends should I falter.

I was also advised how due to the marvels of modern oncology my radiation would be pinpointed with the accuracy of a Stephen Curry three-pointer with *s...l...i...g...h...t...*damage to surrounding tissue. Moreover, such protocol had been successfully transacted a gazillion jillion billion times and was as perfect as could be realized on God's loamy earth.

The device used to provide this life-granting zapfest (featuring Photon Phil in the animated version) is called a Linear Accelerator and looks like some mondo sci-fi Land of the Giants blow dryer; not the cheesy Irwin Allen Land of the Giants blow dryer from the sixties, but perhaps a Tim Burton model, circa 2012. The modus operandi for aiming and evacuating said gizmo is to first take a white, plastic hockey mask-looking thing which holds the head in place by snapping said noggin to the table. Each mask is unique to a patient and the same mask is used throughout the regimen. After the third or fourth daily dose the mask reeks like a dixie cup bonfire and would gag an abattoir rat.

At the risk of sissification, especially in light of admitted LWK status and resultant inferential conformities, by the third or fourth daily dose I realized something was seriously wrong. (Is the skin on my neck supposed to crack open like that?) I couldn't swallow, my gums bled, I suffered from vertigo (many's the time I emerged from the veil to find myself clinging to a door jamb). I ran a constant fever, my eyes burned, my ears rang, and I hallucinated.

I was also intensely depressed. Many LsWK are recurrently depressed and are LsWK because depressives think all the time. More often than not, such an obliquely vague malady is culturally rife, and in yon times was simply called black ass. Depression and other structural maladies were far less understood when I was young, certainly not as prevalent conditions, and treatments were limited.

In 1962, a kid who liked to wear black and read William Burroughs would have been strapped to a gurney and have a hundred-fifty volts of buzz juice piped into his head until he either joined the GOP or forgot who he was through retrograde amnesia. Now such disorders have become *causes celebre*, especially by actors and musicians who are often insulated from the same real-world fallout as the rest of us, and have in fact engendered a bizarre kind of one-upmanship, usually under the guise of promoting a recent project.

"I had postpartum psychosis but wouldn't have traded that period with my daughter, Parallelogram for anything. It was wonderful to just enjoy my nakedness and blue cheese enemas."

"Well I was bipolar *and* tripolar, and had to go off my meds to play Bella Abzug and really get her right, so I was treated with LSD eyedrops and a strict peat moss diet. Plus, I have an ingrown clitoris that makes me hallucinate whenever I sneeze and had to use glucocorticosteroid suppositories. I haven't pooped in six weeks."

Good God!

Notably, there otherwise remains a stigma attached to these psychological afflictions, and were worse fifty years ago when even euthanasia was discussed.

"Timmy jumped in the well and Lassie went after him so we put both of 'em down just to err on the side of caution."

The phrase 'Get the fuck over it' was originally divined for such purposes. Only in sociopathy is such circumvention a natural process.

Nonetheless, and despite the best intentions of fairy-minded social media-loving oblivions, people thus inflicted cannot simply *choose* to be happy—or upbeat or optimistic or any other damn thing—except perhaps through forms of expression and hard-won self-control.

We listen to music.

The opening bars to *Beat It* rumble through my earbuds. Yes, I have a Michael Jackson tune on my playlist. I use it as part of my lawn-mowing *ensemble* to thwart the inevitable ass-dragging in the home stretch. The song has my favorite Eddie Van Halen lead guitar work. I don't have any Van Halen proper. It's hard to explain without sounding like a *grosse bite*, but one only has to see a pony jump through a hoop of fire once to get the gist of it. Repetition is sloth. LsWK are wholly intimate with unrealized potential, succumbing to the soporific gravity of indigenous limitations, and dear Eddie, rest his soul, coasted a lot after the first lick.

Another *grosse bite faux pas* is the precept, admittedly unkind, that Michael Jackson may have moonwalked into the ether at the proper karmic time. He was unsound in body and soul, had squandered much of his fortune, could only hope to echo his earlier musical triumphs, and would have ended his days with a gaping hole in the middle of his face where most of us have a nose.

As barbarously insidious as is unrealized potential, equally damning is peaking too soon, relegated to old soldiers' parades and performing in the lounges of Holiday Inns.

Like most other *kinder* I had dreams as a child. When I was eight, Alan Shepard became the first American in space and most boys went in search of some semblance of helmets and space suits, until piqued moms went in search of their stew pots and Reynolds Wrap. One of my pals was lucky because his dad had a motorcycle helmet but was still smacked for removing the duct hose from the dryer, which he cut into strips and stapled to his old man's long johns—unnoticed until his mater nearly choked to death on dryer lint.

My biggest dream was admittedly vague, and possibly to cover more bases. I wanted to be *special.* I didn't know how or in what way, specifically, certainly not serial killer or flamenco dancer special, though bank robber special had its allure, but being unique—or relatively so—seemed to be of primary importance, and all the imaginings I conjured as a solitary little schmuck was that someday I would be *remarquable.*

Not just to my family and the people who knew me. To everyone. Like the President, the Pope, or the guy who invented Cheetos.

What I grasped in my simple, preadolescent way, is that specialness requires not only a host of tenebrous, almost otherworldly qualities, but advocacy from someone who has already achieved this sought-after distinction in some noteworthy fashion, and moves beyond your Granny saying what a special boy you are, and is, in fact, as remote as it is indecipherable.

Also being a bit of an anarchist, I spent much of my elementary school years facing a corner.

When a wall has been painted and repainted umpteen times and had been around since the time of Jesus, air can insinuate itself into the coating. By the end of my primary education I had counted every pinprick bubble at least a dozen times and knew them all by name.

Crap. I have to pee. I can drag all this godless paraphernalia to the loo or I can call for a nurse to bring me a male urinal and a screen, praying that I can uncoil my pecker sufficiently to safely extend into the hole. Or I could just piss my pants. I rise, drawing the attention of everyone about, scowling at each set of eyes in my own inimitable way to repel all advances, dragging the stand and monitor along like a plantation slave.

Fortunately, a lavatory is nearby and unoccupied. Just before I enter I hear faint music emanating from the nurses' station. *Edge of Seventeen*, Fleetwood Mac, and as I cram into the smallest bathroom in existence, I wonder if Stevie Nicks was one of the Chipmunks before she met Lindsey Buckingham. Yeah, this shit makes me mean.

I started high school in 1968, the same year Martin Luther King and Robert Kennedy were assassinated, the Viet Nam war still raged, the Democratic National Convention in Chicago evolved into riots, and the last production model year for the aforementioned Corvair.

1968 was also the year I learned I was a bastard. My parents back-dated a phony elopement to satisfy my holy roller grandparents. This explains the gap between me and my siblings. They eventually got married, of course. I'm not sure how this affected me, if at all, but ultimately I landed on a single hypothesis. Children should never know their parents' secrets. LsWK understand this implicitly. Why further muddy a roiling river.

Nixon was also elected President in 1968. Yeah, 1968, was a fucking banner year.

I did well in high school if as anonymous as a tick. I was a loyal friend and found my niche as the funny guy.

"Two cheerleaders were catching some rays at the beach and one said, 'I slept with a Brazilian last night'."

"Wow," replied the other one, "my most is three."

I fell in love for the first time my freshman year in college. This was the best thing that ever happened to me. Unfortunately, this was also the worst thing that ever happened to me. She was exquisite, golden hair, green eyes, an eager smile.

LsWK feel and love too deeply. There is nothing ennobling in this. It's not the silver lining, the *joie de vivre* of some unavoidable emotional construct. It's a symptom, the same way sneezing is a symptom of allergies or inebriation a symptom of frat parties. If there is any benefit to over-feeling and over-thinking, and one so meager as to be immaterial, it is a penny in the cache of our souls, another memory to be held if only partially absorbed, another mystery for us to solve.

However ameliorative, and infinitely fuzzy, amour is not a rational process nor does it lend itself to equative analysis. It is analyzed, of course, primarily in the insecurities of the young adult male. Driven by such depth of feeling, I nonetheless found it all difficult to articulate. Believing that should I not at least attempt to convey certain aspects (and effects) of endearment, I would herniate myself, I wrote a love letter.

I was rewarded with such effusion, I thought my insides would burst. Before I could react she flung her arms around my neck, pulling her body against me in such sympathy I've never forgotten the moment or its assuagement.

"I love you, I love you," she whispered.

Yep, I was a goner, a French crepe beneath a *rouleau compresseur.*

Her parents were soon concerned, as parents tend to be, that we were getting too serious too quickly and by the end of the year I was on my way back to Florida with a broken heart and a week-old cantaloupe where my brain once resided.

Who can rightly discern the breadth of such passions amid practicality. Who can quantify a dream of togetherness and growth. Who truly knows what comprises the most fundamental essence of one's identity. We are what we think we are. I was a devotee to the wonder of the unadulterated love I had for another human being. Woe that such is as tenebrous and transitory as any prosaic practice.

Yet... Even then, as a man-in-years-only, I was still capable of parsing all minutiae into polished bits. I knew what I knew and I believed whole-heartedly this was enough. What I did not reckon or even contemplate, was the *other,* that Aristotelian certitude of causality. Whatever prompts a substance to respond to another is easily stymied by variables as broad, as deep, and as innumerable as they are exponential.

Even then, granting every contention its due, some fierce conviction overwhelmed all temperate movement within me—enough to cloak such mighty affection and lay bare a dormant infection suddenly brought to fester. Even as it throbbed, and I was aware of its every ill manner, I could not seem to subdue it.

Persistent Depressive Disorder.

Something within me was broken. LsWK always believe someone will come along to save them, and they are nearly always wrong.

During my treatment and the gross accrual of side-effects, and confronted with my rapid deterioration and some stout consternation from my wife, whose role it was to tend to me while working full-time to keep our chins skyward, my oncologist boldly proclaimed that such results were expected and everything was proceeding as planned.

Back in the late 1700s, doctors called upon to resuscitate drowning victims would take a tube connected to a bellows and blow tobacco smoke into the patients' rectums, hence the term 'blow smoke up his ass'. I didn't need a stogie enema to know which one of us was full of crap.

A nurse pops by to change my IV bag. I'm halfway home. She makes eye contact, sees the earbuds and gestures. She smiles. She's young, not yet jaded by the misery of her charges. I give her a break, if only in my head. Someone *really* wants to be a nurse to work oncology. Maybe it's cyclical. Maybe this was the best possible opening available. Who knows, maybe she really cares.

Another patient a few seats down waves her over and gestures to the overhead television shared by three or four of us. She flips the TV to Fox News. Jesus Henry Christ! I still had my earbuds in and could easily close my eyes and be somewhere else, which is my wont, but I was feeling petulant and ready to launch.

Ignorance used to be quaint. *The National Enquirer* had given rise the *Us* and *People* magazines and the butt cleavage of professional wrestling aficionados. We never considered that ignorance would one day be brandished as a weapon and aimed at our pointy heads, nor would it overtake us and give us Trumpism. Intellectual sloth (and I use the adjective generically as neither am I an elitist) has grown to encompass nearly half our population and we are drowning.

I give the woman the side-eye and...stop. She's my age maybe younger. It's hard to tell. Her flesh is the gray of mica and her eyes are invisible. She's so lethargic she's inert and she's plugged in through her chest like an ET abductee. She is shriveled pate-to-ankle and weighs all of ninety pounds, and her head is a skeletal orb, made even more so with the hospital-issue skullcap betraying the utter absence of hair.

I am not a person of faith. I suppose I'm deistic. I've often wondered why we attribute such *human* characteristics to our godheads, the faults and foibles of querulous personae when these are supposed emblems of *perfection*. Somehow, we don't want perfect unless it's a lot like us.

I grew up a Baptist. Our pastor during my formative years was Lester 'Roadmap' Wooten. He had preached fire and brimstone so hard for so long all the capillaries in his cheeks had ruptured and his face, God bless him, looked like a Rand McNally inset of Orlando.

Where was I? Oh. I am still acutely aware of what traits are required for a spiritually-based perspective, even as a humanist, and have always been struck by a single inviolable premise.

Pain is pain, inclusive, immutable, and requires attention.

We tend to qualify those in pain by various criteria, foremost of which is the degree of perceived self-infliction. We cannot help but think 'serves 'em right' when we view the alcoholic, the lifelong smoker, the homeless, the hapless single mother with too many children (and who may or may not resemble each other) regardless of duration or intensity of extant pain.

To be a truly spiritual person is to deal compassionately with those in pain simply because it needs to be done. The spiritual nature of humankind is not always revealed in words, nor is our limitless potential for goodness manifested only by deeds, but by the willingness to actualize.

If we are persistently unkind, how can we claim to be a redeemed people?

The lady has caught me looking in her direction. My eyes dim and I give her a smile and a nod, and lo, she smiles in return.

When I was twenty-six a co-worker (and good friend in that 'wanna grab a beer' inimitable, fraternal sort of way) asked me if I would escort his fiancée's best friend to the rehearsal dinner. I demurred, at least internally. Well, to be precisely accurate, I ran screaming like a banshee for the door—still, thankfully, internally.

Being a mature adult but pondering the myriad ways things could go south for me, I felt compelled to check her out first. I called her and made a date. Flash-forward a year, give or take, and we got married. Love was not now as virulent as it had been in my misspent youth, but that's progress, right?

Sometimes when we reach a certain age our subconscious whispers 'the next one you meet'...

I got married two days before John Lennon was shot and killed. I was honeymooning on Hilton Head Island, enjoying the felicity of guilt-free conjugation, and did not openly weep. I did, however, as a card-carrying LWK, wonder if this was a harbinger.

Ironically, or perhaps providentially, the medley on Side Two of *Abbey Road* stirs in my earbuds. I become strangely ethereal.

Abbey Road is my favorite album. Harrison finally gets his due. *Here Comes the Sun*, contrived in Clapton's garden in a dawning spring, and *Something*, a sonnet to the woman Clapton would later abscond with, are both his creations. The instrumentation is flawless, the tone paradisaical.

So much has been written about them that anything new would be comprised of such trifle as to render it impertinent, and, perhaps suspect. Besides, even Beatles forget and embellish details as a matter of course. A case in point is the aforementioned medley. Both Mc-Cartney and producer George Martin have been named as instigators of the concept. To me, the most salient point is that they had so much material they could employ snippets not developed into full-fledged songs and not lament its wastefulness.

The longest tune in the medley is just under two-and-a-half minutes long, and the finale, the ambrosial *The End*, is the last time the four of them recorded as a band—August 1969, the same month as Woodstock. Thus ended the optimism of an entire generation, before Charlie Manson put a bullet in its head and left no doubt.

Many people of subsequent generations cannot truly appraise how preeminent the Beatles were in the psyche of those who remember them existent, especially during our teenage years. They glean by osmosis historical relevance in much the same way as the wars that shaped our country—distant, vague, and ultimately disconnected in all but trivia. This is as it should be. Each era deserves its own touchstones, its own heroes, its own brand of nonsense.

At least we didn't conceive or exult Cup Stacking, Tik Tok, selfies, The Bachelor, or Miley fucking Cyrus.

Yet...as I sit, accustomed to the needling pain where the cannula enters my body, vaguely attune to the passage of time, and at great effort to stifle the lingering urge to pee again, I drift back and then forward. Back to December 1980, when Lennon was killed, and then forward to 1985, a foreknowledge of an unmet time I have always held as prophetic.

I posit that The Beatles would have reunited in1985 to fulfill the promise made when they were teens and palely attempted with the rooftop *Let it Be* concert. There would be no new material. There would be no Wings songs, no solo tunes. There would be supporting players, of course, brass, strings, perhaps even shadows to the instruments each so adequately performed.

They wouldn't do it for money. Well, not *just* for the money. McCartney was always game. After the success of *Double Fantasy*, his final album, Lennon wanted to be in a band again. An uneasy peace had settled over each household. Ringo was always a peacemaker, and at that time could no doubt use a boost to his wallet. Harrison could finally step forward as the master adept he had become, bolstered by his later efforts to the Fab Four canon.

And they would play. Not discouraged by the poor monitors and banshee shrieks that had spoiled their earlier shows and driven them off the road, they would play. Clear. Crystal. Harmonic brotherhood. Arrangements previously untenable except in the studio could now unfold like orchids. Egos allayed. Perfected men in their forties now. Husbands and fathers. Sage enough to acknowledge the dispensability of ego.

How grand. How redemptive. How those of us who knew and remembered so desperately needed such a cleansing.

I also think of my ex-wife, apart more than twenty-five years now, who deserved far better than she got.

I failed. *We* failed, due to a confluence of punishing events neither of us could adequately digest, much less expect. A miscarriage. A tubal pregnancy. Another miscarriage. We eventually had children, bright, beautiful, perfect little girls. This should have been reclamation, but they came on the heels of each other, fifteen months apart. I was a non-entity by then, a vast wasteland of accrued despair.

I had left my career, too. I went into business for myself. I had a product I wanted to create and market. It was a good concept, one that would emerge in similar forms from other people a half dozen years into the future. I was undercapitalized. I blew through our savings. I...failed.

The day she asked me to leave—the day I drove away in the murk and mire of my wretched soul, some lightless place I had never before known despite all the proclivities I'd harbored and nurtured to acute perfection in nearly four decades of wan existence, the single overarching thought, ceaseless in my awareness, was that I would not see my children grow up.

Oh, of course I would see them grow up, but gone were the daily mornings of muzzy awakenings, piggy-back rides and the post-bath scents of baby shampoo, and go-to-sleep hugs and kisses.

I had no place to go, no harbor to lick my wounds. Instead, I drove to the hospital and told my sad tale to the ER doctor until he admitted me to the psych ward, where I spent a week numbed to oblivion.

How many times can a person lose and still be who he is?

Fifteen years ago I opened my email one day and was greeted by three innocuous words that nonetheless stunned me to my core.

Where are you?

It was her. *Her* her. My first love. The one who had broken my heart and left me doubting every meager good thing I'd ever believed about myself. After thirty years of silence, here she was, in cyber flesh.

She was the divorced mother of four adult children. And she lived fifteen hundred miles away. We wrote. Eventually we chatted. Catching up, mostly, but there was an ease in our exchanges because there was nothing at stake. We knew early on we were strangers now. How could we not be? But neither of us wanted to relive the past. We just wanted some peace. We both wanted to know there was someone who still believed in us.

Within a year I moved. My children were in college but still at hand and it wasn't easy. Her roots were deeper than mine even though I'd lived in South Carolina for over twenty years. I got a job selling furniture. A year later we married.

Did those old, rarified feelings somehow rebound? Of course not. We had evolved and devolved several times over. She remained focused on her family and bore the stigma of a troubled marriage.

And I...I was still that lost kid always wondering what beastie lurked in the shadows waiting for me to pass.

Once long ago I was able to do a few special things on a small scale, and love on a very large scale, with the belief that I might somehow do very special things on a large scale. And when that ended, when the awful truth of my many strictures came crashing down and ground me into soot, I was able to understand that life itself is lived on a small scale, though I could still love on a large scale. And this was my failure, because I had spent my life trying to claim the magic to do special things on a large scale, and in failing, I was never again able to love on a large scale.

We were content. I could always make her laugh. Then, a few years later, I was shaving and found a lump on my neck.

By the time my treatment ended I was death on two legs. After losing twenty pounds in three weeks they installed a feeding tube. I spent the final two weeks of treatment being wheeled into radiology, hefted onto the table, zapped, then wheeled back out where I slithered into my bed. I did my last chemo in the hospital in the middle of an eleven-day confinement from severe dehydration. I hallucinated dying in a med-evac helicopter crash and that during the night my room went into an inter-dimensional phasing where other people used it until morning.

Even the declaration that I was then cancer-free was met with a vacuous thud.

I am now over nine years cancer-free. Unfortunately, many side effects lingered. My last meal was May 24, 2014, soggy Cinnamon Toast Crunch that I could slide down my throat. Had I known this was to be my last meal I would have forced down a couple of cheeseburgers, a large pepperoni pizza, and a half-dozen donuts. After two years I was able to sip thin beverages again and flavored coffee became my only delicacy. No matter, my taste buds never recovered, either, and everything else tastes metallic.

My salivary glands function erratically and I began to get cavities. How does one get cavities without food intake? Turns out there are enzymes in saliva that protect against decay, so I have to chew gum all the time. I also have hearing loss in one ear, low blood pressure, delayed vertigo (where I still *come to* during somnolent trips to the bathroom and find myself clinging to the door jamb), mild cognitive impairment, and I startle easily. What teeth I have left are yellowed from the inside out and cannot be bleached. And my thyroid is dead.

One final irony, and the reason I sit here with a needle in my arm. The three short rounds of chemo that so relieved me in the beginning reduced my kidney function to thirty-percent. So, twice a year I return to this hall of doom to have my kidneys flushed out—a kind of bootleg dialysis. Well, at least I can listen to my music.

During my annual scan my oncologist, perky as ever, lauds the fact that I remain cancer-free. I don't remind him that I pleaded with him to just cut the damn thing out. I don't remind him that he maimed me or that his protocol is designed for the best-case scenario and not for LsWK like me. No, I give him a pass, because it is not his burden to bear.

Then, with a shy eye and gossamer sigh, he says that my ineradicable side effects happen in only one out of a thousand patients—maybe one out of ten thousand.

I can't help but grin. I finally made it.

Am I special or what? (smiley face emoji)

Two

The Pond

I have thought of her and that summer nearly every day for over fifty years, cached in my most secret place, the sanctum of my most perfect treasures. I suppose I was afraid to ever commit this to the open air, much less paper, for fear that once done, all its wonder would disappear. Such is the lot of all magic in this world.

Yesterday I learned I have Amnestic Mild Cognitive Impairment, an obtuse portraiture for failing memory. I realize it could be much worse. It could be Alzheimer's. My greatest fear, other than to lose all touch with these few holies of holies so long and so assiduously locked away, is that I might fail to tell what needs to be told in time.

This story—this divine riddle—needs to be told. Nothing darkens the face of God more than unmet wonder.

Since learning of my malady, I have vainly wished that my memories contained a menu where I could choose those to keep and those to discard. Like anyone else, I also possess a store of foibles and misadventures, those unpleasant excursions into forests of bewilderment I would have avoided had I been wiser at the time. In the past, even the recent past, I have smiled upon these, and hope to do so again before I am no longer able.

The year I turned fifteen, 1965, my grandmother died and my father inherited the hundred-acre farmstead deep in the bowels of Carter County, near the town of Grayson in eastern Kentucky. A hundred acres, while substantial, is not a large working farm, especially when the land rolled and tumbled like earth primeval. Yet, with all its hidden nooks and niches, a hundred acres can be a whole, sequestered world

Fifteen-going-on-sixteen is a semi-universal cusp of knowledge. Smarter than I ever considered at twelve, yet unaware of the depth of my ignorance until looking backward from eighteen or twenty. Reality is skewed. No worries about food or clothing or career. There are pals, a girl if lucky, maybe some ambition of motorized transportation, and aspiring to be bright enough to get into a good college. There are subliminal parental pressures, curfews and bans on illicit substances. There are more overt peer pressures which are best avoided by maintaining a confined group of friends equally goofy about things, and naturally, a good portion of time devoted to daydreaming and creating scenarios for success as real in creation as they are outlandish. Angst, like baby fat, is a condition to be outgrown.

Above all else, all consideration for *life*, as it exists at that age, is to feel purposeful in self-invention and not let practicality get in the way.

Once the grief of my grandmother's passing ebbed, the ugly business of death concluded, I was informed that we would be spending the following summer at the farm. More specifically, in the old house of faded white boards, metal roof, and no air conditioning or television. My only companions, my little brother and sister. I didn't even have a dog. Naturally, I earnestly lamented.

I was a mistake. Accident is a more generous description, but as my parents were twenty when I came along, unmarried, and only half-way through college (well, from my father's perspective, perhaps a third), it is more than reasonable to presume the stork landed on the roof with a hearty Surprise!

Consequently, there is a considerable age gap between myself and my siblings, and I was more a Dutch Uncle to them than a brother. My sister Austen, named for the famed British author, is ten years younger than I, and my brother Bennet, named after the family in *Pride and Prejudice,* is a full dozen. Bennet grew up with some teasing, the fact that few ever spelled his name right notwithstanding, Austen was luckier and came along when contrived girls' names became *la mode*, even though few got her name right the first time, either.

My father took full advantage of the post-war GI Bill, though he was stationed in California and never saw action. He left school with several graduate degrees and accepted a position at Ohio University, not to be confused with Ohio *State* University, an institution of far greater size, notoriety, and sports acumen. He taught calculus, neither and art nor a science, and a curious subject for such extended study, but he loved problems and was a good teacher. He spent his entire career in Athens—Ohio, not Greece—and was a good father, if remote.

My mother was lucky to attend college. She studied creative writing, which, after a stint at *The Post*, and not the Washington or New York but the OU student paper, qualified her to sell Avon.

Eventually, however, she found a modicum of success writing romance novels under several noms de plume, my favorite being Natasha White Bathurst. She published three books a year but eventually earned a couple thousand dollars per book. My mother was my best friend. She never talked down to me, involving me in everything from boiling noodles to her hair style to if her feet looked big in sandals, from the time I was eight years old. My brain was clogged with the adult mundane long before its time and the preeminent quality of my parents was that they were too easily amused by each other and seemed gleefully resistant to growing up.

All this is confusingly prefatorial, I know, but germane to that season and the enchantment thus evidenced.

It was just after Memorial Day and already sizzling when we arrived. Grossly depressed, I surveyed the untended old house, a ramshackle old barn, and a porous tobacco shed (when had they ever grown tobacco?) that canted a full twenty degrees of bowed wood from the time of Lincoln. I further despaired and heaved a sigh.

"It'll be fun," my father said over his shoulder, oblivious as always.

The house sat far back between two east-west pastures hidden from the road. Between them was a twenty-five acre pine woods. Behind the house and separated by a deep creek bed that filled only after heavy rain and was soon dry again, a field swept upward toward another stand of woods. A wobbly plank was the means to traverse the gully which had, years ago, led to the outhouse, where a bright square of thick green grass still proudly unfurled.

My grandparents always kept a large vegetable garden and a few cows when my grandfather was still alive, though in recent years the land had turned to overgrowth and hardpan. For most of their lives my grandfather ran his hardware store and my grandmother ran my grandfather.

I was rewarded as senior offspring with a room of my own. This had been my grandmother's sewing room and still had a well-used machine and partial rolls of fabrics everywhere. In one corner of the small space was a daybed, a nightstand and lamp, and a three-drawer chest for my clothes. The closet was in the hall, used now primarily for linens and towels.

I pushed the window up to catch some air. It was warped, but after duck-walking it inch-by-inch, it opened. And immediately rattled down. I saw a nearby paint stirrer covered with the ugliest yellow known to man and understood it was a prop. There was a screen covering the opening with a single hole in it stuffed with a cotton ball. Only the most clever mosquito would be able to wriggle through.

The breeze blew in satisfactorily but was too warm to make much difference. Maybe after dark.

My brother and sister were in the room across the hall and my parents' room was just off the back hallway. They had a queen-sized bed with a bowed mattress atop a set of rusty springs that creaked with the slightest movement. My greatest fear was that I would hear my parents in flagrante delicto and die from embarrassment.

The highlight of the house, if such existed, was the porch. It lined the entire front about ten feet deep. There were a couple of bent-wood rockers and a two-seat swing suspended by chains from the ceiling. Perfect for refining boredom to an art form. My brother and sister were lucky. Soon there was a sandbox and a shallow children's pool. The water came from a well and smelled like too long-forgotten eggs.

The first morning I woke to find myself in my briefs atop the sheets. The wee-hour breeze was effective after all and I had goosebumps. Rather than cover up and go back to sleep, I got up. There was only one bathroom. The fixtures had to be pre-Columbian. The shower was a quasi-obscene looking pink hose attached to the spigot and was handheld.

My father had never lived there as a child. My grandfather bought the farm to escape from people after my father had left home. Being a shopkeeper will do that. Even in quaint, bunghole-of-the-earth, Kentucky, dealing with the public could be an ordeal. Echoed whines of overly optimistic do-it-yourselfers—not to mention the universal desire to have my grandfather provide a tutorial on everything he sold—filled the stiff air of the store every open hour.

It was only seven. Three days into my summer vacation, having survived my sophomore year of high school and looking forward to having someone at hand to bully next term, I was lost, marooned as much as Robinson Crusoe. And here I was up at daybreak.

I ate a bowl of cereal and watched daylight shift from coral to gold. Muffled birdsong pushed through the open windows. Then I heard Bennet start to rattle around and I beat it before being shanghaied to entertain a three-year-old. As long as I was here, might as well explore the land. How long would it take to cover a hundred acres?

The dirt driveway ended at the barn. The east pasture lay beyond. The old barbwire fence was sagging in places and completely down in others. Later I learned this is where the bull had been separated, apparently, to give the ladies some peace.

The interior woods thinned here, though still cluttered with gnarled underbrush. The remnants of a path wound around the edge toward the main road. The trail dipped into the trees for a bit, the trail itself long since overgrown, rife with briars and thorny branches. The new sun filtered through the upper limbs revealing a faded, slate-blue sky.

I soon realized I should've worn jeans. My summer wardrobe consisted of T-shirts and shorts and my legs were nipped with every step. City people tend to link small-town people with country people. We are as different from each other as they are. I grew up in a small town but was still within walking (or biking) distance from everything. This was the country, the boondocks, the butt-crack of Americana, utterly devoid of stimulation.

The sun broke through as if the trees had parted, shining on my face. I had worked up a minor sweat but the sun felt good. Farther ahead I saw a clearing, maybe five acres that ended in a narrow arm sticking into the far woods, like a tadpole with its tail backed into the trees. The opening was odd. Completely covered with grass, the undergrowth was thin, as if stunted, with no trees or bushes.

What I discovered only thirty yards inward, hidden beneath the grass, was a large, empty hole. A pit. I walked the entire rim. The hole was maybe half an acre. It was about twenty feet deep in its center, a steep bowl where there was no purchase. I didn't want to climb down because I wasn't sure if I could climb out again.

The bowl was completely bare and nonporous, clay hardened to concrete in the sun. And I soon realized it wasn't completely empty. At the bottom, nearly perfectly centered, was a fallen tree, or large pieces of a fallen tree, massive logs shoved deep and buried. There were six or seven of these mighty arms stuck into the ground like abandoned monuments. The sun seemed to be rising unnaturally fast and the heat was soon tangible. I hadn't brought any water with me, so I made the return trip the same way I came.

I heard the squawking of the two monkeys before my feet hit the porch. I couldn't tell if this was gleeful or angry. I was saved by my father who appeared through the screen door.

"Off exploring?"

I shrugged "A little."

"Well stay on the property if you can. At least until we know more about the neighbors."

I looked around at the empty space as far as I could see. "What neighbors?"

My dad moved toward the car. "About a half-mile down on each side. Across the main road, too."

I had never felt so alone. My father looked at me for a moment, then said, "Going into town for a supply run. Want to come?"

I did not have to think long. Escape of any kind was a gift. "Sure."

I thought to myself how would I know when the town began? I was being snotty, of course. We road for miles and there was nothing but old houses every half mile or so, each surrounded by acreage. A couple homesteads had mobile homes adorned with bobbing wind-vanes and flowerbeds inside painted tires. Some had swing sets and other evidence of curtain pullers. Nearly all had a pickup truck.

"I found this big pit," I said casually.

My father nodded slightly but looked ahead. "Yeah, the old cattle pond."

"What happened to it?"

My father did not answer immediately, and when he did he was far more noncommittal than I expected. "It was drained. Dried up. No more cows."

A pond. A swimming hole. Almost as good as a pool. I had seen its insides. Clean and firm except for the trees at the bottom. My prospects edged northward a tad.

Later, I searched the barn. The smell was awful. Not like cow shit, if I had known what cow shit smelled like, but beyond stale. The floor was still littered with bits of hay, and there was a loft above the far wall. The ladder to it looked deadly. There was an ancient tractor—its age deduced by its appearance, which was rusty and once red, but I found a length of moldy rope.

I tied off to the nearest tree and lowered myself into the hole. Reaching bottom, I moved from one limb to another hand-over-hand, never losing my grip. I pushed, pulled, and shook as hard as I could. None so much as budged. Determined, mulishly stubborn, really, I vowed to overcome. What else did I have to do?

Normally, any diversion requiring physical labor—especially during the summer—would have been met with scowls, grunts, and perhaps even the one vulgarity that was tolerated, *shit*. *Shit* was not a vulgarity in hillbilly culture, or at least no more than *crap* or *hockey*, partly because being descended from solid Scots-Irish stock, the word *shite* was considered only mildly offensive, and partly because hillbillies were not even sure it was the same word, being pronounced *she-at*.

That night as I lay in bed thinking about how sorry the summer was going to be when I could just as easily have had a sorry summer in Athens, where at least there was a decent library and a community pool, I got an idea. A *big* idea. What is stronger than wood? Besides a chainsaw, of course, which I didn't have and wouldn't know how to use if I had one.

Fire. Fire trumped just about everything. The next morning, I made eight or ten pyramids beneath the logs and began. Newspaper to twigs. Twigs to sticks. Sticks to branches. I felt like Prometheus. The massive logs were slow to burn and seemed impervious at first. Should've doused them in gasoline beforehand. Instead, I waited. The dead bark began to smolder and pop. The logs caught. I felt like the smartest Neanderthal in the tribe.

Smoke began to billow and encompassed me. I coughed myself red and climbed out of the hole. Soon, fire began to spread from the center to the ends. My father must have seen the smoke clouds rise and came running. I heard his shouts from near the barn.

"Over here!" I called.

He arrived breathless, relieved when he realized the woods were not aflame. He did not, however, seem to grasp the benefits of removing the detritus from the hole.

"You'll catch the woods on fire. It's been dry all year."

"It can't spread," I said. "It's deep and there's nothing else in it that will burn."

"Cinders," he said, pointing upward. "Land in a tree and whoosh."

I hadn't thought about that. When in doubt, fake it. "I've been careful. I'll be here to watch it."

My father scowled. "Should just leave it alone," he muttered in parting. The words rang woefully hollow, as if some fundamental precedent had been breached. At least he didn't say 'no, stop it'. Of course my father never told me 'no, stop it'. No matter. Permission was implicit.

Eventually, I was down to charred cores. The limbs still thwarted me, stuck deep. Then I remembered the old tractor. Ancient though it may be, it was not dead. There was fuel, but I didn't know if gas spoiled by sitting idle for any length of time. There was a push-button start. That part was easy. And the battery still had some juice because it made that er-er-er-er sound that usually indicates intractability.

Finally, it fired, blue smoke belching through the barn and nearly asphyxiating me. It took me three times to gain any forward motion without popping the clutch and killing the engine. At last, with a skip and a lunge, I was moving. I presumed it was in first gear, so I left it in first gear, moving about as fast as an old lady walking a fat dog, but moving nonetheless. I needed a hat, a checked shirt, and a piece of straw between my teeth.

I wrapped the rope around the first log and tied it as best I could.

I had wisdom teeth pulled a couple of years ago. I was sedated, of course, and what I felt mostly was pressure and tugging on my jaw. Painless, at least for the time being, the dentist worked until suddenly there was a conspicuous hollowness. I felt that in the seat of the tractor. Tension, tension, tension, then pop. I jumped down to see for myself. There the incisor lay atop the dense earth, three feet buried in clay and no cavities. One-by-one the charred timbers yielded to my genius. I dragged them out and stacked the remnants near the far edge of the woods. I jumped into the pit. I had to admire my surgical skill.

The next morning, I popped a soda and moseyed around to the pond site, peeking first into the old tobacco shed. The tobacco shed had a steep roof with arm-sized gaps, where the sun slid inside, producing irregular columns of light. Empty wooden racks high off the floor covered most of it. There were no other rooms or cubbyholes. I heard scratching in a dark corner and beat it out of there. I headed down the tree line and into the passageway to the clearing. I swigged the last of my soda and started a trash pile I would dispose of eventually. For now, I wanted to admire my handiwork again.

I heard it before I saw it, and it was such a foreign sound I froze. Like a toilet running. A very *large* toilet. I moved toward the pit, deliberately now, and craned my neck while keeping my feet as far back as possible. Then I was floored.

There was water in the bottom of the hole, not very deep yet, but enough to cover the holes where the limbs had been. It was also perfectly clear—like tap water in a basin. And there above each hole the water bubbled at the surface. I didn't know much about limnology but I knew a spring when I saw it. With almost no sediment, I wondered how clear the water would remain.

I decided to keep this information to myself, at least for the near future, but was not as disconsolate as before. I had cleaned a wound and returned something to health. I was ecstatic.

We cooked out that night. I thought this was kind of redundant since the kitchen with the windows and back door open was as outdoors as the outdoors. Austen disassembled and reassembled her burger and Bennet gnawed his way down a wiener like a gopher. We sat out and I listened to my parents talk. My mother's book had a lonely kindergarten teacher find true love with someone beneath her station. She wasn't sure if he was to be a folk singer or a janitor. My father talked about probabilities of face cards being dealt with four players, each getting his cards in succession. I enjoyed listening to my parents volley ideas. I thought to suggest that my mother's kindergarten teacher should fall in love with a gambler but sat on it.

Overhead, a red-tailed hawk hovered. Called kiting, so perfectly attuned to the air the bird can float in place, only occasionally flapping its wings. I thought to bring it to everyone's attention but stopped, safely ensconced among my fledgling treasures.

In hindsight, I was entering a transitory phase to learn how to have a life. I sensed the change and even at the periphery, I was a part of everything about me, and I knew there was a living force in the world that was on auto-pilot, and created glory with or without observation, caring not, but was made manifest for any and all to share, to imbibe, to become a part of the cosmic construct and be soulfully altered. I realized that I was an observer. What I was to become, I had no idea, but I had a part to play that was unique to me, and never again would I feel an immaterial part of my own life—a bystander bobbing on the tides of others.

I only had to withstand the awful arbitrariness of life.

I lay in bed that night unable to sleep. I didn't miss television yet but didn't know what else I was going to do with myself the whole summer. I had a pocket radio. I couldn't get any of the local stations, but I got WCFL in Chicago, a good five hundred miles away. Go figure. I loved the Beatles. I had ignored them the first year or so because all the girls in school went on and on about them, and any guy who fell in with that crowd was a pansy. 1966 was different. Their music was changing and I was changing. In the fall, I would turn sixteen. The world becomes a different place when you're sixteen, even in Athens, Ohio. CFL played a new Beatles tune, *Paperback Writer*. Suddenly, I was reminded that there was order and continuity in the world. I slept peacefully.

Morning came and went before I could sneak off to the pond and I half expected the water to have drained out, or lingered in a puddle. The trees stood motionless, like statues of Anubis, the Egyptian dog-man-god, guarding some hallowed tomb.

I thought the pond might be a part of some karmic balance, my reward for being broke, jobless, and held against my will in Carter County, Kentucky, where there were few sources of entertainment that did not involve a fiddle.

What I didn't expect was the girl swimming naked in it. I stopped short, floored. I had never seen a naked girl before in person. Actually, I could only see her backside now. Off to the side I saw shorts and a top in a pile. Who was she?

I saw enough of her face to know that she wasn't pretty by common definition. Her hair was cut too short with blunt ends. Her neck was too long. Her legs were too skinny. She was angular in an overt way. When she turned onto her back I turned my head at first. Her fur patch was surprisingly thin. Her breasts were little more than orange halves and her sternum revealed every bony spur between. Her areolas were the size of quarters and her nipples were tiny buttons. I was stupefied and enthralled.

She swam up to the side and looked at me, placidly, unstartled, as if she had known I was there all along. She made no effort to cover herself. She smiled, her front teeth slightly uneven.

"Who might you be?" she asked.

Every regional accent has shallow versions and broad versions, usually (and unfortunately) resulting from a level of education. Her hillbilly accent was long, elastic, and nearly unending...'Hoo maht you bay?'

"Eddie. Markley. This is our farm."

"Oh," she said with a glint in her eye. "I'm trespassing, ain't I?"

I began to fidget. "No. You're okay."

"Well I'm Melanie. You can call me Mel."

"You live around here?"

"Just up the road. I used to sneak off and swim here before it dried up."

"It was empty when I got here. Stopped up by some big limbs. Must've been that way awhile."

"Prob'ly so . Glad you fixed it." She looked at me and I felt it as if she had poked my chest with a finger. "You gonna come swimmin' or just watch me nekkid ?"

I stripped off my shirt and kicked off my shoes. "Is it still cold?"

"Feels good to me."

I walked over and stuck my foot in. The water was freezing. I sat down and began to ease myself into the water.

"No fair," she said.

"What?" I asked.

"If I'm going to skinny-dip you should to."

I know I must have reddened like an apple. I forced myself to smile and slid into the water, still clad. I felt a jolt right away, goose bumps forming. But by the time I surfaced, the sun bright upon my face, I started to acclimate. I kept my distance. I could keep over fifty feet distant if I needed to.

"You could have worn a swimsuit," I said.

"Never have before. 'Course it was just me most of the time. It's okay. Wear what you want. It's your pond now."

I could see nothing but her head and her hands. I was relieved. I know I sound like a weenie. I felt like one, too. I just didn't know what else to do. She wasn't shy. Maybe she had no sense of modesty.

Besides, being in the cold water kept my nether regions from giving me away. I had to admit, as bizarre as this was, it was nice to finally see someone my own age who I could talk to. I held my breath and sank all the way to the bottom. The farther I descended, the colder it got. I slowly let out my breath to keep from bobbing up. I could feel my ears tighten a bit. Twenty feet was deeper than any pool I'd ever been in. But it was euphoric. I touched the bottom and prepared to push off. I happened to look in her direction under the water and saw her bare legs undulating, and also the fleshy part between her thighs, though with little detail. My manhood noticed, too, cold or not. I swam to the surface and moved to the side again.

"Nice, ain't it?"

"Very," I said. "It's so clear?"

"Spring water's always moving. It's never still enough for any slime to grow. No fish poop, either."

"She pulled herself out, the water cascading down her bare back. Her backside was boyish and flat. I didn't care. She did not look my way or speak. She did not dry herself before pulling on her shorts and halter top. She kept her back to me throughout.

"See you tomorrow," I said, hopefully.

"Yep," she replied. Then she turned again and began to walk through the woods toward the main road.

I watched until she disappeared and made a mental note to sneak a couple of towels out there.

As the senior slave on the plantation, and the only one capable of performing even the most basic task, unless playdoh creatures and building block minarets rose on the to-do list, I knew that any required routine maintenance would fall to me. That afternoon my father and I checked out the lawn mower. At least it was a rider.

Like everything else about, it was old, but it had been used often and kept in decent working order. We changed the oil and spark plug. Checked the air in the tires and sharpened the blade. This, too, was a clown car of maladroit cooperation. For an exceedingly clever man, my father was the Gomez Addams of mechanical aptitude. He upended the mower, gas leaking out everywhere, and vigorously dragged a rasp of some sort across the edge of the blade. I think he actually made it worse.

I really didn't mind mowing and even looked forward to it if I could choose the day and time for myself. The whole point of doing a repetitive task without anyone looking over my shoulder was to surf the muse.

After about the tenth snap of the cord, Dad flicking the spark plug with his finger each time as if to annoy the thing into submission, the engine caught. I immediately engaged the blade and the shifter, causing my father to jump out of the way, and took the petite bête for a test mow.

For so much property there was relatively little to mow. The yard surrounding the house was thin and patchy. On both sides of the driveway were strips about three feet wide. Down by the main road was another narrow plot in parallel, and the old bull pasture had oddly stopped growing on its own.

The west pasture was several acres but relatively flat and empty of obstacles. This made mowing simpler and my ruminations more satisfying as I moved in ever-diminishing rectangles. I couldn't hear the radio over the roar of the mower so I let music play inside my head. There wasn't much else to occupy my attention. Despite all the evolutionary bits in the environment—the buildings, the woods, the undulating hills—every semblance of fractional civilization, even for the mid-sixties, I was ever aware just how remote we were. From the pasture I could only see the corner of a chimneyed roof to the east and a few grazing cows directly across the main road.

I had mowed for nearly an hour and hadn't seen a vehicle on the road.

I thought about ice cream with crunched up vanilla wafers. I thought about whether getting a part-time job in the fall to save for a car was really worth it. I thought about many things in rapid succession, dust motes of awareness too skittish to light.

Most of all I thought of a naked girl lolling in a pond and why breasts that in no way resembled those depicted in my fantasies would suddenly be so intriguing.

Then I saw a flash of black whip into the taller grass up ahead and came full alert.

Anyone who has ever experienced a Rube Goldberg event knows things move in indecipherable ways. A plate is innocently nudged.

The plate bumps a water glass that begins to teeter. The water spills onto the table, the food, cascading onto the floor. The glass then lazily rolls over the edge, breaking as a hand snatches at empty air. All in five seconds.

I don't know what I saw up ahead and freak a little. I slow and peer forward but don't see anything so I resettled. Suddenly, a black snake fired out right in front of me. Instinctively I raised my feet even though they're already a foot off the ground and surrounded by bladed metal, and got a jolt of adrenaline.

Instead of moving forward the stupid creature decided to back-track and I ran over it at three thousand rpms. Snake parts flew out the grass chute. I cringed, and a chill ran up my back. I backed up a few feet, stopped, and disengaged the blade. I took a roundabout route to the massacre site and looked over as far as I could without moving any closer. I saw part of it wriggling in the grass. About half of it to the tail. I used a stick to drag it into the short grass. It became motionless. Dead. I looked again and saw another bloody chunk and flicked it over.

I didn't see the head at first. This shouldn't matter at all, but my mind skittered as puerile neurons fired and I wondered if the head could be hiding, not to mention that I still had to mow that area and didn't want to run over it again. I gritted my teeth and poked around until I found it, its mouth frozen open in shock and disappointment. I used the stick to roll it to the rest of the pile. The snake appeared to be about five feet long. I wasn't dumb enough to reassemble it and measure.

I was still creeped out when I resumed mowing. I shivered every time I passed by the corpse, at least for the next four-or-five swaths. Then I was far enough away to be okay. I still half-expected to cruise by the next lap and see it gone. Maybe snakes can live on like worms when they lose parts of their bodies. And maybe it was just knocked out, which is really, really ignorant because the thing is in three major and a half-dozen minor pieces. It's there every time, all mangled and pitiful. I ain't about to move it again, either, so I didn't tell my father.

I still had to upright the machine when I finished and hose off the underneath. I shivered again as I did this. Luckily, I saw no more snake parts or oozing ick, and realized the thing was completely dispatched. I thought about snakes a lot for many days. I couldn't seem to help it. I was also forced again to recognize that I think entirely too much for my own good.

After I showered, my mother joined me on the porch. Steam rose from her mug and her eyes were red from typing. She sat in one of the rockers.

"Which is it to be?" I asked. "Folk singer, janitor, or gambler?"

"Gambler? I hadn't thought of that. What gave you that idea?"

Oh, yeah. I hadn't vocalized that. "You said you wanted a ne'er-do-well."

"I'm moving away from that. Adds an element of conflict that may prove distracting, since there is so much already."

"That poor girl," I said, teasing her.

"It's not as easy as it sounds, Bucko. It's a formula, sure, but it has to seem real or people will avoid it."

"You mean like a troubled man and the governess?"

"Smart Aleck."

Then she grinned at me. Her eyes brightened as she did, or else glistened from strain. Nearly every memory of my mother makes me smile. She was my lone companion until I started school and guided me with a light touch. She had never let any harm befall me and I adored her.

"Okay," I began. "What about this? A lonely ne'er-do-well hits rock bottom and wants to change his life. But he has no idea what to do. He thinks about suicide but goes to the emergency room at the last minute and is put in the psychiatric ward. There he meets another fruitcake who has hit bottom, too. No wait, that would never work."

Strangely, I had my mother's attention. "Why not?"

"She has to be stronger than him. How about a nurse. Or a nurse's aide? Or a Candy Striper? Someone with a mothering complex who takes this guy in and brings him back to life."

I could tell my mother was thinking, overlooking the fact that I was just being silly.

"You want to romance this with me?"

"That sounds weird."

"Talk it through. Brainstorm. Hash it out."

"Only if you never tell anyone."

Again, she smiled. "Deal."

Just as my dad pulled up amid impatient squeals, I looked at my mother a final time. "Do I get royalties?"

"After I deduct room and board for the past sixteen years, sure."

That night I reversed myself in bed with my feet toward the wall so I could look out the window. I couldn't see the moon or the stars. In fact, I could see little except darkness. Occasionally, a zephyr would whisk among the pine needles and whisper to me.

There was life in the infinite. Of what shape and form, I had no idea. I sensed however, that the spirits of those still grieving their separation from this world were definitely there. I had hardly known my grandparents. Yet I had no doubt that if I listened very carefully, they would speak to me. Life that exists only in the dusky dim must be melancholy, and ache for a willing ear.

I had not fully realized the abject danger of my father not having a project. He had this quasi-demented look in his eye that meant trouble for me. Work. He decided to improve the property. I was suicidal. The house would be scraped and painted. White, of course. The porch, front door, and the two shutters would be painted a nice contrast color. My father chose red. My mother disapproved. Imagine that.

"Dark green would be nice," she said. Dark green it was.

Anticipation is a curious thing. There is the excitement of the unknown, or even a previously satisfying known. There is also a speed bump to safely slow things down, the uncertainty in any environment newly established. Then there is a brake, an overarching sense of worst-case reality that prompts feet to stop and heels to turn around and head the other way.

I had no idea what I was getting myself into but looked forward to finding out.

She was not there when I arrived at the pond. I was disappointed far more than I expected. I jumped in any way to wash away all the sweat and grime. I ducked my head under and scratched the dried sweat free from my scalp. When I surfaced, she was stepping through the last line of trees. She was bright and energetic as she waved and exited the woods. I was already cooling off, the water now warm upon my upper body and noticeably cooler at my feet. She also seemed to be wearing the same clothes as before and I thought her family must be *poor* poor.

"I didn't know if you were going to make it," I said.

"I lose track of the time," she replied.

She pulled her top off over her head. Her small lobes barely moved. She pulled her pants down around her ankles and took a few seconds to kick them off. There was something uncomfortably erotic about the movement that gave me pause. Maybe she didn't care what she revealed because she thought I was a Nancy-boy. Maybe I wasn't her type.

I'd wanted to surprise her. She dove, then surfaced a few feet in front of me, still in deep water. She was sardonic as she treaded water.

"You did it," she said.

I was as naked as the day I was born. "Yep I did. In your honor, of course."

She dog-paddled to the edge and held on. "Well, I think that's just fine."

This was such strange talk, especially since it involved my exposed pecker and nut sack. The reality was simply not addressed.

She turned her back to the wall. "Race you to the bottom and back." Then she plunged, me right after, a pair of white butts glistening in the sun.

We touched the bottom about the same time and pushed off. She sailed closer to me as we rose through the water. Once we broke the surface she put her arms around me, smiling. I felt her warmth from chin to knee. I don't think I'd ever felt better in my life.

I kissed her. I closed my eyes instinctively but opened them again to see her expression. Her eyes were shut. I held the kiss. The gentle motion of our lips seemed natural. It was an old-fashioned kiss, our lips sealed. I hadn't kissed a girl since third grade and got in trouble for that. I broke it off. Foolish, of course, though in my defense I figured there would be more. Of course, the reason I broke it off was because I felt the blood rush to my underworld. Nothing dramatic or noticeable yet, but I was embarrassed. She remained close, her arms around my neck. I rested a hand upon her hip, holding the rim with my other one.

"That was about the sweetest thing," she said.

"Right. I'm sure you say that to all the guys who skinny dip in this pond."

She chuckled low, light, musical, and gently pushed away. She began to slowly move backwards. "Nope," she said. "Only you."

I was glad for the separation, and not just because of potential tumescence. I needed to think. What do I do now? How often can I go to the well on this? How much is too much? Was this merely a fleeting moment and not really the beginning of anything? I was in so far over my head. Am I supposed to say something? God, for a guy sixteen years old I sure am naive.

There she was, watching me as if she knew the gears were turning in my head, eyes alight and perceptive beyond her years.

"Would you ever like to take a walk, or go anywhere together?"

"You mean like a date?"

"Not necessarily. Just to do something different."

"You think we need to do something different?"

"No. Not really."

"Okay then. But it's nice to be asked."

She moved away, treading upright, then flipped backwards and dove. When she flipped, her legs parted and I caught a closer glimpse of her treasure. I dove down toward the vents. The water was still a lot colder and the flow stronger. I was amazed that those limbs, however large, had been enough to clog the spring. Now it felt like an ocean current down there. I saw Mel kick quickly to the surface and I followed.

She was shivering. I didn't know what to make of it at first. She was the practiced one, the erstwhile fish-at-home. She looked at me with a smile but continued to tremble, her arms wrapped across her chest.

"You're too cold," I said.

"Kind of. I don't know what's wrong with me. Can't seem to shake it."

"Let's get out of the water then. Get in the sun."

She nodded, but still shuddered, harder even. Her face was pained, the brightness gone. She seemed paralyzed, unable to move. She could be coming down with the flu or something. I touched her forehead with the back of my hand. I didn't know what I was doing, but I figured I'd know hot if I felt it. Her temperature seemed normal, maybe even colder.

I reached for her and pulled her close, hoping that my body heat would help. She slipped her arms around me and held tight. She continued to shiver. There was nothing sexual about this embrace. I could feel her bare flesh the length of my body, most prominently against my chest, stomach, and groin, but nothing sexual stirred. The warmth penetrated, encompassing both of us, as comforting to me as it was to her.

Gradually I felt her become still. Whatever possessed her had subsided, at least for the moment. I gently stroked her back between the shoulder blades.

"We should get out and put a towel around you," I whispered.

She remained close, firm in the embrace, but not uncomfortably so. "Let's wait a minute, okay?"

She clung to me for a few moments then finally pulled away. I put my hands on the grass and pushed myself up and out. I immediately grabbed her arms at the wrist and helped her up. I fetched the largest of the towels—a beach towel with the faded image of Pepe Le Pew on it, a thin green fog rising from his backside.

"You okay now?"

She nodded. "Just a little woozy, I guess."

"Then let's sit down."

She shook her head. "I'll be fine. Let me get dressed."

She opened the towel and patted herself dry. I turned away as if she suddenly needed privacy. She dressed quickly and walked up to me. The color had returned to her face and her eyes were livelier. She reached to hug me and I returned it. Just before she left she gave me a kiss on the lips, a small millisecond kiss. I took her hands in mine and after a minute she headed for the trees.

"Can I walk you home?" I called after her.

She looked back. "I'm okay."

Then she disappeared into the trees.

I didn't know what to think or how to feel but pity was not any part of it. She was Nereid, heiress to the sea. She was a force of nature, powerful and wise to anything I could certainly throw at her. She was also vulnerable somehow. And she was more real than anything or anyone I'd ever encountered.

Instead of going home I stretched out on the towel, searching the empty sky for meaning. A blue jay cackled unseen and the heat soon became oppressive, and I moved into the shade. The air was still turbid, an invisible nebula that seemed to press in from all directions, making it hard to breathe. Even so, I smiled. The kisses had been sweet.

My mother was sitting on the porch when I returned.

"I thought we were going to do this together," she said.

"Let me get something to drink," I replied. I fetched a soda and sat down in the swing opposite her. "How come you want my input but don't want to pay me?"

"Tell you what. If I use your ideas, I'll give you a cut."

"You've already used my ideas."

"True. Okay. Anything over five thousand dollars I'll give you ten percent."

I knew this was no bargain. "Where are you?"

She always squinched her face when she was deep in thought and chewed on the end of her pencil. The eraser always remained intact but was wet, and the wood beneath displayed deep teeth marks. I would remember those details the rest of my life.

"I need to add another element of tension."

"He's a psycho who killed twenty people."

"Kinda ruins the element of romance."

I thought hard. It was fun in a balloon-animal sort of way. "How about this? He's in the Army. No wait. He works for a company that makes weapons for the Army. They have a new missile. Smaller, easier to move, but very powerful. He's the guy who designed it. Everything goes great and this company is going to make a jillion dollars. They do a test for some honchos—generals or whoever— some place on a base. They fire the missile. Something goes wrong and it crashes on the base and kills a bunch of people. This is bad. Maybe it's not really his fault but he's so far gone with guilt because of it he decides to kill himself."

My mother sat straight up and looked at me. "I may have to give you a raise," she said.

The weather was strange that evening. The sky was sunny and bright until nine o'clock, though thunder rumbled in the distance. No dark skies could be seen, but in the faraway bellies of clouds, flashes of lightning were trapped. My parents were tag-team teaching Laurel and Hardy the finer aspects of Candy Land. Bennet was going through that stage when he would scream at the top of his lungs if he didn't catch on right away, which was often. Some people haven't shaken that habit even in their thirties. I had to get out of there or I would explode.

This was that wonderful time of day when the sun was down but daylight still reigned. It was just as hot and humid, but without the direct radiation of the sun, it felt cooler. Even so, I had broken a sweat by the time I reached the main road. I headed east, walking at a leisurely pace in my comfy old tennis shoes. I wasn't headed anywhere in particular. There was no place I could walk, specifically. Just checking out the neighborhood, such as it was.

A couple hundred yards east of us and across the road, I stopped at the house and looked up the driveway. I had seen something that didn't register and I had no idea what it was. I retraced my steps. An old dog lay motionless on the porch. That wasn't it. There was a new Thunderbird in the driveway. Ford had gone from the small sports models to a much larger one. 1964 had brought a new body style, more luxury-oriented. But no, that wasn't it either. There was a smokehouse out back made of old boards like our tobacco shed. Did no one ever update those things? That must've been what caught my eye. Then I looked again and noticed that the driveway split. One part curved toward the front of the house and the other part moved deeper into the property. I bobbed my head and thought I could see part of another building between the trees. Then I noticed there were two mailboxes across the road.

I was not anxious to go farther. I would be trespassing, I might wake up the dog and provoke it, and it was nearly dark. I also knew that I could be seen from the house if anyone was looking. I moved to the far edge of the driveway beside a chain-link fence, at least partially concealed by trees. I followed the path deliberately, eyes straight ahead, as if I had every right to be there. I passed the dog and the house without any growls or 'hey you, what are you doing there?' The road began a gradual sweep to the left and I followed it until it straightened again.

There I saw an old ramshackle house overlooked by a pair of age-old pines. There wasn't much to the house. It was barely livable and small. There was a post missing on the front porch and the roof sagged. The paint was worn. I could have peeled it clean with my fingers. A couple of window ledges looked rotten. Blankets hung in the front windows instead of curtains. I saw no one, though there was a light on inside. I turned back and left. Somehow I knew this is where Mel lived and it saddened me.

Fully dark now, I moved toward home at a quicker pace. As I walked I felt ill-at-ease, as if I had breached some unspoken covenant between us even though no one else knew or would know. I was restless for a long time that night, even as the rain fell in gouts and lulled me to sleep.

The wire brush had worn a blister on my palm, but I finally finished scraping. All around the house looked strewn with confetti. I removed the shutters and set them aside for painting. Sanding the porch had been easier. There was far less chipped paint, creating smoother edges. The paint glided on smooth and my technique was improving. I didn't enjoy painting, but I made good progress. I was relentless, my head full of woolgathering and naked hillbilly girls. Even they are as graceful as swans in the water. If my father left me alone, I would finish the whole thing inside a week.

Dad seemed pleased by the progress. My mother was happily—and furiously—working on the new book.

Any implication that my father was fundamentally inept or that our relationship wasn't close, would not only be specious, but would wound me. I loved my father. I have spent many scattered hours, oft times fleeting moments amid demanding routine, contemplating our seeming distance. Fathers have particular expectations of sons, happiness, safety, security, certainly, but bend toward adequate preparation and life-accomplishment. A mother's expectations are more amorphous and center around a satisfying, worthwhile existence undefined except as fundamental peace of mind and goodwill.

One thing about my father, he would try anything. I did not inherit, nor acquired, this personality trait.

In fact, he was a brilliant mathematician. This is not hyperbole. What most don't understand is by teaching math, even advanced math, one loses the freedom to explore theory or delve into research. Impetus abates, replaced by routine. Ohio University is not a school for dolts and underachievers, however. Advanced math is advanced math. He taught something called quantum calculus. I can't even make change for a pack of gum.

After his P.H.D., he applied to NASA, who was determined to send people to the moon by 1969. My father was informed that NASA was full-up, except for certain engineers, but would he be interested in taking an exam to be kept on file with his resume and other information? He was able to do this from home because these were essay-type questions and not true mathematical solutions. It's like asking, how much does a fart weigh? He leapt into it, however, even though he knew there wasn't a job at the end of the rainbow. I could hear him whooping with excitement and accenting every-third-whoop with Yes! as he completed each part. I was maybe ten or eleven then and had no idea what was going on.

Later I learned that while on a caffeine-and-Snickers bender, he wrote a summary based upon Einstein's work on the real potential of manipulating space. It was all fantasy, of course. His idea was to create an artificial sphere, a moon, actually, with a different gravity and magnetic field than Earth. Its proximity, or relative nearness, to Earth, would then allow the space between to fold, so someone could travel from one point to a far distant point without occupying the space between.

He never heard from NASA but was asked to apply for several positions over the years. He turned them all down, going the way of nearly all others whose relative comfort and security kept them grounded where they were. I don't fault him for that. It doesn't mean he isn't as brilliant as the next highbrow and was always endearing in a Gilligan sort of way.

Sometimes being *more* is a choice that involves something other than ambition. I understand the nature of contentment far better now. Risk-taking and derring-do always shines on the page or the screen, but the simplicity of life calls us to safe harbor, where we might find ourselves at peace, and enrich the world about us with the calm, loving kindness of certainty.

The fourth of July was fast approaching. I had survived the first month, and now became aware of just how quickly the days were passing. Now I wasn't so thrilled. I would leave Mel behind. My father informed us that there would be fireworks in town when it turned dark. I wondered, not aloud, of course, if these were comprised of jars of gasoline tossed up in the air and detonated with a shotgun. Maybe there was some red, white, and blue food coloring in the gas for oomph.

The fireworks were surprisingly entertaining. In a poor, or moderately poor area you either get colossal fireworks and shorten the program, or you get mediocre ones and make it last, just as in life. The village squires opted for the former. The entire program lasted an hour. There was a ragtag band playing patriotic tunes and a speech from the mayor about how the greatest country on earth was going to Hell. There was a reading of the Bill of Rights by the President of the local Daughters of the Confederacy chapter, and there was six-and-a-half minutes of fireworks.

Every afternoon I thought of Mel's kisses as I walked to the pond. I also thought about other aspects of her anatomy I have touched with my body but not my hands. Perhaps this should be remedied. I was still deathly afraid of going too far and risking a good thing. I also began to admire my handiwork in passing, the painted house and the aroma of freshly-cut grass. These are the things that comprise a sense of satisfaction and purpose. For lack of a better term, I, too, was content, and it was as unexpected as it was obscure.

What occupied me the strongest was the fear that I could still screw things up. That's what happens with apprehension. Our own actions sabotage something worthwhile, and once done we may even feel relieved we don't have to worry about losing any longer. I had never been confident in the unfamiliar.

I was there first again that day. I still expected to show up one afternoon realize she wasn't going to come.

I'd grown accustomed to swimming naked, and had to admit it felt good. The pond had warmed a great deal but was still cold enough to shrivel LeRod et Reel. I had a ritual for every time I arrived first. I'd hold my breath and blow it out as I sank to the bottom. Then I lay there face down in the cold until I was forced to surface. Sometimes when I resurfaced I'd see her approaching. That day was one of those days.

She always greeted me with a smile or wave or funny face or some combination of these. I have seen her quiet and thoughtful but never sad. That day she stuck her tongue out at me and dove in. She surfaced halfway across. I saw this as a sign that she didn't want any romance. She paddled around and lapped the edge until she stopped a few feet from me on the opposite wall.

"Feels so good today," she said.

"You, too? Wonder why that is?"

"It's perfect," she answered. "Hot but not a cloud in the sky and the water's not too hot or cold."

"Yeah, the pool I use back home would be like bath water by now."

"And good company," she added.

"Yeah. You are still the strangest girl I've ever met. But incredible."

She floated toward me but stopped short. "How am I strange?"

"You skinny-dipped that first time and you didn't know anything about me."

"You walked up on me, remember?"

"But you didn't cover yourself or ask me to look away or anything like that."

"I didn't believe you would hurt me."

"I wouldn't. But you didn't know that."

"I know things. I see things. I hear things. I know what kind of heart you have."

I don't know if I blushed, but I was not used to flattery. "Maybe. But you couldn't have known for sure I wouldn't take advantage."

She smiled broadly. "I'm stronger than I look and could probably outrun you. Plus, I know where to put my knee if I need to." I smiled at that and she continued. "Besides. You brought me here."

I didn't understand. "How did I do that?"

"You fixed the pond."

As I was still processing what she said, she swam into my arms. She held me with unseen strength. I felt balm in every pore. I turned my head to kiss her. She responded. Again, this was more embers than flare, and I could not believe my good fortune. Then, tragically, the monkey jumped and there I was. I pulled my hips back but that only made things worse. Now I was poking her belly. I should have shouted en garde to her navel. I pulled back again and got clear, but she held me firm and it was uncomfortable. I knew I couldn't stay in this position long.

Then she reached down and took it in her hand, gently, without any pressure. It was all over now. No way could I avoid making a dispshit of myself.

"It's okay," she said softly. She let go and looked at me. We were so close I could see nothing but her eyes. They were deep, fathomless, understanding all things without collapsing under the weight. "Come with me," she said.

She climbed out of the pond and waited. I was reticent about this because junior was still saluting the flag. She didn't move her eyes from mine. She didn't make a face or rib me. She took my hand and walked toward the shade near where her clothes were piled. She snagged a beach towel on the way and spread it out. She lay down and pulled me with her. Once there, we lay on our sides and kissed.

My anticipation was manic. Even a little scary. Now that, beyond a doubt, qualified me for the pansy hall of fame, but it's the gospel. She didn't seem to notice and pulled me closer. Sex may be a natural process. We could probably figure out that the key goes in the lock and had to be jiggled to work. Foreplay, or anything you want to call it, is not natural. Far from it, especially if there is more than one step to it. I slid away from her and began to work my lips around her tiny breast. All the while my hand stayed low. She stroked my hair and my cheek. Everything was far more perfect than I expected, and less furious.

"Come lay on top of me," I heard her say.

I did. She saved me from further shame by guiding it toward Nirvana. I heard her groan and stopped.

"Did I hurt you?" I asked.

"You're fine," she answered. "Go ahead."

I have thought about this a lot, and still don't know how to describe that first feeling. I already felt a tingling and the pressure around my poker was perfect. I had never felt anything like it. Every nerve alight, every sensation elevated. As I began to move I made sure to go slow. I figured that might be my only saving grace. She locked her knees against my hips and squeezed. Inside her I had found a solution to every mean thing.

Sadly, however, I couldn't last. I slowed more and tried to hold it but after about forty-five seconds I felt a glorious tension in my marbles and then the release in several huge spasms. It seemed to go on forever until finally it stopped, and my outer self began quivering. I moved to withdraw but she held me firm.

"Stay," she whispered.

So I did, and after a few seconds I began to kiss her cheek to her ears. She brought my head to rest against hers and stroked from my hair to the base of my neck. It was the second best feeling I'd ever known. After ten minutes of gentle petting she reached down again. A miracle occurred. I became stiff again. Ah, youth.

This time lacked the hypersensitivity but was still ambrosial. And this time I was able to go on and on. This time I felt her tense. And with a single gasp she shuddered, then was still. I didn't know if I was supposed to keep going or not. I definitely did not want to stop. I thought she would tell me if she wanted me off her. I kept on. She locked her ankles around my waist. I let go again and the feeling was electric all the way through to my gut. Then I rolled off. She did not let me go and I did not want her to let go. We rested face-to-face again, so close we shared the same breaths.

"Thank you," I said. I was a little hoarse but managed to speak softly.

"You belong to me now," she said.

Such an odd thing to say. I didn't care. She was right. I did belong to her and that's the way I wanted it.

"Should I bring a blanket from now on?" I asked seriously.

She chuckled low in her throat and gave my neck a sharp squeeze. "My, aren't you confident."

"I didn't mean anything by it."

"Shush," she said. "Just let me feel you for a minute. And yes, you can bring a blanket. A mattress even."

Far too soon, I watched as she moved into the trees along a path I could not see. I remained somewhere in the upper atmosphere, but my primary thought was how to snatch a blanket without it being missed, and without being interrogated. I relaxed to an airy amalgam of pleasure and heat. I still felt every bit of it, every tiny touch in every moment. I hoped for many delicious returns.

I took a hot shower before bed. I had not gotten back into the water after our adventure and wanted to wash off. A shame, really, as the faint, musky odor lingered, a prized secret. I searched my closet for an extra blanket but found none. I would have to check the other rooms when everyone was gone. I knew I would figure it out.

We had sex every day after that first time. I would love to say I got better at it. I sure thought I did. Mel never seemed disappointed. I had no frame of reference. I found an extra blanket on the top shelf of the closet in my parents' room and hid it in the barn. Only on certain occasions did I see the hunger in Mel's eyes. This was not the look of need. More like a petition.

An hour, maybe two, was all the time we ever had together. Once, we coupled three times during those two hours. We never left the blanket. We spoke with our fingers, our lips, our bodies. We never declared anything. Yet whenever I would ask to see her at any other time, or at any other location, she always made excuses. And I always let it drop, afraid I'd push her away.

Mel was already in the pond when I got there. As soon as I jumped in she put her arms around me and hugged me tightly. Then she buried her face in my neck and stayed there.

"What did I do to deserve that?" I asked.

She nuzzled me and whispered in my ear. "You treat me like I'm a real person," she said.

This was puzzling. "You are a real person."

"To most people, I'm just a girl."

"You're not *just* anything."

"There's your answer."

"Well is it okay if I'm really glad you're a girl?"

She wrapped her legs around my waist and Shorty snapped to. "I'm glad I'm a girl, too."

Then she kissed me. I'd always thought that this kind of relationship would be dangerously passionate, that it could be no other way. Ours was not. In ours there was heat, still incendiary, but would not flame up then die. She seemed to know me instinctively.

The first drop of rain hit me in the head, more than a drop, actually, a plop. The sun was still shining as if unconcerned, so I thought it would pass. Then the roof caved in. Water fell as if the top of the world had been pulled back. I saw no storm clouds. Still broad daylight. But the thunder rumbled and we scrambled out.

"Grab your stuff, I said.

She grabbed her clothes and a towel. I grabbed mine and the blanket. I began to run toward the barn. I realized we were both naked. We covered ourselves in the front as we ran but didn't stop to dress. The door of the barn couldn't be seen from the house. I did a quick look over my shoulder. She was right behind me. We dashed through the door and I pulled it closed and barred it. A thousand-to-one shot anyone would show up, but I wasn't taking any chances.

We looked at each other dripping wet and laughed. I dried her hair. She rubbed herself down then wrapped the towel around her. I did the same then hung our clothes on a couple of nails. I grabbed the blanket.

"Come on," I said.

I led her to the loft. It was dusty but breathable. I spread the blanket on the floor. The boards were hard underneath, but not as bad as if we didn't have the blanket. We lay side-by-side with the towels loosely covering us. It wouldn't be long before our skin ceased to be cold.

"Listen," Mel said softly.

I did. The rain beat a steady cadence on the roof, loud, but somehow soothing.

"Music of the storm," I said.

"Poem of a summer's day."

"Good for sleeping, too."

"The best," she agreed.

"You wanna take a nap?"

"No," she said, and moved her hand to my groin.

I think it's already been established, and multiple times, that I'm a moron. When we joined, I was so afraid of her getting bruised by the floor I barely moved. Finally, she said "It's okay."

I had edged a tad away from utter ineptitude by gaining slight control over my glands. Mel seemed to appreciate it, her arms and legs tightening as the moments passed. I still had no inkling as to what she felt or her own satisfaction, but I waited until she locked her ankles around me and hoped for the best.

I held her with her head on my shoulder and listened to the rain.

"I have to go in a minute," she said.

"If it's still raining?"

"Don't have a choice."

"Why?" I asked.

"I'll be missed," she said, "and there will be Hell to pay."

I knew she wouldn't explain further. I would often think about where she was, what she did, whose rules she followed. Maybe someone mistreated her.

I got up and followed her down the ladder. "Why don't you let me walk you home?"

She hugged me and kissed me sweetly. "Maybe before it's over with," she said.

How unfortunate it is we are aware of those lesser grains of our becoming only when we are made aware of our own mortality. Our reasons for being can change so dramatically we forget the more inconspicuous steps whisked clear by time. It is the lot of every sensitive soul to wander the corridors of recollection with a sense of faint despair even when memories are flush with promise, if only because they are gone and will never come again. A thousand startling, glimmering events cannot dissuade the backward look of a sentimental heart.

I watched through a crack in the door as she headed toward the pond. Once she was out of sight I closed the door and returned to the loft. I lay there and stared at the cobwebs clustered on a rafter and listened to the ballad of the rain. The next thing I remembered was waking up two hours later.

I knew beyond a doubt why I had never read romance novels, other than having it spread around school and getting me killed. This wasn't true love. True love exists. *Amour* can even be more romantic than the greatest novel. True love encompasses all of life but doesn't have to weather misfortune to prove itself. True love is when two people are devoted to each other, and choose to remain devoted to each, and enjoy each other's company. No one in these books ever says, "Will you go to the drug store and get me an enema?" Or "Will you look at this thing on my foot?" Or even "Does salmon patties sound okay?"

It probably wouldn't be very entertaining if these books did relay those incidental truths, but what people are really buying is fantasy love. That's okay. I get it. Everyone fantasizes about everything. But if we must fantasize about love then we are far poorer than we realize. There are qualities of love that exist beyond our imaginings, tiny, seemingly irrelevant morsels that create and embellish life. When my mother asked me to ride into town with her, I went eagerly.

The manuscript was neatly packaged with a typed label. I still thought the whole thing odd, but I had come to believe that there was something at stake for her with this book beyond anything she'd felt before. Maybe she believed I was her good luck charm. Even so, why such impatience.

"I still don't understand why you aren't waiting until we get home," I said. "It would probably get there the same time."

"You mean because it'll have to wait for the Pony Express here?" she said.

"Or gets sent to God knows where before it lands in New York."

"Once it has postage and is in the box, it's over for me. I'll worry about it. I'll hope. And if they take it I'll have to do some rewrites. But I've done my part. I've done the best I could—well, everything can be better, but you know what I mean—I've given it as much juice as I have."

"I'm starting to get excited, too," I said. This was meant to be sarcastic but held more truth than I would admit.

"You're pulling for your old mom, huh."

"That and I own a piece. We get home, I start looking at cars."

She smirked. "I wouldn't count on that just yet."

"Hey. Anything with my input is bound to be great."

"True," she said. "We looking at Lincolns or Cadillacs?"

"Stingray," I said. "Convertible. A black one."

There was a smidgen of angst flitting about my head, like August gnats, but that is the beauty of this age—to unknow the unknown in an ignorant state of grace. Only in hindsight, that delicious and terrible robber of life, does meaning matter. I knew that my emotions were far more powerful than my rationality. Yet perhaps for the first time, I could think in a clear-minded fashion without diluting it with raging fears and paralysis. I would force myself to relish each remaining hour without spoiling it with uncontrollable doubt. Subjecting Mel to any kind of morbid countdown would rob us both of relish. Besides, I could always fall apart later.

Mel and I had made love with unspoken longing. We were in the shade and neither one of us wanted to move. Mel had developed this habit of resting her hand on my package. It didn't hurt or anything. I just thought it strange. After a few times, it began to feel natural. I'd asked her at least five times if she was ready to get in the water. She had said yes each time, but we hadn't moved. She was so soft I didn't mind the heat, though my stomach was sweating.

I asked her a sixth time if she was ready to get in the water. This time she said—

"How do you think your life will turn out?"

What? Dear Lord, I have to think now? "I don't know," I said finally. "I haven't thought about it."

"Sure you have. You've thought about it a lot."

How long would it be before anyone else knew me so well. "I'll finish high school. I'll go to Ohio U. Somewhere in there I hope to figure out what I want to do and try to prepare for it."

"I know," she said.

"What?"

"Storyteller. You will be a storyteller."

"You can't make a living as a storyteller," I said.

"I don't know about that. I just know that's what you will be."

I didn't know how to respond. "What about you? What will you be?"

She didn't answer for several moments. "I'll be Melanie Bowers, just like I've always been." She stirred. "We get in the water now?"

"Sure."

As I lay in bed that night I thought about what she'd said to me. Maybe at some point something inches to life within us that is more attractive or creates a new mindset. Maybe other things wither, like the cocoon of a larva, and we must devote time and energy to healing and emerge wiser or more sensitive or more in tune with the feelings of others—or more bitter or damaged, or simply less alive. All I knew was that turning sixteen didn't mean as much to me as it had at the beginning of the summer. Nothing did.

I surprised myself. I wasn't depressed. I wasn't effusive, either, but I didn't mope around. Somehow, I believed in possibilities. Sometimes they come out of nowhere. Sometimes they shine, as magnificent as they are unearned.

Mel and I had promised each other the impossible. We wouldn't say or do anything to treat this as a parting. She was waiting for me. She smiled and waved as she always did. She took me by the hand and led me into the shade. The sex was sweet and satisfying as it had always been. If there was any variation it was that I caressed and kissed her forever. I did not enter her for a long time. Once done, it would be over. And I didn't want it to be over.

We laughed as we splashed around. It was August and the water was pleasant even to ten feet deep. But sink below that and the chill of the spring was still there. The spring still flowed, creating shifting currents near the vents. I don't know how many times the water had cycled, had been completely refreshed, or even if that had happened at all. Perfect was perfect.

One day, the water would sour with algae and insects, and this unblemished pool would be just another memory. But not that day. That day it was precisely pure, an emblem of its most unequaled self.

I held Mel's hand under the water. We hadn't separated beyond arm's reach. There was no such thing as a proper good-bye to someone who had remade everything. Without ever declaring a love for each other, we had discovered a transcendence we had never sought. At the time, I didn't have a clue about how truly special this was.

We went to the shade again without speaking. This time there was an awful yearning about us, but this, too, was surrounded by affection.

When we finished, we lay side-by-side, staring through the upper limbs of trees. As usual, she had her hand on my genitals and this time I had my hand on hers. Only my hand moved. I lovingly stroked and kneaded that fuzzy patch as if it was a beloved pet.

"You ever coming back?" she asked.

"Of course. As soon as possible."

"Can I use the pond while you're gone?"

"Sure. Treat it like it's yours. But you know in a few weeks it will be too cold to use."

"I know."

"The screen on the window to the left of the back door doesn't latch. We were supposed to fix it but we never did. It's wedged in there pretty good, but if you ever need to get into the house just pull the bottom of the screen out. I'll make sure I unlock that window after my dad has gone through and checked all of them. You would need a ladder though."

"Okay." Then she added, "Don't say good-bye, okay."

"Am I allowed to say this is the best summer I've ever had?"

"Yes."

"Am I allowed to say you're the most wonderful person I've ever met?"

"Once," she said teasing. Then, as quickly as it all had begun…"I have to go. I'm sorry."

I wanted her to make an exception. I wanted her to choose me over whatever else she was supposed to do. I didn't. I knew she would have stayed if she could. I believed I was being level-headed, but inside I thought I was going to throw up.

She stood and moved toward her clothes. I followed.

"I'm going to leave the towels and the blanket here."

"Okay," she said meekly. She pulled up her shorts. She pulled the top over her head.

Once done, I reached for her. We held each other close, almost as if we were dancing. Then we kissed, a long, slow-burning kiss. When we pulled apart we didn't let go. No tears fell but her eyes gleamed wet. She reached and kissed me a final time, then turned on her heels. I watched after her as she neared the tree line.

"Mel?" I called after her.

She turned and looked at me.

Suddenly I didn't know what to say. Everything had been said but I couldn't let go. "You just don't know," I muttered.

That incredible smile blossomed. "I know."

We had a quick breakfast and finished loading the car. My mother was getting in a last swing as my father did a final check through the house. I stood by the car door with this indescribable feeling, as if I were coming undone, as if at long last, something critical was at stake for me. I knew I risked breaking the spell but couldn't help myself. My father appeared at the door.

"Sorry, but I need to do something first." I said. "Give me a half hour, okay?"

Both parents eyed me as if I'd sprung a leak, but I took off at a run toward the pond before they answered. I figured there was a shortcut to the road, but I didn't find it. I snagged bits of flesh on the branches but made it quick enough. I jogged down the road to the driveway. Fortunately, there was no one outside to ask me my business or anything else to slow me down. The dog napped. I slowed to a walk, not because I didn't need to hurry but because I needed to catch my breath and didn't wanted to stand at the door like huffing like a boob.

The yard was a weed patch and the walkway had been overcome long ago. I knocked without hesitation and a worn, haggard woman, old beyond her years, came to the door. I stepped back to show I was no threat.

"Who might'n you be?" she asked.

I could see the resemblance in the teeth and the set of the eyes.

"Eddie Markley," I said.

"You the ones been at Skinny Markley's farm all summer?"

"You mean Woodrow?"

"He was always Skinny to us."

"He was my grandfather. My grandmother died. My father inherited the farm."

"I heard she passed. Sorry. So what do you want?"

"I wanted to see Mel."

She looked at me as if I'd assaulted her. Her entire face seemed to shrink. "Go now," she said tersely.

"I only need a second. I just want to say good-bye."

Strangely, her lip quivered slightly. "Boy, if you don't leave this instant I'm calling the law." The she turned to go inside. I took another step back.

"Aren't you her mother?" I called after her.

She turned and gave me the same odd look, though now it lay beneath a mask of torment.

"She was my baby sister," she said.

I had fallen into a deep, empty space. "I'm sorry?"

"Are you that hateful to come here and stir such bad things up? She was my baby sister. She drowned fifteen years ago in that very pond on your land. Go on now, git!"

The door closed and the bolt caught. I was across the road before I could even comprehend what she said, much less her meaning. I didn't remember moving or any physical elements around me. I wasn't even sure I still breathed. Mel had drowned when I was a baby? My Mel? This was insane. This was impossible. This wasn't some ridiculous ghost story. She was flesh and blood. I knew this without any doubt. I had savored her flesh, rested beneath her touch.

Suddenly everything inside me broke at the same time. I began to sob, and so violently my ribs hurt. I could barely see but I kept stumbling forward, feeling that if I stopped I would die. I made it all the way to the barn oblivious to everything but all-encompassing pain. I paused and wiped my face with the hem of my T-shirt. I fought with every ounce of energy I had to pull it together. They were waiting for me. I put on my sunglasses to hide my bloodshot eyes.

I got into the car and muttered thanks. As my father pulled away, my mother looked at me. "You're as white as a sheet, Eddie," she said.

"I ran all the way," was all I could manage.

I leaned my head against the window glass and closed my eyes. Hopefully they would think I was trying to sleep, though I couldn't sleep even if this was somehow possible. The terrible tandem was in full rebellion. When we crossed into Ohio they were fast asleep. My dad looked into the rearview mirror.

"Hey, Buddy, I've been meaning to ask. Whatever happened with the old pond?"

I nearly broke down again. "I gave up on it."

My father paused.. "Just as well. Girl used to live around here sneaked in all the time and swam. About the time you were born. One day she drowned. Daddy found her. Said it nearly killed him. Pumped out all the water and cut up that tree to plug it up."

I could feel my throat close. I was shattered and rested my head against the window again, pretending to sleep.

I don't know how I made it through the school year. How does a kid process something like this. I don't remember a lot of details. I certainly didn't tell anyone. Sometimes I would hide and cry. This was the only way I could survive. I hit the off switch, hung out the closed sign, completely shut down. I played dead, became a non-entity.

I kept myself occupied every moment of every waking day and thought of nothing for fear those fragile seams would split far too wide to ever heal. When any stray thought would wriggle in I read and listened to music. I dove into my courses and became a good student. But in my dreams, I swam with a phantom.

The next year, I made sure I had a summer job lined up that would keep me home. I became an intern for a graduate ornithology student. Who the Hell gets a PHD in ornithology, anyway? I spent ten weeks traipsing around the woods with him cataloging birds and their habits. My parents would take the imps to the farm. It took some convincing, but at sixteen-going-on-seventeen I could fend for myself.

It would be years before I could get past the grief and look dispassionately at the reality. I had spent the summer loving an entity that couldn't exist by any human reckoning. I couldn't spend my whole life wondering how such a thing was possible. I couldn't alter the truth of it, or even recall those days without savagely torturing myself. I lost something in myself for a time—the will to dream, perhaps, but I didn't kill myself, either. There is value in the passage of time if one dares to look ten feet past his own shadow.

I always made some excuse to stay put. It got easier. I went to Ohio U and majored in American Literature. A pointless major, I know, especially from a prospective earnings standpoint, but as it turned out, this didn't matter. Serendipity had cast her lovely gaze in my direction, perhaps some divine equilibrium for stealing my soul.

My mother's book became a best-seller. Now, a best-selling mass-market paperback, with the complicated reserve accounting, and pitiful per-copy royalties, wasn't exactly easy street. Mom ended up making about seventy-five thousand dollars. Even so, that was ten times the average salary at that time and much more than my father.

True to her word, I got my cut. Naturally, it didn't come in all at once but with my part of the advance I bought a brand-new Honda S-90 motorcycle with my mother's admonition not to break my neck ringing in my ears. I saved the rest. She suggested we try a real partnership. She would continue to crank out the smoochers and we would write the more involved books together. She was spread pretty thin but flourished in this new opportunity.

We went back and forth about a nom de plume the entire time we wrote the second book—about a missionary kidnapped by the very people he was trying to help, eventually falling in love with a native girl and gaining the trust of the tribe. He chose to remain there and lived as they lived. We narrowed it down to one name each and in the end settled on a combination of the two. We became Elspeth Loveland Walsingham. Bess for short.

The second book sold better than the first, and by the third book the first edition was published in hardback. We got some foreign language rights. Who knew there were so many lovers of romance in Thailand? Circulation grew. Our readership grew. The fourth book was sold to ABC who made it into the worst TV movie in history. But by the time I graduated from college, four-and-a-half books in, I was making a decent living, and Mom gave up writing the boilerplate books for good and all.

Years later, when she wanted to slow down, we reversed roles. I became Bess and she became the consultant. She's still with us. She's ninety-three and has kept all her faculties, though she is slower and smaller than she used to be. My father retired at sixty-five. He died of pancreatic cancer when he was seventy-two. Over the years, I've fought to remember every noble thing about him. Maybe he made it into the far ether after all.

I did not return to the farm until ten years after that first summer. I came in the spring and I came alone. I went to the pond before I unpacked. The pond was covered with leaves and grit, but when I stirred it, the water beneath was crystal clear. I saw no sign that she had ever returned. I honestly believed I would know if she had. Regardless, I had it pumped out, plugged with concrete, and filled with dirt until it was level with the surrounding land. I planted grass and in a few seasons not a trace of the original pit could be identified.

Here is the truth of it. I have lived a fulfilled and contented life. And as I said in the beginning, I'm in a good place right now. I'm just afraid that one morning I might wake up and not know all about myself anymore. Another thing, this story is a part of my legacy. I wouldn't have made the effort if I hadn't wanted to tell it all. But make no mistake. This was and is my story and should a million people claim it, it will still be mine. Always.

Why does any of this matter? In the mid-sixties, before the hippies, Woodstock, and the worst of Vietnam, before Charlie Manson and the men on the moon, there was a kid who spent a very real summer loving a puff of smoke. Where she was, or is, and how she returned to life in her original form, I never knew. I stopped brooding about that long ago.

I know why she came. I freed her just as I freed pure crystalline water from the earth. She returned because something waited for her.

I was merely a beneficiary of her presence. For the first and last time, I knew life enchanted.

I spend as much time on the farm now as I can. With technology constantly improving, I was able to research Mel's entire family. I learned nearly everything about her life before the accident. I visit Mel's grave and do my best to keep it up. The reality was deadening at first but is oddly comforting now. When Mel's sister died, there was nothing left of her immediate family but headstones and words. It's just as well. I only want to remember that summer as we were, uninhibited and with no regret.

The farm is a lot different now. I updated the house and made it livable for someone who doesn't want to rough it. All the old fences were torn down and replaced with a single perimeter fence that encircles the entire property. I had to tear down the barn due to neglect but kept the tobacco shed as an homage to the past. Those ragged old boards must be petrified or something. I had an arborist come in and thin the woods, so I could walk through the pines on new grass without getting poked with a branch. A waste of money, sure, but I wanted my signature on the old place.

Oh, and I kill every damn snake I see.

Now, I sit in the swing and sway up and back. It's not the same swing. That doesn't matter, either. I had a strip of carpet installed beneath it. I dragged my feet so much I skinned the paint off and got tired to repainting. I write in this swing. Modern technology again.

On one of the rare occasions when I was asked to address a group of aspiring writers, a darling girl not yet a truly intellectual being, asked, "What is your fondest memory?"

Who asks that? What an asinine question.

I knew instantly, of course, even though I hesitated. Surprisingly, I found relief in reply.

"It was a scorching summer with a girl I loved with all my heart, and the pond we swam in—skinny-dipping. Neither exists any longer. But then, neither does that boy."

Amid a sparse chorus of titters, I suddenly felt that old familiar thud inside my gut, and recalled how painful is love when there's no happy ending. Hell, no tomorrow for that matter. Some things I hope to God I never forget.

Then I kicked the swing into motion again and opened my laptop.

Bess calls.

Three

JUNIOR'S AT THE Y

This is the transcript of a cassette recording from 1986

Hello Franny, my sweet girl.

I know hearing my voice is peculiar and maybe a little hurtful so please let me explain. See, I've been doing this ever since we got married every five years or so. First few times I wrote it all down. This recorder made it easier. Ruben kept the tapes in his law office under lock and key and got rid of the old ones every time I made a new one. Whichever one was the last he would give to you. I told him to wait six months so maybe the hurt wouldn't be as fresh.

There are things I shoulda told you all along but I guess I was afraid of what you'd think. There's also things I probably should have said more often but still wanted you to know.

This one—I know it's between 1986 and 1990 and I am between fifty-seven and sixty-one years old, and something's happened we weren't expecting, so I am dead, which is a damn shame, pardon my language. Too young to die no matter how you look at it.

No way for me to know what it was—heart attack, stroke, accident—of course. I know it wasn't a disease that would have gone on for any length of time or I would've had the chance to redo some of what's said. It's a mess, I know, but I got my reasons, if you bear with me.

By now you've already seen the will and all that and know I left you in pretty good shape. The farm is paid for and there's plenty of savings and more to come. Butch is a good store manager and pretty honest, and except for the time he looted the Red Man for that turkey hunt to impress his in-laws—and who'd a thought he'd worry about such a thing married to that big ol' woman who's allergic to the broom handle and the dust rag and put those kids in daycare two months in so she could watch the Price is Right and sit on the phone all day—but all in all, the store'll be just fine.

So...as I was saying, Ruben didn't charge me extra for this, which is hard to believe in a lawyer, friend or not, but I've done for him a time or two over the years. Paying that worthless girl of his to work that one summer has to be more than the good Lord could've expected from me anyway. Not to mention she ate her way through about a hundred dollars' worth of Slim Jims without chipping in a nickel.

There is a lot I want to say, so I'll get to it. But first I have to tell you the worst of it. I promised myself I would. It's one of the main reasons to do this tape thing. I should've told you in person, but I guess I'm more a coward than I let on. It has weighed on my heart all these years. Now, it's got nothing to do with you. And it's got nothing to do with other women or drinking or any kind of carousing. But it's still awful. Worse than awful. Bad awful.

(pause, background noise, then a sigh)

I know I've told you I love you thousands of times. I meant it every time. But there are reasons why I love you I've never said, and I think maybe I should if I can find the right words.

You made me believe like I had won something. A big something. I wasn't much use in school, Daddy's whole family was no account, and I really didn't have many prospects starting out. I believed you were my reward for staying clear of trouble and being a decent man as much as I could. Weren't much chance for me to win anything any other way. So's no matter what came after, I still had you—a reminder that I had really good luck at least once.

Now you might be thinking, if you were such a prize, why wasn't that enough for me? Why'd I have to spend all my time and effort at some broken down old gas station? Other than making a living, of course. Well, a living was enough of a reason in the beginning, money being as scarce as peaches in December. Weren't no good jobs to be had when we was that age.

But it was mine, Franny. I would love to say it was for us, and in a lot of ways it was, but any man with a heart pines for something all his own. Maybe it's something simple like a little piece of land, or a house with a nice yard, or a truck. For me it was not being anybody's working man. I wanted to be on my own. God forgive me, but I wanted that almost as much as I wanted you, though I can't say I ever actually loved it. But it was a part of what I wanted, and after that, I made sure to never ask for anything else.

June twentieth, nineteen-fifty-five. I know you remember. You looked like a little china doll in that dress. Something from a story. Not even real. Your daddy never believed in me. I know that, and there never was any hard feelings. And he never said nothing to make me feel bad. But I knew he had grown up with Uncle Pete and Delbert and knew that Daddy was a rounder. Guess he figured I was the same deep down.

But there you were. And without saying too much since I'm not there for you to smack, those three days in Atlanta after our little wedding in the old church were like heaven. I'd never felt anything so good in my entire life. I was always afraid I'd smush you during relations, please excuse my being blunt, but I got over that pretty quick once we got started. Enough of that now. I know I embarrassed you. Silly talk from a silly man.

Remember living over Addie Blood's garage? Three rooms and a bath. You in that tiny little hole while I was out there pumping gas. But you did okay. You made it homey and pretty. I hated those days when they were happening. I remember feeling so bad that that was the best I could do starting out. Now, I look at them like I look at the Army—something I made it through and overcome, I guess you could say. Something I lived through that won't ever come again. Lord, we were all of what—twenty-four?

I know I hurt you many, many times. Took me a long time to figure out what bothered you with you being so quiet. But I got to recognize the signs. If you squinted just a tad, or huffed once out loud or through your nose, or cleared your throat before you smiled again, I knew I'd said or done something foolish. I know I was dead wrong about babies. That one still hurts, too.

You wanted to have kids and I kept saying wait until the business was going real good and we had a house and a stake. But that wasn't all of it. Maybe not even half of it. I didn't want to give you up. I knew being a mama is a full-time job and I wanted you all to myself. So there's the truth. I wanted you all to myself and I'm sorry.

Was thirty too old? Did I make you wait too long? All I know is that baby tore up your insides so bad before it died and you couldn't have any more but I honestly don't think waiting those extra few years made any difference about that. Lord, I hope not anyway. You were tiny and he was big and they didn't figure that out until it was too late to do anything about it. So I hope you never held the waiting against me, even though it meant we were a no-kid family. I know a part of you had to be disappointed, and I know I'm to blame, and I thank you for not saying so out loud or treating me like I was just a selfish man.

We did okay, didn't we? I knew life couldn't always be good. I was at least *that* smart. Life has a way of turning on people like me who get more luck than they deserve. So the day I hear about I-sixteen going in my heart goes flat. When was that, sixty-eight, nine? I just knew I was a goner. That highway was going to do me in. I started thinking that maybe a dozen or so years in business is enough for any man. What chance did I have to keep the station going? I mean, the roads were going to be all torn up. We weren't even sure the Y would be there anymore. Junior's at the Y is a pretty stupid name if there ain't no Y. Oh, it was a holy mess of mud and dirt for all that time. When it rained I had to wade through slop just to get in the front door.

But the Lord was ready to teach me about having real faith. The people in town still came out. They still bought their gas. They still bought a snack. They kept me going. Maybe part of it was because I let people loaf and kill time without running them off, even if they were in the way. But my good luck held. When they said an exit ramp was going in right past us, so close and easy to just loop around, I would've done a jig if I'd known how. Added two more pumps and a big sign all lit up a mile up the highway. Redid the building. Added a few more shelves. Made nearly as much money in cigs and pop than I did in gas, especially all those Yankees who were used to paying through the nose to smoke.

Even after such a mighty revelation of God's goodness, I backslid. Seventy-three. You remember. Damn A-rabs shut the oil down and people were scared they couldn't get no gas. And I panicked. What was it, even numbered license plates on Monday, Wednesday and Friday, and odd-numbered on Tuesday, Thursday and Saturday? People in lines to fill up. But I only ran out of gas once. Came close a few times. Got down to the suds coupla times, but only hit a dry bottom once.

Now who the Hell ever thought we'd have self-service for gas, pardon my language? Glad I didn't have to predict the future. Glad I had those six acres of pines out back, too. Land wasn't worth burning down. But I could build on it. Made the store five times bigger, had twelve pumps—all you-pump-it—the repair shop and tires. Added the Dairy Queen not too long after and it made money hand over fist. Yeah, in some ways those smart-alecky OPEC boys made me a rich man. All under bright lights you could see for miles. Open twenty-four hours. Thirty employees. I'm not bragging. It's like I said before, the Lord and good luck had more to do with it than I ever did. Whatta the kids say...I's blown away.

I didn't ever have to get dirty again if I didn't want to. Bought us our place outside of town. Built that gazebo down by the pond. Put away a goodly amount of money every year. Didn't owe nobody nothing. Could've kicked back and not hit a lick at a snake and still had more money than I could spend if I lived to be a hundred— Well, anyway, you know what I mean.

You remember all those nights sitting in that swing in the gazebo, sipping some of your good coffee and looking out at those foolish ducks? I got to where I loved the quiet. No need to talk when all was right with the world. Nobody could ever say that Junior and Frances Betts didn't have it made.

I still get offers for the store at least twice a year. Usually from one of those big oil companies. The last one just over two million dollars. We could have retired. Hit the road in a camper. Go see the Grand

Canyon and California. Yellowstone. Mount Rushmore, maybe. Or just go to Myrtle Beach for a few weeks and sit under an umbrella. But I couldn't. It wasn't the money. It wasn't even that I was afraid of going stir-crazy or bored out of my skull.

It was fear of bad luck. Why mess with good luck? When good luck comes around you don't shoo it off after a few years. You ride it until she hits the wall. Then you duck and run, maybe, but you don't quit til.

Good luck stayed with us from Day One, mostly. Oh, there were worries when a new convenience store would pop up down the road, or the exit ramp was being worked on, or gas went sky high and everybody thought it was my doing. But folks still came. Still bought our gas. Still had the cheapest pop and smokes around.

I walk through the store and it's always "How are you, Mr. Betts?" "Have a nice day, Mr. Betts." Shoot, the only people who call me Junior any more are you, the few boys around who knew me coming up, and the people at church. Even they call me Jerry in front of new people.

But I would have loved for us to have done more of the things we could afford to do. Because now?...

Yeah, we owed it to ourselves to go on a cruise or fly up to New York and splurge some just for the heck of it. Now I reckon it's up to you to sell out or not.

I sometimes think about how I never asked if you were still happy. I always promised myself I'd spend more time finding out some of these things, but I didn't. Maybe I'm too scared of rocking the boat when so much is going right. You always seemed happy.

But were you really happy, Franny? Did you love your life? Everybody says it's a new world for women. They have their own hopes and dreams aside from everything else. Did you ever feel I held you back?

I know how smart you are. Did you want to go to college? You could have. You're the only person I know who can work the Sunday paper's crossword puzzle without cheating. Was there a job you wanted? You could have done most anything. I was so happy the way things were I never asked. People today talk about personal fulfillment. I never thought a lot about it. I was lucky to have a job I liked. Did you ever feel unfulfilled? I know it's a little late in the game to bring this up now but I need to make sure you know I'm trying to cover as many bases as I can. I know that if you made sacrifices for me it was done from the heart. But if there was anything you wanted to do we didn't do, I'm sorry if I got in the way.

I liked that you were quiet and never said much. You wouldn't have gotten a word in edgeways with me anyway, ha-ha. But did I ever make you feel that you couldn't tell me what's on your heart, even if it wasn't all rosy? Did I take for granted you were satisfied without ever asking? Did I get in the way of any of your hopes and dreams? Did I love you wrong sometimes?

I can only say this. You made me. Whatever good is in me is because you put it there. Whatever kind heart I have is because you made it easy for me. Whatever kept my temper from ruining everything is because you healed me and wouldn't let me be discouraged. This isn't just talk. I'm nothing like I was before I met you. You gave me a chance to be better than I was cut out to be.

You have a different kind of faith than me. How did you know I wouldn't turn into something ugly? That I wasn't just mean? How did you know that I would work to give you a home and wouldn't let you down? How did you know I was the one? You didn't just help me. You loved me into being a decent man. I know you've seen me impatient or stomping around irritated at something. You've even heard me yell. But not very much. How did that happen when before I met you I was mad all the time? I'd even grit my teeth in my sleep and wake up with a sore jaw.

I'd cuss as soon as say boo.

I wasn't a better man *for* you. I was a better man *because* of you.

Oh, Franny. I know I will come home after I'm finished with this and take you in my arms. And you won't know why. Now you do, and I'm so sorry I'm not there to hold you again.

Well, I reckon I should quit stalling and get down to the rotten apple. I'm not putting it off deliberately. Just let myself get sidetracked. There's a big sin hangin' over my head and I need to get out with it.

I wanted to say something about when you were sick. It was what—ten years ago? Now that's hard to believe. Seems like last year. Never smoked a day, never breathed anything but fresh air, except around your Daddy, and you get emphysema. How does something like that happen? Three weeks in the hospital. On oxygen for months. Even now I know you have times when you can't breathe and go for the air tank.

Here's something I never said. I was scared to death. I was afraid for my life, Fran. Because without you I knew I wouldn't make it. I couldn't take losing you. God help me, I'm glad I went first.

After we were married, I started believing the station would take care of us and that we would be able to live without worrying where our next meal was coming from or picking the meat off a chicken back to put in a stew. I had you. I had a life. I got saved. We had some bad times, I know. Our folks passed over the same five-year stretch. I put most of our early money in re-doing the station not thinking it might not fly. Maybe it was my famous boiled peanuts that kept customers coming, ha-ha.

I live free knowing we don't have to struggle with bills and things. My mother struggled 'til the day she died. She couldn't afford food some of the time. I ate oatmeal for supper more than once. That's why I joined up right after I graduated. War or no war. All through basic I ate like there was no tomorrow. Sarge asked me if I had a tapeworm. I'd never had my fill before.

I was just thinkin'. I sure hope what happened to me wasn't anything bad you had to see. I hope it wasn't a wreck with you in the car and you're all laid up. I didn't think about that. Now I'm worried. Oh Lord. Maybe I ought to erase that part if I can figure out how.

Like I said, if you decide to keep the store you can always talk to Butch or Pauline to get the straight skinny.

(pause, background noise)

Oh. Pauline. I know there's been talk ever since I promoted her to head cashier. People don't want to believe in Christian charity when it comes to a boss and a woman he hired. Three kids and no husband. She didn't have a pot to piss in.

Forget about how much I love you. Forget about all the years we've had. You think I'd be so stupid as to risk my luck for a woman who wears too much makeup and bleaches her hair? Not to mention come Saturday night she's out juking and looking for a man. Besides, she earned it. Never late, never lays out, never has to report missing cash. She has done as much for my peace of mind about the store as I ever did for her, that big tattoo on her arm or not.

You know, sometimes I think I had another life all laid out for me. I was supposed to be a no-account like Daddy. Maybe my best shot would have been to stay in the Army. I wouldn't have gotten a decent job otherwise and I would have been bitter about it. I wouldn't have found the Lord because I'd have felt I'd been hoodooed. And if I ever did find a woman to settle in with, she'd of probably been hard and mad just like me. And if we'd had kids they'd be hard and mad kids. Who knows, I might have ended up in jail. I know you think I'm just carrying on. I admit it's not like me to say such a thing, but it's true.

Having good luck makes you think it'll go away if you don't think you deserve it. So I tried to stay humble and be grateful.

I just went back a long ways thinking about the Army and those boys I knew in the war. We lost some of them at the Imjin River. Hadn't thought about that in thirty years or more. That was before I got pulled off for special duty. I know I never talked much about it. There are reasons for that above what you might think. But, anyway—

It was right around Easter, fifty-one. The Chinese were coming after Seoul. Everybody knew that. It was the Brits mainly held the line. Not many Americans in the beginning. The Chinese were going to throw a quarter of a million soldiers at us. In the beginning, it was mainly the twenty-ninth brigade that had to hold 'em. The Brits, like I said, and Belgians. I'd never even heard of Belgium before then. I'm sure those boys were wondering what they were doing in Korea with no stake in the fight except to keep South Korea from going communist. They were outnumbered by a ton and the fighting was fierce. But they held the line for three days. One of those English battalions, still the twenty-ninth, I think, got stuck up in a place called hill two-thirty-five. They were surrounded. Now that was a real do-or-die war. I don't know how they got out of there alive.

The whole thing didn't last long and we got orders to move out again. Part of the way we had to retrace our steps and passed that hill again. My unit was near the lead and we were the first ones there. And I saw it. Now it wasn't like there was a thousand men or anything. But there were thirty or forty bodies laying out there on that slope. The sun was out and it was actually a pretty day. And there were these dead men scattered around. If you're in the Infantry you see people die. Some pretty close up. Sometimes you could take aim at a particular helmet and actually see him drop when you fired. You don't think anything about it right then. Too much going on. You find something else to aim at. This was different. These men weren't going home. They hadn't seen the night pass or the day come. They looked like little bushes or something laying in that grass. A detail was already there to gather them up and thank the Lord we kept moving. But I couldn't shake it for many a day. Glad I didn't have to look in their faces. All of a sudden, I knew that it was real, and so many wouldn't be going home except in a box. Don't know why it hit me like that. I had been in close battles before and would be after that, but usually we were on the move before all the dust settled. Those boys who had family fretting and praying over them every day, and soon they would know the godawful truth.

Anybody who has ever been in a war, no matter who or what he is, will tell you the same thing. Unless there's somebody on your doorstep trying to hurt you or take something from you, it's not worth it. Never. No war has real glory. No hero really wants to be one. God bless England. They are due something for that.

I know I'm not college-boy smart but sometimes my thinking goes way out there. I thought the other week about how much of yourself do you think you keep in heaven? Heaven's supposed to take away all the bad, right? So wouldn't you be a completely different person? Would you even know yourself? Would you remember some of the important things that happened if they turned out wrong? What about lessons and such you learned from such things?

And why get rid of all the bad, anyway? Guess that sounds crazy, too. But sometimes it's the bad things that make us good. Nobody wants to hold onto things like meanness and spite, but what about sadness? What about being sorry for things? What about being afraid?

Sadness sometimes tells me how much I love you. I guess you could call it yearning. You have given me so much it makes me want. Now I know I have you and all I have to do is pick up the phone or come home, but a part of being grateful is fretting about losing something. Just like luck.

They say the point of having life at all is to get to heaven. So be it. You and I were far from perfect, but what good would it do if we ended up as strangers? I sure don't want my soul to burn in Hell, but if I can't think or have feelings or know what it was like to live in this world, or what it was like to have you for a wife, then who I really was don't mean a thing. And if who I was decides if I get to heaven or not, then what's the point of being somebody else, even if the Lord says you're a better man now? You give away everything that got you there in the first place.

Well...like I said, I think of the oddest things.

I really don't think about death that much but I do think about my soul. I've had some close calls before now, too. Not just in Korea. Car slid off a jack once while I was kneeling beside it. This was before we rebuilt and got the new lifts. I could've had my head under the wheel well.

People always say they're afraid of dying. I guess that's so, too. I'm not afraid of dying. I'm afraid of death.

In my thinking, we either have to look at life as something we survive or what time we have to really be alive. Cause what we have is all we've got. I am so grateful for life. But looking at it real close, you have to start giving it a different meaning. I'm just a plain man who owns a convenience store. My whole world is you. We've been together for thirty years. Some of those years I barely had time to say hi and bye. But no, that's not near long enough. I could've honored God without being on earth at all, if that's all he really wants. And I could've enjoyed life so much more if I'd had more time and less distractions.

So if God Almighty is going to use our life as the way to decide if we're worth it for all eternity, it seems to me like we've all been shortchanged some.

Like I said, I have foolish thoughts. We are born into this world knowing nothing, believing nothing, doing nothing. We grow up and we learn to do for ourselves. And we spend many, many years making a living and trying to get by. If we're lucky we have someone who loves us and the chance to be a family. We deal with all the bumps and bruises along the way. But no sooner do we get a good running start than our body comes back on us bit-by-bit. Then, our mind starts to go. Then, we're gone. That's why death scares me. Too little life here. Too much to ponder over about what happens after.

I got lots of regrets. I've made more than my share of mistakes and acting contrary to what the Lord wants. It would be a true blessing if most of these things were swept away. But what if some of these mistakes taught me about trying harder to be the person I want to be? They have done me some good. You can't argue about that. Because if you take away the nudge, you take away being somewhere you ought to be. Like your car breaking down and you find out your brakes were shot and you could've hit something hard before too long. So you know to look after your car more. If you don't break down, you might not know your brakes is bad until you run off the road or up against a truck.

I still feel bad about the cat. Now I know that having that thing brightened your world. I don't know why that animal hated me so but the feeling was mutual. Sneaky thing would hide and wait 'til I walked by and blindside the back of my legs. Yeah, it hurt, and made me just about poop my britches more than once. Got on top of the refrigerator once and slunk down. Then when I reached in to get a pop it clawed my head. I must've jumped a mile. Good thing it didn't pounce from up there or I'd have wrung its neck. Had me a nervous wreck, looking at every chair and plant and at every corner wherever I walked. Had me wearing work boots at the supper table. That cat was from the Devil. Can't believe you named it Fluffy. Should've been called Hellcritter or something. Even so, I was truly sorry about what happened. I know you had to think I did it on purpose. You said not, but it had to cross your mind because you knew me and that cat were mortal enemies.

I had no idea it was sleeping in the dryer when I threw in those towels. I was just trying to help out with the chores. Didn't make any noise, at least that I could hear, when I pushed that button. Maybe it broke something and expired before the drier burned it up. I don't think it suffered. Least I hope not.

You know I don't like the new pastor much. Maybe I'm really backsliding and will end up being a flunky in heaven for saying that, but it's true. It's not that I don't get anything out of his sermons. I do. He's a good preacher. What really bothers me is that the committee went to hear him and came back saying he was the best thing since cheese grits, so we made him an offer. And he said he just didn't feel *called* to be here. So they looked around some more but couldn't find anybody else who stirred them the way he did. Then we all had a meeting and sweetened the pot a goodly amount, plus a car. All of a sudden he heard the call! God was just holding out for more money.

Well. A man has a right to earn a living but if he wanted more money he should have said so in the beginning and kept God's call out of it. I'm not sure God calls anyone to be anything. Was I called to own a gas station-convenience store-car repair-tire sales and ice cream place? I doubt it. People have a knack for things and enjoy things more if they're lucky enough to find something like that, but I'm not sure God cares one way or another about what a man does for a living if he follows the rules and tries to be a good person.

Like in the Army. One of the guys in our platoon was a crack shot. The best I ever saw. He could hit a quarter at fifty yards, I kid you not. We had a tank column come at us once and shells were going off everywhere. We had anti-tank, of course, and were dug in waiting for air support. Well a couple of halftracks with machine gunners in the back tried to slip around behind us. So we turned and started firing, but it was like shooting at a brick wall. Then this old boy lined up and shot out the tires of the first one. Bam! Bam! Bam! Bam! They were supposed to run flat but he tore them up good. They bogged down. Now they were sitting ducks. They could still fire those guns but we got the jump on them. Blew those things to kingdom come. Air support came in and took out the tanks before any of their feet hit the ground. And everybody close by came to give this boy a pat on the back.

I really didn't know him very well. We weren't buddies or anything. As we lit out we ended up side-by-side. He doesn't even look at me, but says real low, "I hate guns. I've always hated guns. If I make it out of here alive I will never touch another gun as long as I live." Actually, what he said was, "I hate effin' guns,", but I wasn't about to repeat that. Cussing has never been one of my problems, mostly. So here is this man could shoot his rifle like it was a part of him, and he didn't want no part of it. I don't think God made him a good shot or didn't make him a good shot. I can't really see God would give a man such a gift whose main purpose was to kill people.

I don't mean to harp on about the preacher, but that wife of his sings so loud and shrill it hurts me in the privates. Okay, maybe that wasn't as funny as it was mean, but just because you're a good preacher don't mean you're beloved. Lots of men who came before weren't nearly as silver-tongued but everybody loves them.

He does do a good baptism, though. Almost like he was on a stage with a spotlight. Once he blesses and dunks you, you know you've been blessed and dunked. I half expect to hear violins after.

Well, here I am, still waving my gums, knowing when I'm done I'll take this to Ruben, swap it for the old one, and won't even think about it very long. I won't remember half of what I said. It'll just sit there for the next five years. I know it's peculiar. Can't help it. Something you need to know and I want to make sure you do in case I don't get around to it in person.

(pause, sighs)

I know I keep saying I need to tell you something important. I know you probably think I'm stalling. I'm not. Just made a coupla left turns is all. I said it was bad and it is and is the hardest thing I've ever done. Well, enough of that. Time to ante up.

You know how I was a plain old infantryman in Korea? That part's true, of course. I got that shrapnel scar on my back to prove it. But that ain't all of it. Toward the end of my hitch in fifty-two, I was part of a small group who were sent on secret missions near enemy lines, and even across the border into China. See, everybody from Truman on down was really peeved about the Chinese butting in. They had like a million soldiers and we spent more time shooting at them than we did at the North Koreans. China had gone Communist and they wanted Korea to be Communist, too. Anyway, it wasn't their fight but I reckon they didn't think it was our fight either.

I don't know if you know anything about germ warfare or not. After the first war there was a big ruckus 'cause gas hurt so many people who survived the war only to die slow from it. People in the second war was sneakier about it, but it still happened. Well, it was pure taboo in Korea. We weren't really doing gas in the same way anyway. We were doing diseases. We were trying everything from VD to measles. Not all of it worked. Couldn't get smallpox right. Had a kind of he-man chicken pox but it was mostly cholera, meningitis, and different kinds of the flu. It was all deadly. I'm not saying it was right but we weren't about to buck orders. We would spread out across enemy lines and sneak near Chinese camps and set off little canisters. Wasn't no smell or smoke. We tried to follow the wind. We wanted to be sure the wind was going toward the enemy. Sometimes we would have to sit for a couple of hours. Sometimes it would rain and we scrubbed the mission. We wore masks, naturally, and gloves and rubber leggings. Looked like one of them movie monsters. And when we got back they hosed us off with some kind of spray and scrubbed us down. Hard. Hard enough to chap skin. But it was worth it to be safe. Like I said, nobody else knew what we were up to, and there were only six of us. None of us ever knew if it worked, or how many got sick, but we figured it was doing some good or they wouldn't keep sending us out. I reckon we did about twenty missions the last three-and-a-half months I was there. Then I was mustered out. I never saw or heard from any of those fellas again. Tell the truth, I didn't really care if I did or not.

So I did my part. I was told to never speak about it to anyone and never did. I was never asked about it either. Later they even got the United Nations in on it, but that was for dropping stuff out of planes, which I never knew about anyway.

You and me got together soon after I come home. You were such a pretty little flower. My heart ached every time I saw you.

I know you remember that Ernest Smith was going to sell me his little gas station at the Y for twenty-five hundred dollars. It was a great location even then, where sixty-eight veers off from thirty-six. I'd hire a mechanic—maybe somebody who'd been in the war—and then I'd have gas and repairs. Add another pop machine and I'd be set. I already had almost four hundred dollars saved, some of it even before Korea.

So I talked to Earl Jukes down at the bank. He said no. Flat no.

You never knew that but it'll make sense in a minute. It tore me all to pieces inside. Here I was, an honorably discharged soldier with a good down payment in his pocket and they turned me down like I was trash. Maybe I didn't come from the right family but I'd seen that bank piss away money on far worse ideas. Don't know if you were living here then, but old Ed Shepherd had a soda shop in town for a couple of years. This was when I was a boy and he was about twenty-five. Root beer floats for a nickel. Couldn't beat it. But he went under. Blamed it on the depression but FDR was already in by then and we were on the mend. He was married to Sarah Johnson and her Daddy owned that peach orchard so the bank lent Ed the money. Maybe old man Johnson made good on it but you see my point. The bank either thought Ernest's station was worth less than the twenty-one hundred dollars I wanted to borrow or that I was too stupid to make a go of it.

Lord, it's been what—thirty-odd years? I brooded on it for over a month. I knew all along I should've just let it go but this idea had ahold of me good and tight.

Just before I came home from the war, me and this other guy were moving these canisters we'd been using when he fell out. Fainted dead away. One of the men who came when I called for help was some kind of doctor or scientist or something. They said not to worry he'd be okay. I asked after him and the man in the white coat told me a few of those canisters were filled with knockout gas. Trouble was it didn't work. Not in the open air. Too thin. They'd used mixtures with ether, nitrous oxide—which is laughing gas—chloroform, and stuff with dozen-letter names. Nothing would work except in closed up spaces. So we were going to take them out in the middle of nowhere and blow them to kingdom come. Good riddance. Well, I did the dumbest thing. I kept a couple of them. I don't know why. Later I thought it was probably the Devil already working on me.

You might not remember this either, but before they remodeled the bank it had this humongous old fan in the back wall. That thing must've been five-six feet across. When it was on full blast, like in the summer, it sounded like a freight train. Don't know how they could talk to each other.

I spent a little time around there. Snooping, you could say. Getting the layout. Looking at streets here and there, just to see what I could see. Every Friday morning, they got an armored car.

My guess it was for people to cash their paychecks and I saw that around nine-thirty, ten, only Jukes and two tellers were there, and they cranked up that old fan like clockwork.

So...well you may have guessed where I'm headed with this.

One Friday I just decided to get on with it. There wasn't any way I was going to come to you empty-handed like that. I leaned over and uncorked the first canister right behind the fan. There was so much suction it nearly pulled my sleeve in, so I knew if there was anything in it, it went in. Then I did the other one for good measure. I was worried about those high ceilings and that big empty space.

Was I afraid somebody would get sick? Yeah. Was I worried somehow they'd trace it back to me? Sure. But right then I was more concerned if it'd work. Weren't no cameras then and nobody really on the lookout.

After a few minutes I went around to the front door. I was lucky nobody had come to do business yet. I stuck my head inside, holding my breath. Sure enough, Earl was laid out across his desk snoring with his mouth open like just off a bender. The two girls were on the floor behind the cashier's counter. Both of them had been counting money and it was scattered everywhere. Not to mention stacks piled up waiting to be counted. I went back outside and huffed good air as much as I could. Then I held my breath again knowing I had to be quick, too.

I knew if I took twenty-five hundred, Earl might get suspicious. If I took twenty-one hundred, he might remember I had a down payment. So I took three thousand. Didn't think they would suspect me. I also knew that the police would wonder why a robber wouldn't take it all, but maybe they would figure whoever did it was in a hurry and got scared. I was sweating like I was in front of a firing squad anyway.

First part went perfect. Nobody came in. Nobody saw me. I walked out like I owned the place and around and up the hill, the money in my pocket. I talked to Ernest the next day and asked if I paid him five hundred good faith money would he let me make payments. He said he would. That let the holdup calm down before any big chunks of cash floated around.

The second part was a miracle. Since it was a sin and a crime, I knew it was Satan's power. But a man from the power company said it must've been a gas leak and Earl never reported any of the money missing, either. Later I realized that he didn't want the bank examiner to do an audit because maybe he had been up to some funny business himself. He was never caught, so maybe he wasn't guilty but the main thing was, I was home free. I paid Ernest five hundred dollars a week until it was paid off, and still had nine hundred in case things got slow. I hired Bobby Sickle who had been a mechanic in the Navy, paid him a good wage and a commission on all his repair work.

Business was good. I sat out front in that old rocker until somebody pulled up and I would go pump the gas, check the oil and clean the windshield. I loved it. Didn't much like working six days a week, especially after we got married, but we made do until we were doing good enough for me to hire somebody else to help out.

I'm not trying to justify what I did but doesn't a man who's lived clean his whole life and goes to fight in a war and gets his shoulder sliced open to the bone, and risks his life with God knows what kind of chemicals, deserve a stake? One simple stake. That's all. Do or die. Fail and you're working for the railroad or the flour plant. Why didn't the people who have money see that? Isn't gumption worth anything?

Now. You see I was scared to tell you. I was scared to death you wouldn't love me anymore. I know you had faith in me and trusted me to make everything work.

I know, I know, it was a godawful thing to do. It still eats me up. Thought about it near every day since.

Of course, I never forgot what I'd done, but the business grew and grew and I was happy in a prideful way that Earl and his cronies had been wrong about me.

Years later, when I started going to church with you, I knew Brother Wellman was working on me. I know you and him were in cahoots but I know my immortal soul was in danger. That lesson about the fallen woman about to get stoned tore me up. Sure, he was talking about how those men were all phonies. But he also told her 'go and sin no more'. I knew right then that I didn't want to go through the rest of my life with that sin hanging over my head. I was saved and forgiven. Now, the hard part.

How was I going to get the money back to the bank? I didn't think spilling my guts out to anyone but the Lord was necessary. Maybe I was wrong about a lot of things but I didn't think I should have to go to jail, either. I thought if I paid it back somehow we'd be even. But I had to make it right.

I figured that money at ten percent interest—a lot more than the going rate—over all those years was about twenty-one thousand dollars. I about ripped my britches. Not that we didn't have it, but how in the world was I going to get that much money back to the bank without anybody noticing?

Well, I decided to do it straight up. I started putting back cash a little at a time so nobody would notice. Didn't want to have to go into any of our accounts. It took me the better part of a year.

I went up to the night deposit with one of their bags I had never used before. I knew they had a camera by then so I wore a sweatshirt with a hood. You couldn't see my face or tell it was me in any way. To throw a little more sand in there, it was a Georgia Tech shirt, who everybody knows I hate and wouldn't be caught dead in one of their shirts. I put the bag in the regular slot. I never used that deposit slot, either. I used the bigger one you got to have a key for.

I thought there might be something in the paper or some kind of story. Or even loose talk and scuttlebutt. Maybe Earl's boy and that second-time wife of his kept it. Went to Mexico or somewhere to lollygag in the sun. The point is, my soul was finally clean, except for keeping it from you, which was dead wrong.

This is pretty cowardly, I know, telling you something this bad this way, but the truth is, I don't want to have to see how you look at me now that you know what I did. I just couldn't stand it if you looked at me disappointed. So now you know. That's that.

Well, dear dear Franny, I'm going to close this out. More than likely I'll have to do it again in a few years anyway. Everything I said is from the heart. Most everything but my big sin is easy to say. People say there are no guarantees in life. That's pretty true. But near everybody will take love when it's offered. No man will deny himself if there's the slightest chance of happiness. No man will turn away from gold once it's within his reach. You were those things for me. I always hope I would marry someday. It didn't fill me with joyful expectation. It was just there, like getting a job or having a place of my own.

Something that's a part of life that just happens. So I figured I would love and be loved just enough to get by.

Before you, my ideas about love tended to be more toward the practical and not much about the romantic. I don't know what makes someone love another. It may be a smell that sinks in deep and you don't even realize it. Maybe it's a voice or a way of speaking, or the way somebody laughs. It could even be that you trust your head more than your heart and it feels like love. What we all want deep down, and never believe is possible once we get to a certain age, is the love that heals all the damaged pieces, and keeps us steady as we go on. A love that teaches us without words. A love that makes us feel we belong where we are and have a purpose. A love to keep us all our days.

I don't know how you wanted to be loved. You never said. But as for me, thank you and God bless you. I never lost those wonderful feelings. Thank you for the wonderful years you have given me. Thank you for never holding back, even when I was cranky. Thank you for being sensitive to my moods and my ups and downs. Thank you for listening and for always being there. Saying I love you just doesn't seem enough. It's like saying your pumpkin cake with the cream cheese icing is okay, when it's so good it's miraculous.

I am so glad I didn't have to spend these years without you. You kept me from believing the world was a sad place. You are the prize I didn't deserve.

Thank you for saving my life.

I am, as always, your devoted husband.

Junior

September thirtieth, nineteen-eighty-six

Four

The Goat Man

Nick Hirsch was a reasonable man, more than willing to let the other fellow have his say even when it chafed him like an over-starched collar. He was also a stickler for accuracy, and when confronted with its inverse his eyes would grow small, his lips would tighten into a thin smile, and he would beg off with a quick glance at his watch. No point in being rude simply because somebody else got it wrong. The world is full of blowhards and dopes and he figured it had always been that way.

Case in point, he was lost, and the fathead who gave him directions was due a size nine in the caboose by all rights, though Nick also knew by the time he got back into town he'd be over it.

Even so...the world may be rife with divine mystery, sure, but only a fool ignores the thin line between fact and fiction. Right or wrong may be subject to interpretation, like the tenor of a man or the beauty of a woman, but some things simply *are.* Laws. Death. The strike zone.

What was subjective, at least in his mind, was viewed as such without alibi. Nobody likes a know-it-all. He, too, was intimate with the yin and yang of life in the sad old world.

He loved September, that golden season when the balmy sun soothed the soul. He hated August, air thick as fog and heavy enough to smother. He loved his job, baseball, sweetest game ever invented, a game of perfect pauses. Hated wasting time, as in being lost. He loved a good chat, especially about baseball. Hated braggarts, pinheads who didn't know the subtle but elegant difference between a brushback and a beanball. He loved intricacy, that incorruptible ballet of motion and the utter grace of the hop on the infield. Hated the dust on country roads, suffocating on red smoke, as he was now, factually and unhappily near the ass-end of Oneonta, Alabama.

Back to Huntsville and try again tomorrow. And August was just around the bend.'Had God thought twice, he might've backed off on the clay and iron oxide that painted the ground red in south Alabama, squirming to the surface like bait worms after a rain. All Nick could do was roll up his window and bake.

He pulled off the hardpan and swung the nose of his '38 Ford back the way he came. He unbuttoned his top button and loosened his tie. He undid his cuffs and rolled his sleeves up a few laps. Not many would bother with a shirt and tie in his heat. Nick wouldn't have it any other way. To him, being a professional was on the black side of the line.

He stuck his pinky in his left ear and scratched, irked that it itched when it wasn't good for anything else. He cursed his luck on the inhale and thanked the fates on the blow. So what if he was deaf in one ear? What did that have to do with shooting Krauts or Japs or Wops. He could hear everything he needed to hear and here he was, a 4-F. No decent woman would get within ten yards of a 4-F, even if he was near the top of slim pickin's. Then again, he wasn't getting shot at, either.

He was lucky to have a good job, even a payback job, also thanks to his ear.

He'd been a rookie for the Indians, a third baseman with a magic glove and a decent arm. A little light on the stick, but he was coming around. Sixth big-league game after being called up. First and third, one out. Anything on the ground meant a run. The pitcher had a tell. He flicked his elbow a tad for the gas. Nick tightened his forearms but eased his grip. Waiting. All he had to do was get solid wood on it. Then—

Wham! Ninety-miles-an-hour flush against his ear. He went down like the curtain on a bad movie. They said a bit higher and he'd be dead. He was out cold for nearly a whole day as it was and all the parts inside his ear were busted. He could've still played. Nothing wrong with his arm. Except he was ball-shy now. No matter how hard he tried, he would step in the bucket on a pitch two feet outside. Damn it all! His playing days were air.

So, the Indians made him a scout. No hard feelings. He was still in the game—still on the field, though now in the bleachers.

Many of the baseball stars had joined up within a week of Pearl Harbor. Baseball was forever. Teams needed players until the big boys came home. He liked the job, even the long days on Podunk roads in Podunk towns watching Podunk players. He scouted the boonies. This wasn't even A ball. Some were mill teams with men playing for wages plus meals. "There's an arm like a rocket you gotta see down there," the boss man said. "There's a bat like a sledge hammer over there." Yeah. Okay. He'd check out the arm. He'd check out the bat. But he was still a long way from Cleveland.

Anywhere from east Texas to Georgia, Louisiana to Kentucky. He was to measure the moxie of every piece of white trash with a chaw. He had a good eye, but real talent was rare and putting a man in a uniform, even in AA ball, was rarest of all. Besides, every man with a set was in the war. What were these retreads doing here still playing ball in the first place?

The next day he was off by ten for a three-hour ride to an afternoon game in no-man's-land. He made it eighty miles on blacktop, though there wasn't much to see. Molehills, green and lush and empty, large open expanses with small houses set back against the trees. Could've been Tennessee or Kentucky. Then, invariably and inevitably, he would hit old dusty, past shacks and shanty-towns of coloreds, withered old women covered neck-to-ankle, rocking on their sloping porches, ugly dogs and a few gaunt cows, small patches of corn, cotton, or tobacco. People worse off than the Russkies being hammered by the Fuhrer. He wondered if they even knew how bad off they were.

He saw a sign for the field and followed the arrows. The field had been carved out of the pine woods and orange dirt, one of Uncle Frank's WPA projects during The Depression. Nicky hadn't seen a house or a building within five miles of this place.

There were fewer than fifty people there. No one was there to greet him. No one even knew he was coming. Better that way. Get these boys playing natural as if nobody was watching. He swatted at a mosquito as big as a mayfly and found a spot in the bleachers. He needed to be right behind home plate to get a real feel for the arm.

He knew he was in trouble inside thirty seconds. First, the arm had a gut the size of a beer keg, which was probably how he got it. Nobody said a man had to be skinny to play for the Indians, but he had to be able to last nine innings, every third day, for a hundred and forty games. Even as a reliever he needed to be able to run in from the bullpen without having a stroke. The second reason was worse. They were playing a colored team. The fact that they could play each other at all was a miracle but manpower was short. Nick knew he couldn't get a real feel for any prospect against Negroes, unless the arm was whiffing the lot. Some of these nameless colored boys in shitholes like this were as good as men in the bigs. Now if he mowed down the side there might be something.

Big belly was on the hill. His windup was implausibly smooth. Wait and see. He looked at the scoreboard. It was already nine-to-two in favor of the crickets. Well, he'd had a nice drive in the country at least. Ninety degrees if anything, half the road all over his clothes, his face, his hair. He watched a couple of innings anyway. Just because he loved baseball. He left the way he came without a word to anyone, an invisible figure in a loose tie and a hat tilted over his face.

He was short with rusty hair and freckles. He looked harmless, except he scowled most of the time. Squinting in the sun had molded his face into a perpetual look of disdain—or petulance. He hated looking like an overgrown kid. He was twenty-five, for God's sake, and had earned his manhood, 4-F or not. Well, what could he do about it.

Huntsville was not a big town as big towns go, but it was big for these parts. More importantly, it had a couple of nice hotels, a few bars, and more than a few greasy spoons. If it had been fifteen hundred miles north, without hillbillies or goobers, Nick would have said it was a great place to be. His bed was comfortable, and on the outskirts of town was a dive that had the best chili he'd ever tasted. He couldn't have cared less about the bars. He was a Dr. Pepper man.

Finding good grub and a good bed was crucial. More now that he would be around for a couple of weeks. He had a couple more crackers to look at, a stick and a catcher. He washed his face and neck in the sink in his room and combed his hair. His mop had a natural wave that slid back over his right ear—the good one. He changed his shirt and dusted off his hat. Then he aimed the Ford at the diner. Fully sated, he took a walk downtown. The onions were giving him the gripes.

All the shops were closing and daylight was starting to nod. Air raid signs hung on every lamp post. People clung to the shadow puddles on the walkways but didn't hurry. Huntsville had been a nice quiet town before the war, and as safe as a Baptist church. Then in '41 the government bought five square miles of clay, sand fleas, and pinecones to build three chemical munitions factories. If the Krauts and the Japs ever grew the stones to fly in from the Gulf, Huntsville would light up like the fourth of July—if some bonehead didn't toss a butt in the wrong direction first.

It was muggy as he lay out on his bed for the night, atop the covers in his drawers with a fan rattling in the window. Maybe tomorrow would be better. No reason not.

Another day, another dusty road, another small-time ballgame in sweltering heat. He already had his shirt sleeves rolled up to the elbow. His hat made his head sweat but kept the sun out of his face. Poor odds if the trip was worth the trouble but his job required optimism and he wasn't a shirker. He was hoping to see both players today. Tricky business. Watch one for a couple of innings, drive fifty miles and catch the other one. At least he would be closer to Huntsville when he finished. He saw the catcher first. A stick was easier. Sure, the pitching was lousy on the whole. He'd seen sticks pound the horsehide at every at-bat but couldn't hit an A-baller's sweeper at seventy miles-an-hour. Nick knew he could factor in the pitching for a good stick. There was also bat speed, body control, hitting the ball hard every time, hitting line drives, hitting the opposite way, not over-swinging, and sacrificing to move a runner up. The absence of any two of those things were deal-breakers.

Catchers might seem easy to measure, but weren't. There were a million details. Suppose he calls the pitches himself. How many mistakes did he make? And is a mistake sent over the left-field fence from calling a bad pitch or his hurler tossing up a melon? If he's always alert and has plate presence, look more. If he has an accurate gun and throws out a high percentage of base-stealers, go from there. If he can fool the ump into calling a strike on a pitch two inches outside and not grin about it, give him the high sign.

Everything depends on the eye and more than a few hunches. Work the numbers, too. Too many maybes and the club says pay better attention. Too few and the mojo's gone or else somebody's pissing in the wind. Nick had been doing this for three years, since before Uncle Sam joined the war. He had reported seven possibles. There was usually a trip to Cleveland or Florida, where they had spring training, and a look-see from the big shots. One out of the seven was signed. The lucky one was doing okay until the war came along. Somewhere in North Africa last he heard. One-in-seven in three years may not sound impressive, but it was topnotch in those circles, especially if the prospect lasted more than two years. Nick should have felt good about himself, but no one remembers what happened last season.

He needed to give himself a talking to, stop being a crank. So what if his life hadn't gone exactly the way he wanted? He had played pro ball. He had a good job and a car only five years old. The 4-F still stung, even if the war could've taken an arm—or worse. Yeah, he hated being mean. Whenever his thinking turned sour he always told himself that he was only twenty-five. Plenty of time yet to make his mark. Then again, he was twenty-two when he started, and the years weren't slowing down. Time was on the fast blacktop without a stop sign. No wife, no kids, no real home. No roots. He was just another leaf on the tree.

He tried not to think that maybe he was scared. All that time alone in a car, an unknown man on an unmarked road, and chasing down long shots was no way to live. Even if the good lord himself knew the straight dope and asked him what he was afraid of, he couldn't say. Maybe he couldn't put it into words. Deep down, he knew. He was afraid that the life he had was all he would ever have, and it wasn't enough. Not by a mile.

The catcher looked good behind the plate. Steady glove, good arm, his head in the game, especially with men on base. Good hitter, too. The opposing pitcher might not have been a fireball, but he was ahead by two runs. The catcher was one-for-three, a solid single. He might have had another hit—a hard grounder on the grass at shortstop, but he was too slow. Catchers were nearly always slow from crouching so much.

And that was the problem with this guy. He had a hitch in his left knee. Not many people would even notice, probably no one around here, but Nick knew. The knee was gone. A lot of the cartilage had been ground down to nothing. Probably bone-on-bone in a couple of places. Even baseball fans have no idea just how much damage is done to the legs because of squatting for nine innings. It's an unnatural posture, like driving nails overhead all day. Too damn bad. Nick would like to get one decent prospect on this trip. Make eating all the dust worthwhile. As for the catcher, the knee kept him safe from the draft.

He was lost again. Hell, he was always lost but this time was his own doing. What was lost anyway but sight-seeing? There were rarely any signs on these country roads. There might be a mile or more between houses. He told himself that he would rather drive past the dumps in the worst slum on a paved road than live the high life on the dirt. He only carped to himself, never out loud, so it didn't matter. One road led to another road and eventually he would come to a main road on the map. Now he was on a long-ass feeder looking for the next long-ass feeder. Maybe that's why there was so much boondock baseball in those parts. Not much else to do, and too hard to get anywhere else.

He pushed the Ford up a long hill, dropping it into second and bleeding the crap out of the transmission. As he topped the hill he saw a connecting road a half mile or so away. Lips to God's ear this was the right one. He coasted down the other side, gaining speed so as not to ride the brake. He had to baby these wheels as much as he could. The godawful mileage and sick air was bad enough. He hit sixty near the bottom and tapped the brakes. Something caught and he spun through a sand pit. He ended up crooked, facing the opposite direction. He wasn't hurt. Maybe a little rattled but nothing that hadn't happened before. There wasn't any traffic. He hadn't seen another moving vehicle in half an hour. He backed up a few feet and swung the car around.

A sudden sound assaulted him, enough to make him flinch. Not only the volume but like nothing he'd ever heard before. He'd only been a block away when a brakeman for the railroad slipped and severed a leg. That had been as terrible a cry as he was ever likely to hear. This one was worse, soul-wrenching and stretched past the breaking point and hanging in the air like an air raid siren.

He'd heard a lion roar on the radio. Add that. He'd heard women scream in monster movies. Toss that into the mix. Add the squeal of a P-51 diving down full tilt, just like in the war pictures. Then, what, a wolf caught in a steel trap? Yeah, that, too. Then make it as rough as a buzz saw as it caught the wood flush.

On and on and on. Thirty seconds. Forty-five. The jeebies snaked up his spine and dug in. He let off the clutch and eased along slowly to see if he could figure out where it was coming from.

The next house was on a little rise behind a couple of crooked old oaks, a dingy little shack with shingled walls and a burnt-up stovepipe sticking out of the tarpaper roof. Across a dirt driveway was an old barn. More like an over-sized shed. Half the size of a regular barn with a wide door closed tight. The godawful ruckus came from the barn. He was sure of that.

He was so unnerved his hands quivered like a palsied old man. He dropped the shifter and hit the gas, wear-and-tear be damned. He took a right onto the next road. He was miles along before that sound left his head. An hour later, he still brooded about it, but it finally gave way.

The next field was a shithole but Nick liked it immediately. There must've been a hundred people in the bleachers. Baseball craves a restless audience and edgy static in the air with every thump of the catcher's mitt and the call of the umpire. The players were just kids. Maybe high school players—or just out—who wanted to keep sharp. There was a little hut with a window where this boy the size of a bus sold pop and popcorn. He had a soup-bowl haircut shaved above the ears and looked like a cartoon character. Nick bought an RC and went to find a seat. The only way up was to climb the bleachers but no one paid him any attention, just the way he liked it. No one would know he was a scout anyway because he looked like most people, except maybe he had nicer trousers, a long sleeve dress shirt (the sleeves rolled up), a clean Homburg, and good wingtips. He quickly scanned the crowd. Maybe they would think he was a banker or an undertaker goofing off for the afternoon.

His boy was playing right field. People who don't know any better have said that they stick the duds in right field. Not true. You have to have a bazooka to play a decent right field, cat feet and good depth perception, and the timing of a sniper.

The sun was in his eyes and he tipped the brim of his hat down in the front. He looked at the rusted-out scoreboard. Third inning. Naught—naught. The pitcher was a string bean with a rubber arm that threw slow benders. Batters moved all the way up in the box and still swung too early.

His boy didn't bat the next half-inning but made a running catch behind second base that was a lulu. Not just raw speed, but an instinctive reaction to the flight of the ball. He'd started running as soon as the ash struck horsehide. He was up third next inning. Nick sipped his RC and thought about days like this when the sun was too bright, the air too hot, and the wind dead as Pete. Perfect days. He hadn't forgotten. Stand there in that lime rectangle with the stick and watch for the ball to come out of the sun. That's the trick. Some say to watch the pitcher's release. True and all, but find that instant when the ball straightens out and comes flying out of the light of day, then you've got it. Watch for the twirl of the seams and get the bat square. Nothing like the music of the bat on the ball.

This pitcher chunked heat and had some zip, too. But he had no control. He had two balls on nearly every batter. He was habitually high and tight. Hitters were so gun-shy they would duck on anything box-side of the middle of the plate. Nick flinched a couple of times himself. Bad memories of a month-long headache and a deaf ear for life.

His boy took his practice swings and stepped up. He had a good stance but Nick would've shortened it by three inches. Let him take a longer stride into the ball. His swing was all shoulders and back. The real power is in the legs. He had a good eye. He took the first two pitches. One was inside off the plate but he didn't move. Maybe he'd faced this guy before. Small-time usually means small leagues. The next pitch was on the outside corner, a sneak pitch after a brushback. The boy saw it coming. He lined it between the shortstop and second base for a hit. Problem. If he tried to pull everything he'd hit into a million double plays at a higher level. He needed to learn to go with the pitch—to hit the ball where it is. Time would tell.

At the crack of the bat most of the crowd cheered. Hometown boy. The biggest whoop came from a girl—a young woman, actually—down front. Maybe she was his wife or girlfriend. He'd handled this before and was a pro. Women were always good for info on the qt. He could snoop without anyone being the wiser. Any woman would talk to him without going into the clamshell, and without her man getting hot. Women wanted Cary Grant but would settle for Jimmy Stewart. Not Jimmy Cagney, unless, of course, it was the real Jimmy Cagney. Nick was smart and could put on the dog when he had to, but he would always be short, about ten pounds overweight and with a face like Mickey Rooney. Being a 4-F just put the nuts on the sundae.

Later, his boy charged a single and threw out the runner trying to go from first to third. Another checkmark. Nick waited until the next at bat before moving. The boy tried to pull a pitch on the outside corner and flied out to short center field.

While he was batting, the woman down front shouted, "Come on, Donnie!" During the changeover, Nick moved down front. He made sure he approached in an arc so that she would see him before he got there. No shock in being spoken to.

She had honey-blonde hair, side rolls, bangs, and short flips above the collar. She was smallish, petite, well-kept yet casual, with a plaid blouse, tan trousers and saddle oxfords. She had no obvious blemishes and round cheeks. She was more cute than pretty, more June Allyson than Rita Hayworth. Cutes make you feel comfortable and are squeezable. You want to walk holding hands with June or share an egg cream. She looks like a mom. You want to settle in and cuddle with June. Rita is gorgeous, sophisticated, wonderful—untouchable. You can't imagine her ever eating a hot dog or sweeping a floor. She's out of your league, anyway.

He smiled as he neared and waited until he caught her eye. When she did she flashed a shy smile but didn't jerk her head away. Nick was sure to sit with plenty of space between them.

"Nick," he said, holding out his hand.

"Alice," she said, shaking it. It was a man's shake. Not one of those limp things with fingertips only.

"Sorry to cut in on you, but you seem to know number twenty-seven."

"Donnie Bell. Yes."

"I try to keep up with all the local baseball, but I don't remember seeing him play high school." It was a bluff, but harmless, and nearly always worked.

"He's been out of school a couple of years. We moved here from Texas. He's trying to keep in shape so maybe he can get a tryout in Florida next spring."

Nick nodded. "Makes sense. You his wife, girlfriend?"

She grinned broadly at that. "Twin sister. Can't you tell?"

Hirsch laughed with her. Enough for today. He stood to leave. "He play with anybody else?"

"Just this summer league now. Playing a team from Gadsden tomorrow."

"Away?"

"Here."

"Thanks. He's a good ballplayer. Sorry to bother you," he said. He tipped his hat for good measure, waiting to hear the magic words.

"It's fine," she said.

Donnie Bell had promise. He would have to watch him several more times. Nick never broke the ice until he was at least half-sure. No point building up some greenie's hopes when he just might be taking a flyer, even for a tryout. Nowadays his thoughts always began the same way. Boy is twenty and in good shape. So why isn't he in the war?

The road was in the hinterlands and it was nearly dark. Nick was sure he could find his way. Something about that awful shriek haunted him, gnawed his bones to the marrow. Bits of gravel pinged against his car and he slowed down. Damn thing already had more scratches than a mangy dog. A professional's car had to look decent, too. He made the turn and saw the steep rise in the headlights. He recognized the trees that stood atilt, buried on the slope where the yard ended—defying gravity. He let his car idle to block out as much noise as possible. No way he was going to cut the engine. He needed to git in a hurry if it came to that. He hung his head out the window and aimed his good ear. Nothing but a breeze and bugs, quiet as a hiccup. The old barn was high off the road not more than a hundred feet away.

Then he saw movement. A shadow that didn't belong at the corner of the barn and he'd missed it. He heard a grunt. He'd heard a boar once make a sound a little like that. It was short and sharp, a huff with a bite. Then he heard the rattling of a chain and in the shadows he saw the thing move and instinctively leaned back.

It couldn't have been a real animal. It was long and shaggy, and it reared up like a horse. It was as black as a midnight sky, blacker even than the shadows, though the shadows hid it well. He couldn't be sure but it looked like it had horns. And when he hit the headlights again to beat it out of there, they caught two big, gold eyes, flickering evil in his direction. He moved out and held his breath until he was clear.

He realized he was shaking and that vexed him. He was a grown man, for God's sake. There wouldn't be anything wild and vicious right out in the open like that, pitch-dark or not, chained up or not. Then he snorted at himself. If the boys in the clubhouse could see him now, ripping-your-skivvies scared, they would have something funny to chew on all the way into September.

He hadn't eaten anything except a box of bone-dry popcorn since breakfast. He needed a BLT and a Dr. Pepper. Maybe some apple pie warmed up with a scoop of vanilla. These were long days. He didn't have time for silly adventures. If he did, he'd have tried harder to fake hearing in his left ear and gone to Europe or the Pacific. He sighed out loud. Not even the Navy would take him, and that duty was as loud as all get-out anyway. Who set these slack-happy rules in the first place? Maybe he should have tried the Navy first.

He resisted going a roundabout way to the park, telling himself to stay off that country road. Just wasting time. Just wasting gas. Acting foolish. But he couldn't seem to help himself. He hated mysteries, so he went the long way anyway—drove by the old rundown farmstead—and there was nothing. Nothing chained up outside. No sound. All he saw was an old colored man toting a bucket toward the back garden. Lord, was he that hard-up for a kick? He slowly pulled away, chiding himself halfway to the park.

He still got to the field before the first pitch. The crowd was a bit thinner, but not by much. Alice was there, too, sitting in the same place as the day before. He walked toward her, taking his time. As soon as she looked his way he threw up his hand. She waved back and smiled. No, he wasn't a creep at all. Just a nice guy who liked baseball. He pointed to a spot a couple of feet away from her.

"May I?"

She slid her pocketbook closer to her even though there was plenty of room already. "Sure," she said.

Top of the first the visitors scored twice. Today's ace had a wide ass and a fastball a girl could hit. Nothing came Donnie's way but he looked easy in the field. He was batting third. Leadoff man struck out. The Gadsden pitcher had a hard breaking ball. It looked like a fastball and got there quick but whipped down and away at the last second. Easy to whiff for free swingers. Second batter crouched so low he was almost bent double. Made the strike zone about six inches high. He drew a walk. Donnie dropped the second bat and stepped to the plate. Nick focused. This would tell him something. The coach would make the call, sure, but it was up to Donnie to get the runner to second if the bunt was on. If he had a hero complex he could slop his way to two strikes, forced then to swing away. Power hitters always want to swing away. It's who they are.

Donnie took a couple of hard practice swings and stepped in. His bat was cocked and ready to fire. The first pitch was a teaser, outside. The second was a perfect snapper, looking to split the plate before diving away. Just as it began to tail Donnie dropped the bat and laid down a bunt up the first base line. He played the bat like a glove, pulling it back at contact to deaden the ball. It ended up about a foot short of textbook and the catcher played it. He didn't even bother looking at second. He threw Donnie out easily. Donnie did his job. He did exactly what the numbers said he should do. Two away now, but a man on second.

The second time Donnie came up there were two outs and nobody on. Nothing to lose so you swing like a woodshed whipping. Foolish ninety percent of the time, but every hitter did it. Hard to get a ball diving away from you up in the air with anything behind it. This is where a good hitter would look for it outside and inside-out it to right field. Trying to pull was a sure out. As expected, nothing the pitcher threw was more than two inches over the outside part of the plate. One ball, one strike. The next was an inside fastball, high and hard, to make Donnie take a step back. He did, but nonchalantly inched his way in again, sandbagging the pitcher by pulling his head back about six inches. During the windup Donnie stuck his chin close to the plate, right where he wanted it.

The pitcher got sloppy. The ball broke sharp but when it snapped, it was fat over the plate. Donnie bent his knees and leaned into it. He tried to pull it. He couldn't help it, that's the only way he knew, but he caught it flush and sent it toward the gap and the center fielder had to play it. Good arm, though. Straight as a Kansas mile. Donnie still slid in for a double.

Alice cheered and whistled like a sailor. "Nice lick, Donnie!"

Nick was infatuated. After the inning, he excused himself to stretch his legs. The day was hot but dry as toast. He got a couple of pops and brought one back to the girl. "Thanks," she said, and gulped about half of it. If she burped he'd be in love.

After the game, he threw down a wild card. "I'm new here, too. I would be obliged if I could take you and Donnie to supper."

She looked at him noncommittally but nodded. "Let me see."

Nick watched as she went over and spoke to her brother. He glanced over in Nick's direction. Nick turned away, looking at nothing that might look like something. After a minute, Alice returned. "He promised a couple of guys he'd go out with them later. Besides, he's got to go home and clean up. There's no locker room or anything."

"I see," Nick said. "Maybe some other time." He took a beat. "The offer is still good if you might join me."

She looked as if sizing him up, but didn't take long. "Sure," she said.

Alice seemed the type who would like the café—meat, two vegetables, homemade soup—but Nick took her to a steak house downtown. He had never eaten there, but heard it was nice. He parked, then went around and opened the door for her. She looked at the place as they were going in.

"This place looks fancy," she whispered.

"It's okay," he answered. "I've seen where the cows live."

It was pricey, too. No problem. He didn't exactly rake it in, but he didn't spend much either. Meals, gas, hotels, and occasional entertainment—usually plying a prospect or his mama with movie tickets or a lap around the local department store—were paid by the Indians.

They ordered. Mainline eats. Steak, potato, beans or corn, toast. Coffee for him and milk for her. She would look sweet with a milk mustache. Both were at ease and that made everything kosher. Alice fired the first salvo.

"Do you work?"

Ah. Weighing the prospects. Nick nodded, eyes aglint.

"Yes. I check the tracks for the railroad. Walk a stretch, check for anything that might need to be fixed, then move on to the next stretch." He could lie like a dead dog when he had to.

"Sounds nice," she said.

"How about you?"

"I'm looking into something part-time. Going to start secretarial school this fall."

They were served. Everything was steamy. Alice brought a spoon-edge of spuds to her lips and blew on it.

"So what brought you to Alabama?"

She held her finger up until she swallowed. "Mama's sister lives in Decatur. We got a place just this side of it." She paused and took a sip of milk, drinking it as delicately as you would a cocktail. "Daddy passed. We had a little ranch in Texas but Mama didn't want to fool with it anymore. She sold out and here we are. She's fine. She's set up pretty good."

"Donnie play ball in Texas?"

"Oh yes. His whole life. Born with a glove on his hand. Used to throw a ball on the roof of the barn and catch it when it came off. That roof was high, too. He'd gather up buckets full of rocks about the size of a quarter and knock 'em into the hayfield. Daddy used to holler at him because they'd get swept up and make the awfulest racket in the baler." She chuckled to herself.

"Family is a great thing."

She peered at him across the table. "Yes it is. You got a family?"

"I've got an older brother stationed in England. You won't believe this. He keeps books for the Army. Oh, he gets nervous because the Krauts are still bombing London, but he's pretty safe on the base. What you'd call one-in-a-million duty. My old man works in a tire plant in Akron. Mom is a housewife."

"You think Donnie is any good?"

He measured her a second but it was a straight question. "I'm no expert but he seems pretty good."

"All he ever talks about is 'making it'. 'Making it in baseball'. I try to keep him down to earth. He is most of the time, but when he plays he gets wound up."

The steak was tender and had a peppery flavor he didn't recognize. "He'd improve his chances if he learned to hit it where it is."

She had nearly finished her meal and hadn't wasted a bite. Maybe she had a hollow leg. "What do you mean?"

Now Nick had gotten caught in the middle of a chew. It was only half-chewed when he swallowed. He knew a catcher in the minor leagues for the A's who choked to death that way. "He's a pull hitter. Got power. But when you try to pull a ball on the outside part of the plate you lose all your power. But if you learn the timing, and get into the habit, you can still swing hard and drive it into right or right-center. You ever see him hit a ball to right or right-center?"

She thought for a moment then shook her head. "You know a lot about baseball."

Hirsch shrugged. "Been a fan all my life."

They settled. He finished and pushed his plate away. "How about some pie or ice cream?"

"Might have some coffee."

As soon as the waitress passed he ordered the coffee. The waitress brought it with a short pot on a tray and refilled his at the same time. Then she gathered up both plates and took them away.

"Say. This is none of my business, but how did Donnie stay out of the Army?"

He saw her face redden but didn't know if it was anger or embarrassment. "Long time ago he and some kids were playing and daring each other to do something foolish and he stuck a stick way down in his ear. Burst his eardrum. He's nearly deaf in that ear."

Hirsch gasped a laugh. He couldn't help himself and continued to chuckle as he set his cup down. Alice was openly irritated. She hated being laughed at or taken for a fool. Nick shook his head as an apology.

"No. I'm sorry. You're never going to believe this. I got a bum ear, too. Silly way to run a war if you ask me."

She smiled broadly. "Donnie hates me or anybody else telling that."

"So do I. A man looks like he could take on the world and he's got something nobody can see. So they think he's a fruit or a psycho."

Her eyes twinkled over her coffee cup. "Well I know better."

It was a little more than a twenty-mile drive to Decatur. Alice had excused herself just before they left the restaurant and smelled of lilac when she returned. She was good company, even without speaking. He rolled his window most of the way up to cut down on the noise.

"You ever play baseball?" she said.

"I did," he answered.

"How come you didn't try to do anything with it?"

Hirsch smirked to himself. "I did try to do something with it."

"What?"

"I played in the minors for part of two seasons then spent part of the second year with the Cleveland Indians."

"You're kidding."

"Nope."

"Donnie would pee himself."

Hirsch chuckled at that. "Got beaned. That's what caused my bad ear. Wasn't the same after that."

"I'm sorry," she said. "Do you miss it?"

Hirsch had a stock answer he hid behind anytime anyone would ask. A casual "sometimes". The truth was far more telling. He missed it all. He even dreamed about the noise of the crowd, thousands of people speaking at once and no single sentence heard. He missed the smell of hot dogs and sweat, the lime in the batter's box and the hint of cut grass. He missed the chatter of the guys in the infield. He missed the feel of the ball being snagged in the webbing of the glove. All because he didn't see the track of the ball soon enough. In those early months he would wake stark in the faint hours with a gnawing in his belly.

"Sometimes," he said, now more genuinely. "I do."

Mother and the set of adult twins lived in a small white house in a nice, quiet neighborhood. All the lawns were trimmed and the sidewalks swept. Not a dirty car in sight. Some windows bore a blue star banner for a service member far from home. One bore a gold star banner for a boy lost long before his time.

Donnie was in the street playing three-handed catch with a couple of kids. Nick opened her door and walked her to the porch. She stuck out her hand and he held it instead of a quick shake.

"Thanks for the supper," she said.

"Thanks for the company," he answered.

She reached in her purse and pulled out a pencil and a slip of paper. "This is our phone number. Let me know if you're ever in the neighborhood."

Nick folded it and put it in his shirt pocket without looking at it. "When's the next home game?" he asked.

"Next Monday," she said.

"Maybe I'll see you there."

"Okay."

He walked down the sidewalk, making an effort to move at a normal pace and not skip or kick up his heels. Alice called out from the porch.

"Nicky?" He stopped and looked. "You should be a coach or something."

"I'll think about that," he said, and touched the brim of his hat.

This was the best day he'd had in a long, long time, an age since he last had female company. He kept his cast aloft and his impulses in check. He knew Alice would be soft and warm, with no airs. Her bangs danced when she laughed. How often are you within driving distance of here? Well, actually probably eight or ten days a month, not counting weekends.

He knew she was special. But the farther he drove the easier she shadowed away. His mind kept rolling to some nightshade beast and banshee's call to doom. Before he knew it, he was parked a hundred yards up from the property with a good view up the hill to the barn.

He rolled his window down, cut the engine and sat. It was graveyard still and silent, the night a blanket. He could hear the engine pop as it cooled down. He had just begun to settle, his muscles liquid inside his skin. Maybe he had exaggerated the whole thing.

The sound leapt like a riot of brass. Jagged, punishing, inhuman, and when the wail began to abate, several short bursts sounded like a rifle shot, and as raucous as the cry had been. Nick started so badly his body seized, and he winced. He clenched the steering wheel so tightly his hands turned white. Then it came again—up to the breaking point, then that wicked bark like Old Scratch himself fighting for breath. Two, three, four times it went, almost exactly the same every time. Then, as suddenly as it began, it stopped. Nick held his breath and counted the seconds and waited. The world became as it had been.

The barn door pushed open and the old Negro man brought out the monster on a chain and wrapped it around a post as thick as a telephone pole. Nick involuntarily leaned back as if he stood two feet from it. The creature was as black as death with a shaggy coat. It must have been four feet tall at the shoulder, six feet long as it stood on four hooves, and as sturdy as a heifer. Its bearded face was evil incarnate and two black horns a foot long protruded straight up from its forehead, curving back at the end.

The nearest thing he could figure was a goat, but this was a goat from some other world, some Hellish world. No goat had ever been this big or this black. No goat had eyes that glowed gold at night. No goat had horns that stood like spikes reaching skyward, thick enough to impale a man. And that unholy sound, like all the voices of the damned squeezed in sinister chorus. He started the car and fled.

He wanted to talk to somebody—needed to talk to somebody. He almost stopped at the nearest pay phone and gave Alice an Ameche. He asked the night man at the hotel if he had anything to help him sleep. He didn't. He went upstairs to his room and washed down. He put on a fresh undershirt and dress shirt and went downstairs to the bar. Light crowd on a weeknight. He felt strangely relieved. Maybe it's better to talk to yourself as a fool than to anyone else. He sat at a booth in the corner. He would move if a group needed it. For now, he wanted to sit with his back to a wall.

He ordered a Schlitz. It was brought to him in a chilled glass, a thin layer of ice bubbling as it slid down the side. He never had been much of a drinker. Whiskey could have put him under but he hated the taste and didn't want to wake up sick. He didn't much like the taste of beer, either, but maybe a little lube would help him relax. Sinatra started belting *All or Nothing at All*, and Nick jumped a foot and nearly choked on his brew. There was a speaker in the corner behind him though the jukebox was across the room. He resettled enough to pull his heart down out of his throat. Jumpy as a rookie.

He spent the next few hours scrubbing his mind clean, failing, but relentless. He walked the block. He took a bath as hot as he could stand it until he was pink. He read last Sunday's *Birmingham News* and finally dozed off sometime just after reading that the Indians' eight-game winning streak was ended by the Washington Senators.

The next day he decided to have a quick supper at the café. Maybe call Alice after to see if she wanted some company. It was early for supper, not yet five, but he was hungry. There were people in a couple of booths and at the counter, and in the corner was a trio of old roosters jawing because they had too much time on their hands and couldn't do much else but jaw. He'd met a couple of them in passing.

One of them looked his way and Hirsch waved. The codger waved him over.

Nick went grudgingly with a painted-on smile. He wasn't about to eat his supper listening to war stories from these rusty old liars. The trio was interchangeable in their button-down shirts and suspenders, gray hair with a hint of Brylcreem, except for their expressions. The man who waved him over was Kyle, he thought, pleasant with an affable smile. He was introduced to the others as Nate and Tim. Tim had that watery-eyed, stoic mien, but Nate looked like someone had peed on his shoe.

Nick took a seat and immediately looked at his watch, smiling the whole time.

"I heard something about you," Kyle said. It was a jovial tone.

"That the reason I'm not in the Army is because I'm queer?"

All three laughed at that. "That you was a baseball man," Kyle continued.

"I am. Sort of."

"What do you do?" Tim asked.

"I'm a scout for the Indians," he said. Kyle and Tim pursed their lips and nodded in appreciation. Nate looked him head on, stern-faced.

Nate made 'hello' sound like 'kiss my ass'. "Baseball ain't as good as it used to be. Branch Rickey, Cy Young, Honus Wagner..."

"Moses," Nick interjected, knowing he'd get a rise out of Nate, especially after Kyle and Tim busted a gut, but want to nip the guff.

"No," he added, apologetically, "they were all great players. I would have liked to have been around when they played."

Nate nodded appreciatively and they were all pals again. Hirsch ordered meat loaf with green beans and cabbage. When the waitress brought his food, he was stuck. They all gandered at his plate and he waited for the punchline. It was Tim this time.

"Don't let your meat loaf."

The others laughed as if they hadn't heard it a thousand times and Nick played along. The trio got back to where they had been before, allowing Nick to eat in peace. Most of the talk was about people around town who were up to no good in some way or another. They were worse than yentas. Just then they were onto some pretty young gal about twenty who had taken up with a man at least twenty-five years older. A well-to-do man obviously.

"Made his clams in sheep or some such," Nate said.

"Now she's got an old goat," Kyle added.

They roared again but Nick had a floater in his head now. After the laughter died and the old roosters resettled, he spoke up. "I ask you fellas something?"

"Sure," Kyle said.

"I was looking at a player the other day way out in the country. I was just driving, minding my own business when I saw this colored man in a ramshackle old shack chaining this—"

"The Goat Man," Kyle said, barely above a whisper. Tim nodded ominously, and Nate looked fit-to-kill. The air was unnaturally still.

"That what that is?"

"Cursed," Nate spat. "That nigger and his old lady, too."

Nick hated the word and eyed Nate for a second before Tim spoke. "You hear it? Bad as bad can be. That whole side of the county is all coloreds now and no account ten miles around."

Kyle raised his hand like a deacon at a prayer meeting to become the voice of reason.

"A lot of bad history out there, true. And maybe some voodoo or whatchu call it, too. I's you, I'd just let it be and stay away from out there."

Tim nodded but Nate flushed red and clenched his jaw. "It's a blasphemy."

Nick paused. "How's that?"

Kyle waved his hand again and chuckled nervously. "They got their strange ways and I reckon we do, too. We're all better off just leaving it alone."

"Nigger magic," Nate grunted. "Pure and simple wickedness."

Nick pulled up in front of the tidy white house and parked. He drew a couple of comb strokes through his hair, then bit down on a mint. Peppermint flavor filled his mouth. He wore a crisp white dress shirt, the sleeves down where they should be, a pair of gray dress slacks, and black dress shoes. He looked as good as he ever would. He left his hat on the seat, though he would have been more comfortable having something in his hands.

Alice came to the door in a pretty floral summer dress cut to just below the knee. The hem was wide and flowed outward like sunshine. Not a hair out of place. He hadn't gotten close enough for a whiff but would have bet two paychecks she smelled like bath powder.

She stepped out on the porch and closed the door behind her. "Mama wants to meet you and learn everything about you," she said apologetically. "I didn't think that would be on your hit parade."

"If it makes her believe that I'm on the up-and-up, fine."

"Thanks. Let's save it for the next time, okay?"

So there was going to be a next time. Hot diggity dog! "We walk then?"

"That would be nice."

Grace had kissed Nick on the head. It was a pleasant night, even a bit fresh when the breeze kicked up. Seventy degrees, tolerable humidity.

They walked shoulder-to-shoulder down the sidewalk. The whole neighborhood was picture-perfect, a dog here and there and a few noisy rompers.

"Great neighborhood," he said. "Peaceful."

"If you like that sort of thing."

"You don't."

"No. I do. I don't mind a little night life now and then either."

"But when you're worn out by it you can go back where it's quiet."

"I guess so."

Their hands bumped together and he took hers in his. She didn't pull it away. In fact, she interlocked her fingers. Nick felt it in his solar plexus and let it simmer. Nothing to hurry to or from. Nothing to fret over. No dilemma to chew over.

"So tell me about playing for the Indians," she said.

"I spent most of my time in the minors. My big league days were short and sweet."

"But you got there. That's something."

"Yeah, I did. And it is. Hard to let it go, though."

"I can imagine. I've never done anything that special in my whole life."

"Give it time. You're not even old enough to drink yet."

"Will be in a couple of months."

"I'll treat you. What'll you have?"

She giggled. "I don't know. I've never drunk anything before except beer."

"You'll have to try a bit of everything then."

"So when are you going back on the road?"

Nick went to sea for a moment. "Pardon?"

"The railroad. When are you leaving to check more tracks?"

This had been easy so far. Suddenly, it wasn't. He could sling a white lie, blue lie, or black lie with the best of them. But he didn't lie to friends. And he didn't lie to women, even those who asked for it. She wasn't some Kewpie Doll straight off the farm, but she was what she appeared to be. He had no doubt about that. The time had come.

"I need to tell you some things," he said, a trace of sadness in his voice.

"Okay," she said cautiously.

"But first, if I ask you to keep a secret can you do it?"

"I think I can."

"Even from your brother?"

She had no idea where this was heading. "Unless it would hurt him, yeah." She paused and pulled away. "Lord, you're married, aren't you?"

"No. No. Nothing like that. In fact, it could turn out good. Maybe."

"Okay," she ventured again.

"I don't work for the railroad. I work for the Indians. They gave me this job after I got hurt. I work all the Gulf States. I'm a scout. I couldn't say anything because I was there to scout Donnie."

Her mouth popped open, then broadened into such a great smile it made dimples as big as olive pits. "You're kidding. Wow, Nick."

"You can't let on. I'm not ready to talk to him. I need to see him play a couple more times. Sorry."

She pulled her hand free and raised both of them to her face. "I can't believe this. Oh, he'll be so thrilled." Then she turned and embraced him. Nick felt it all the way down to his feet.

"I hope you know this isn't why I wanted to get to know you better."

Alice smirked. "You mean if you asked me to a movie for Saturday night would I go just because you might help my brother?"

Nick grinned . "I just didn't want you to think I was on the make or anything."

She chuckled. "I'm not easily fooled."

They walked on. She took his hand this time. "What time?" she asked.

"For what?" he asked curiously.

"What time are you picking me up for the movie Saturday?"

He laughed softly and shook his head.

Nick had never believed in Fate. He didn't believe in a Master Plan, either. He believed in luck, but not as the end-all be-all. Mostly, he believed in action and reaction, like Newton's famous law. Actions can give a man a sense of control over his life. Reactions are what happens when he loses that control, and how he reacts tells what kind of a man he really is. Not always, of course. Not a hundred percent of the time. But, a lot. You pick a direction and head that way. Even if things turn south, you can adjust if your head is in the game. You panic or freeze like a lost kid you might as well fold. You've lost. Sure, you can come back, maybe pick a different road, start over, but the longer it takes, the farther down the line you've slipped.

When he was offered the scouting job, his only choices were yay or nay. After that, he called most of the shots. Sure, the team sent him on some fool's errands—the woods are full of wannabes—but it was their dough. It was his eyes and ears—ear—and his brain and his gut telling him what to report. He hadn't made a serious mistake yet—an arm or a stick or a glove that had been a teaser and got past him—a loafer who went to camp and embarrassed him. Not yet. So did he ever think maybe he was better off with a bum ear, a better scout than a player? Nope. Nor did he believe it was any kind of design working for him to see some greater potential for himself. He did wonder, however, if some—thing—beyond his purview might've looked at him, trying for all he was worth just to be a decent guy, took pity on him and nudged Alice in his path. He could've ignored it or stepped away. That was his call, like everything else. She could've been a brat or a snob or a flirt. She was a peach, the real deal, and for a moment he let himself be grateful to whoever or whatever might be hidden in the clouds for two good legs and two good eyes, and the gumption to see what was there right in front of him.

Nick had a day off and found himself out in the country again, as if the car had its own sense of direction. It was a good three hours until dusk and the beast was not chained to the post. The shrieking began as if on cue. Nick didn't flinch this time but it was unnerving. He tried to analyze the sound, separate the layers without giving in to his spine, but found cold fingers scratching its way up from the small of his back. It wasn't the devil and it wasn't some hoodoo but how could such an animal exist? How did it make that sound in the first place? Pretty soon the old Negro emerged from the barn with the demon on a chain and latched it to the post.

The goat seemed docile, tame even. It shook its mighty head and the chains rattled. Nothing added up, but Nick drove off because of what he was thinking, and how foolish and reckless it was. There was only way he would ever know what was going on out there. He would have to come back after dark. Late after dark. And take a peek inside.

Nick inhaled an omelet with a side of hash browns for supper, and coffee so strong he had to put three cubes from his ice water in it before it was drinkable. He was standing at the cash register when Kyle came in and stopped.

"Hey. Nick."

Nick nodded and gave the cashier a fin.

"Listen, I feel kinda bad about all that loose talk the other day."

"No, it's okay. A puzzler, though."

The old man shifted and stared at his feet. "Nate's got some past out there and I guess it still eats at him, if you take my meaning."

"Sure. I'll avoid the subject in the future, okay."

"Yeah. Might be best."

There was an American Legion game being played on the main field in the city park. Nick wasn't all baseball, but when he was solo, which was most of the time, he enjoyed watching a game more than movies or nightclubs.

This was Junior American Legion. Thirteen to seventeen-year-old kids. These older boys, so close to graduating high school, could end up fighting in two years if the war was still on. They would also find out pretty quick if they had the stuff to play at a higher level when they turned eighteen. Many colleges had teams now. Independent leagues were springing up everywhere, and small-town baseball was king. The future for diamond dogs looked bright if wars didn't put the quietus to it all.

Nick grabbed a hot dog at the snack bar. This was an eat-or-die-trying dog. First you had mustard and catsup. Then the frank, fat and oozing greasy water the color of sweat. Then you had chili sauce (without the beans), all topped with a layer of Cole slaw. Getting through one before the bun fell apart was proof positive of a charmed life, but either way, every bite was worth the mess. Nick ate the dog wrapped tight in a napkin, revealing only a mouthful at a time. This worked until the napkin soaked through and his hands got so sticky he couldn't stand it. Most of the time he kept a chunk of ice wrapped in another napkin for such occasions, rolling the wad around the tips of his fingers, drying them on the backs of his trousers. If the ice—or ice water—held out until he ate his way through both dogs, life was on his side.

Some of the players were already men. Their chronological age hadn't caught up with their adult bodies. Some still looked like boys, acne and bicycles with streamers on the handlebars. Some were talented, focused. Some were awkward, with two left feet and two paws for hands. But one thing remained the same. They all loved this game. Whether they were fighting grounders or fighting for a future, they spent their summers just like every other ballplayer on earth. And someday, when they were old men, the yarns they spun would involve a stitched ball and a bat.

Nick remembered himself at that age. He had played ball of one sort or another since he was eight years-old. He wasn't very good until he was in high school. Small school, so most anyone who wanted to play got to play. He got lucky. One-in-a-million lucky. After high school, he went to an open tryout for the Indians and got signed. Went from A to AA after only twenty games. He could snatch anything hit within ten feet of him. He charged every ball, even those he would probably have gotten just as quickly if he'd stayed back. His signature, or forte, not that it made any difference, was throwing the ball on the run. He rarely planted his feet and threw. He leapt at balls hit in his direction, his glove already within an inch of the ground. He snatched and tossed in a three-quarter, looping manner, and most of the time he hit the target flush. His throwing motion was better for his arm. Maybe it could be argued that planting and throwing put more zip on the ball, but he got to the ball quick and unleashed it just as fast, with more mustard than anyone realized. 'Deceptively fast' is what one of his coaches called it.

Of the five double play opportunities he had in the bigs, he made four. One got away from him but was still on the money. It hit the dirt three feet from the bag and the second baseman muffed it. Nicky got tagged for the error, though—the only one he ever had.

He doubled up two men at first on line drives. They didn't see the throw over until it was too late.

He only hit .260 in the minors. He took batting practice until the coach quit throwing, claiming his arm was worn out. Nick rarely struck out, and he could hit the off-speed pitch as well as anybody. He just had bad luck. He believed that luck was the main difference between .260 and .280. He always hit the ball hard...but too often right at somebody. He may have set the all-time record for hitting the ball within five feet of a fielder. He tried everything—lighter bat, heavier bat, shorter bat, longer bat. He tried moving up in the batter's box, back in the batter's box, crowding the plate, backing off the plate. He even tried bunting his way on just to prime the pump, and had some early success, as quick as he was, but as teams caught on, his odds climbed the ladder.

His hitting wasn't disgraceful, but there were so many times he hit the ball flush with ducks on the pond, only to see failure in not advancing the runners, or more commonly, hitting into a fielder's choice. Once, with men on first and second, he got the sign for a hit-and-run instead of bunting them over. Coach knew he could make contact. Both men took off at the pitch, and Nicky clobbered one that would have busted bricks, but the shortstop didn't have to move an inch to snag it. It was the first—and only, as it turned out—triple play in the league that season. Worse, he got thrown out of the game, for the first and only time of his career, by slamming his bat to the ground, which tagged the ump in the knee on the rebound.

Still, he had stories to tell, too, and maybe—just maybe—he would have grandkids to hear them one day.

Despite every inner voice he could rally screaming in his head, Nick found himself parked just down and across the road from the demon's barn. It was too dark to make out many details, but he knew the beast was not outside. Rattling chains made a very distinct sound and there was none. It was after ten, but he wondered if he should have waited until later when the whole world was asleep. The darkness was stark and absolute.

Anxious about noise, more about what he might find, he slowed his breathing. He pushed the driver's door closed as softly as possible. He could not close it completely, but the latch gripped and held. He tiptoed across the old road, pausing every time he accidentally kicked a stone or stepped on a twig. He knew he was being ridiculous. The night was peppered with ambient sounds, though he moved as stealthily as a thief. There was a shallow ditch between the road and the edge of the property. He traversed it easily. There was a two-foot berm he had to shinny up, and he knew he was ruining his pants. Up the slope to level ground the dewy grass muffled his footfall. Across the dirt driveway was a path circling the barn.

As he moved, he looked for any kind of opening in the walls. He found nothing until he came around the back. The back door was closed tight, but about halfway down there was a gap in the wood, part of a missing board. His toe touched something and he stopped. A mountain of tin cans blocked his way. Food cans. Why so many cans? A single can rolled free from the pile but made no more sound than the crack of a twig. He froze. Nothing. The blackness fell still.

Through the gap he heard the chain rattle. Just before he moved his eye to the hole, the shriek blared—the siren of damnation, the discordant scale from low, mean blasts of air to the shrill, ear-bursting pitch. Startled breathless, he spun around and stumbled into the heap of cans—no louder than a drill press in a bell factory. As he freed him himself he heard the front door slam and a voice roar, accompanied by the rack of a shotgun.

"Whoever you is, you better git!" Nick already had two feet moving.

And the screech wailed for relief.

He couldn't go back the way he came. He'd be in clear sight when he passed the barn. He ran east along the back property line, listening for footsteps. The yard was covered with small dips and bumps, and once he lost his footing and took a header in the dirt. He knew the next house was at least a quarter mile away, so after a couple hundred yards he stopped and listened. The old man hadn't followed him. He cut toward the road. At the edge of the grass he half-jumped, half-slid down the bank and across.

He couldn't see his car yet but pounded in that direction. He heard nothing but his own heavy breathing. He opened the door and slid in one motion. He started the car and pulled a U-turn with the gas pedal on the floor, the wheels spinning everywhere, but he got the car righted and pointed in the proper direction. He heard a shotgun blast, loud but too far away to do damage. Even so, his trespassing days were over.

He was so glad to see her he nearly wept. Her smile made him feel human again. He sat beside her and gave her a quick peck on the cheek. The teams were warming up. He saw Donnie playing catch along the first base line. That's when he knew Alice had kept her word. Donnie looked in his direction without recognition.

She squeezed his arm. "I'm so glad to see you."

"Me, too. Sorry I didn't call. I got stuck downstate."

She looked toward the field. "This should be a good one. Number one and number three."

"Which one's which?"

"The Mavericks—Donnie's team—is third. The Flycatchers are in first place."

"What's a flycatcher?"

"A kind of bird."

"Oh. Clever."

The game started and Nick got what he came for. In the second Donnie threw a man out at the plate trying to score from second on a routine single. He chunked a perfect one-hopper and the mitt thumped.

In the third he hit a liner on a rope past the third baseman for a double, driving in a run. The Mavs were up by one. In the sixth he flied out to short center field on an outside pitch he tried to pull. Out three with two ducks on the pond. Not good. In the seventh he let a ball drop in front of him instead of diving for it. Poor Alice shrunk but Nick knew it was a smart move. Kept the runner on first from going to third. If he had lunged and missed, the man would have scored and the batter would be standing on second. A double play got them out of the jam. In the top of the eighth he came up with a man on third. He couldn't bunt. Two outs. He took a ball away then settled in again.

He squared as if to bunt anyway and the pitch was in the dirt. The catcher made a good save. Donnie had strike one. The third baseman and shortstop inched in and watched for the bunt. That's what Donnie was hoping for. The next pitch was a fastball just off the plate outside. Donnie squared again. The third baseman and shortstop charged. Then Donnie slid his hand down the bat into the swinging position, though choked up about four inches. He stuck the bat out and gave a little half-swing. The ball popped up right to the shortstop—except the shortstop wasn't there. He was standing by the pitcher's mound watching the ball bloop over his head. Run scored. Donnie was on first. They won five-to-three.

Nick and Alice sat in the shade for a minute before heading out.

"Just thought I'd let you know I'm going to talk to Donnie when he gets home."

Her face brightened like a lamp. "That's great. He'll be so excited." She paused and frowned. "What if he goes out with the guys and doesn't come 'til late."

Hirsch squeezed her hand. "Well, if Mama won't let me sleep on the couch I guess we'll do it tomorrow."

She reached and hugged him, her arms tight around his neck. "Thank you, thank you."

He pulled back and kissed her. Short, but a real kiss. "You're welcome."

She sat closer to him on the way home. Once they left town and made it through all the gears to cruising speed, he held her hand. He thought he'd been content before, but this was new. He'd grown more wary over the years, not completely trusting when good things came his way. He was living proof that good things never last.

If nothing else, Alice had a calming effect on him, part gentleness, part humor, part loving-kindness. He was becoming at ease with being at ease and this was as alien as it was redemptive.

Yet he had an itch that had burrowed in and settled.

"You used to raise cows, right?"

"Cattle, yes."

"Do you know anything about goats?"

"A little, I guess."

"Are there breeds that are as big as a calf, maybe?"

"Not that I know of. Mountain goats can get pretty big."

"How big?"

"Three feet high. Hundred twenty-five, hundred fifty pounds. Something like that."

"Nothing bigger?"

"Not that I know of."

"Long, black shaggy coat?"

"No. Not black."

"So you don't know any goat that's say two hundred pounds, four feet high, six feet long, long black coat, two horns right out of the forehead a foot long, curving back at the end?"

"No. You sure you're talking about a goat? Not some kind of exotic ox or buffalo?"

"I don't think do. What about sound? Any of them make this long banshee-like cry?"

"I don't know what a banshee sounds like."

"Like a fire siren. Then throw in some yaps and make it rougher."

She thought he was spoofing her. "No. And neither have you, I'll bet."

Nick mulled for a long moment. "How 'bout I take you to brunch tomorrow and then for a ride in the country?"

"Sure," she said. "Sounds like fun."

Nick said nothing more about the beast. The next morning, they had flapjacks and bacon, juice and coffee in the hotel restaurant. It was a weekday and guests were thin, the overhead lights purposeless against the rising sun. She smelled of roses. He didn't let his mind wander to thoughts of her taking a bath. Something might rear up and shame him.

"I didn't get to bed until two," she said.

"How come?"

"Why do you think? My brother couldn't be still. Stomping around the house with a big grin on his face, stopping every so often to whoop. Worse than a kid at Christmas."

"I told him he would have to be patient. There's a couple of months left in the season, and they still have a shot at the pennant. They'll meet up in early October, probably in Florida. I didn't give him the 'once in a lifetime' speech, but I told him it had to be all or nothing."

"He knows, Nicky."

Nick had been here before and now there was something more at stake. "Lookit. You gotta know he might not make it. Say he has a good tryout. Next spring they'll start him in A ball, maybe AA. He's not going to make any money."

"Donnie knows all that," she repeated. " Doesn't bother him. He'd work a night job if he had to. He's done it before." She squeezed his hand. "Wouldn't you take the risk for a shot at your dream?'

He looked at her. "I would, yeah. I did."

Soon they were out of the city. He grimaced, as if involuntarily, an edge to the drive as they drew nearer. There was a smidge of relief from the heat—if eighty degrees and stiff air was relief. Alice still sat close and watched as fields and rolling hills passed by. Occasionally she looked up at him but didn't say anything.

"You're just going to have to bear with me on this," he said. "I don't understand exactly what's going on out here."

"Where?"

"You'll see."

Alice was more than curious. She was antsy. Because he was antsy. And that scared her a little. "Will we be getting out of the car?"

"No," he said. "It's a little harder in broad daylight to see and not be seen."

He found his customary place, hidden by the trees and the angle of the slope. He could only see the left side of the barn door.

"Can you see that?" he asked.

"What am I supposed to be looking for?"

"A rundown old barn."

"I see the corner of something."

"Here. Scoot over closer."

She slid to the left as far as she could. Nick moved as much as he could, wedging himself against the door. He put his arm around her shoulders and tapped her to move in as much as possible. She was nested against his ribs, his arms holding her in place.

"I know it's not comfortable."

She grinned. "Oh, it's not too bad."

"See it?"

She stuck her neck out as far as possible. "I can see part of a door to the end of the building, and a post."

"Good," he said.

"You got any binoculars?" she asked.

"No."

"Thought you would."

"Why would I need binoculars?"

"Watch ballplayers, I guess."

Hirsch grinned. "Most of the time I'm too close as it is."

He spent a few more seconds organizing his thoughts. He wanted to explain what-was-what without exaggeration. His concern proved unnecessary. At that moment, the screeching began. He felt her entire body tense again him. She did not have to strain to hear the cacophony of shrill cries, like a choir of alley cats, separated by a trio consisting of a braying donkey, a very large tubercular man hacking his head off, and the high-pitched bark of a small dog—all in staccato unison.

"What on earth is that?" she said in disbelief. "I thought you were just teasing."

"Don't I wish. This thing is glued to my head."

"And you don't know what that is?"

"I told you. It's the monster I was trying to describe. Just wait."

The cries seemed to rise in volume as one replaced another, six or seven in a row. Then the old Negro trudged across the dusty yard. He opened the door and shuffled inside.

"Now watch," he whispered.

As he predicted, the door reopened and the old man led the beast out on a heavy chain and attached it to the post. The riotous noise had already died.

"What on earth?" Alice muttered.

"So, do you know what it is?"

"It looks like a mountain goat, only I've never seen one that big. And they are never black."

"Where do they come from?"

"Montana. Wyoming. They live in the Rockies. Only place I know of. They're very agile. They can climb those mountains. People hunt them. It's not easy."

"So, it is a goat."

"Technically, they're in the antelope family."

"Yeah, yeah, but is it a mountain goat?"

"I think so. But not like any I've ever heard of."

"Do they make that sound?"

She vigorously shook her head. "They kind of baa like any other goat. Nothing I know could ever make that sound."

"Spooky, I know. Do you know how long they live?"

"Not sure. Twenty years, maybe. Less in the wild."

"Try fifty. And then some."

"You're kidding."

"People say they've seen that thing for the last fifty years."

"The only thing I can think of is that it's a freak of nature, like a cow with an extra leg or a two-headed calf."

"I thought something like that, too."

"What do you think it is?"

"The old loafers think it's evil. Like a demon or something."

"Well, I believe in the Devil. And I know goats have been associated with him sometimes. I just never thought I would ever see something like that in real life. And that old colored man. He seems harmless."

"He knows which end of a shotgun is which."

"What?"

"Never mind."

She sat up, removing herself from the line-of-sight, but not leaving his side.

He continued. "I don't believe in all that demon stuff, but I tell you. I can't figure out what it's doing here. Something's going on in that barn and that animal is part of it."

"Might just be a pet."

"Could be. But why hold on to something that makes a racket like that?"

"I don't know. Maybe voodoo."

"You don't really believe that."

"I don't know what to believe. Maybe something happened to its throat and that's the sound it makes. Spooky, though."

"Yeah, maybe. Seen enough?"

"Yep."

Nick got all the paperwork done for Donnie and sent it in, including a picture with him grinning like a weasel. Nick's part was over. Donnie would probably wear himself out before his tryout, but this wasn't necessarily a bad thing. He would eat, drink, and live baseball until October. He was in a league until Labor Day anyway.

Nick also decided that his trips to the country were at an end. Yeah, he'd said that before and had never been a welsher. Whatever this was, it was none of his business. Besides, the more he thought about it, the sillier the thought of anything sinister became. The monster was big, but most of the time he just lolled in the sun, chewing through a bushel basket of greenery and hay. He also sensed deep down that the old Negro just didn't have it in him to be Devil-kin. If he was up to something naughty, so what? Even when he charged in the dark with a scatter gun, there had been as much trepidation in his voice as there was intent to harm.

This adventure had been a grand diversion, though. Now he had a new story to tell. Everywhere he went there were stories. He had always done his share of bullshitting, but this one about the goat man was a doozy. If he could put a sharp-pointed end to it, he would never again be outdone. The tale would spread so wide that in a few years it would come back to him from total strangers, and with so many new embellishments he would have to bite his tongue to keep from laughing out loud.

Time to put it aside. Now, there was a girl. Maybe *the* girl.

Except for the wail of that thing. That, he wouldn't forget so easy.

Alice held the crook of his arm as they exited the theater. Hirsch was nearly blinded by the sun. He stopped for a minute to let his eyes adjust, then repositioned his hat to protect them.

They walked toward the next cross street. Matinees as the first course were sublime, because such early entertainment was simply a preview of nicer things to come—if he didn't do anything stupid.

"I love Henry Fonda," Alice said

"I do, too," Hirsch replied. "Well, not *love.* You know what I mean."

She grinned and patted his arm. "Good movie," she said.

"Cold air. I'd pay two bits just to get out of the heat."

"Then you should wear short sleeve shirts."

Nick made a face. "Unprofessional. Short sleeves are for tourists and teenagers."

"And not a man-about-town such as you."

"Well, I'm not so snotty about it as that."

"I know. I was giving you some gas."

He grinned. "I figured. I like it."

"Lord, I'll bet you'd never wear a pair of shorts."

"Not in public."

"What, you got skinny legs?"

"At the very least."

Several of the buildings had awnings reaching far over the sidewalk. They provided some relief, but not much, and only for a few seconds at a time. They walked from shade to sunlight several times, the air suffocating throughout.

Nicky grew a thoughtful mask. "Did the movie make you mad?"

"Isn't it supposed to? I just remind myself it's only a movie."

"I had part of it figured out pretty quick," he said, but not in a boastful tone.

"Which?"

"I knew Henry Fonda's character would end up delivering that letter."

"Did you think those men were going to be lynched no matter what?" she asked.

"I don't know. I was pulling for them even if they were bad. You know, there was a lynching near where I grew up. I must've been ten or so. Colored man was accused of molesting this woman and stealing her car. They found the car all torn up not too far away."

"That's so awful. Lot of colored people in the cities, but not out where we were."

"I shouldn't have said anything. It's not fit conversation."

"You should remember those things. The more people remember them, the less likely they'll be free to do it again."

"True in that case, anyway. A few months later guy asked the husband if the wife was okay. He had stopped to help, see, but she shooed him away. So the husband knew she had lied about being molested and the car being stolen. Truth was she had been putting on lipstick when she ran off the road and wrecked the car and didn't want her husband to find out."

"That's terrible."

"Didn't helped the man they lynched. None of them were ever charged. I think the man beat his wife pretty bad and did a month in jail, anyway, but that's a far cry from what he would have gotten for murder."

"It's been almost eighty years since that war and whites still hate colored people. We aren't going to have any peace until we get over that."

"Yeah, they'll be in the bigs eventually."

"You think so?"

"Too much talent to ignore forever."

They stopped for traffic. The light changed and they walked across the street toward where his car was parked.

"What is an ox-bow anyway?" he asked.

"It's a bend in a river that makes it flow in the opposite direction. Like a U."

"Anything you don't know?

"Sure," she said. "What's going on at that place you showed me with whatever-that-is."

"Well, that's over. Try not to let it bother you."

"I will if you will."

Nick told the old coots at the café he was headed to Florida just to get a rise out of them. They mentioned the beach, lollygagging in the sun, the college girls in their swimsuits. There was also fresh seafood, countless lakes, and orange trees. The truth was far less elegant. He was headed for the panhandle—pine trees and mosquitos and the rank smell of paper mills—rattlesnakes and dirty sand and moonshiners with guns. There was a possible in Marianna, not too far east of Mobile. Marianna is where the Florida School for Boys is located, and said to be the worst reform school in the South. It is also the largest, and a place for beatings and torture and death. No kid removed for a time from polite society had a chance, regardless of how tough he was. The School was far more dangerous than many prisons.

The prospect, a recent release and a survivor, was rumored to run like the wind, could cover left field and center field by himself, had a cannon arm, and hit with power. Nick just knew he was too much a hard case to take orders, or ready to fight at the drop of a hat. Too good to be true is nearly always too good to be true.

Nick knew all about weaknesses, his own included. When he had lain in a darkened hospital room with one side of his face swollen and the color of an eggplant, he'd known he would never play the same again. When Julianne Morrow began to complain about his absences during every date, he knew they were quits. And when he became expert in finding the merest fault in a ballplayer, he knew to leave well enough alone.

Geographically, Marianna, Florida, was indistinguishable from Alabama and Georgia— plain, sandy, and thinly green. A person could stand in a certain spot and drain the radiator in three states in one go. The air was leaden with clouds, but the rain held off. He passed fields dotted with people working. Dark people, aglow with sweat. The streets of Marianna were stippled with large palmetto trees. Marianna was also the home of Florida Caverns. Eons ago, the land that became Florida was underwater. Most caverns remained underwater but Florida Caverns was a dry, airy system with huge, open rooms. Well, he wasn't here to sightsee anyway.

He had another, legitimate reason to doubt. This was going to be a tryout. He hated tryouts. Nothing to show game sense. Nothing to show how a player responds in the clutch. There were no teams, no true source of challenge. Tryouts were exercises and could easily be staged. Game action revealed more about a player than a dozen tryouts. The game is everything, even when it's bad. At times Nick felt that some coaches figured him for a chump.

They were to meet at the high school field. The school was closed for the summer. Hopefully, there would be no spectators, especially Dad, Mom, or Grandma, shouting as if the kid was in the World Series. He hated their expectant looks, their swelled chests of pride. He especially hated talking to them, especially if Sonny was a dud. "No, Ma'am, sorry, but the boy should learn to be a bookkeeper or something."

His first look at the kid surprised him. The boy wouldn't turn seventeen until October and had a year left it high school. But he was lean-waisted and trim, with heavy thighs and shoulders two-feet wide. He was over six-feet tall, too. His hair was cut in a burr, and he did not look as capable of violence as he did a bit overwhelmed by it all. Nick knew the feeling intimately.

The kid's name was Freddie Boggs. A couple of things in the coach's favor. His co-conspirators were players from Florida State

University, which made them fairly legit. There was no small talk, and with a nod from the coach, he took the field. A couple of different hitters stood at home facing the field, another man ready to glove the return throws at whatever points were desired.

"He's got some he-man shoulders," Nick whispered to the coach.

"He had to swing a shovel or sledge every day at school." School was a kind description of the kid prison at Marianna.

"What did he do, if you don't mind me asking?"

The coach didn't hesitate. "Put his stepfather in the hospital for six months. Broke bones from head-to-toe. Told the law the old man was beating on his mother."

Nick nodded noncommittally. Worse things to do time for.

The coach whistled at the batters. The pair stood about ten feet apart, a lefty and a righty. Both tossed the ball to hit, but only one actually swung. Freddie wasn't supposed to know where the ball was going beforehand. It was a bit over-done, but sincere. After shagging a couple of lollipops and leisurely tossing them in, they got down to business. Flies down the line. Flies toward the gap. Flies so short an infielder could have taken them. Line drives he dove and caught. One-and-two hoppers hit on a rope he snagged with ease, each ball hurled into the cutoff like a rifle shot.

Then there were a few throws to third, each one like a missile. The coach whistled again and waved him in. "Take a few swings now, Fred." Boggs picked up a bat and moved to the plate. He was breathing hard, but he should have been sucking vapor after so much running.

"Pitcher is FSU's best," the coach said lowly. "Freddie's never seen him."

Hirsch had an 'uh-huh' detector but believed the coach. The man seemed to be doing everything on the up-and-up to make the kid stand on his own. Nick got a feel for the pitcher during a dozen warm up tosses. He could blister the ball. The pop of the mitt told how fast the horsehide was moving.

Boggs had a good stance and focus. The first couple were over the plate. He pounded both of those into the outfield. As the pitcher moved the ball in and out, the boy went with them. He nubbed a couple, but could go right, center and left. Then the pitcher began to mix in breaking balls with no discernible pattern. Boggs swung and missed badly on a slow curve to the outside and everyone snickered. Except Boggs. His demeanor never changed, jaw clenched tight enough to chew nails. He made contact with everything else thrown at him. The pitcher was close to A ball level. Nick was impressed but showed nothing.

Then, unexpectedly, Boggs moved to bat lefty, and with the same results. Even more power with the off-hand. Not quite the same bat control, but he could still spray the ball, and with authority. Nick couldn't help but smile. He didn't talk to the kid that day, but said to the coach, "You may hear from me. Make sure he finishes school and make double-sure he plays ball next year."

Even on day trips Nick started to miss Alice, picturing her every facial nuance in his head. It wasn't just the time away. It was being in unknown territory and feeling detached from everything. Where was home? Where was his heart? That night they had taken a walk down the street near her house. They left the neighborhood and found a quiet street leading toward town. He needed to escape Donnie and a thousand-question onslaught. At a cross street, he stopped at the edge of the streetlight's shadow, held her and wouldn't let go.

"My, my," she said. "What's that all about?"

"Just missed you is all," he said quietly.

She could have teased him or made a joke, but she had a good sense about such things. She spoke without a hint of levity. "Missed you, too, Nicky."

Nick was sweating and could feel the dampness beneath his pits. He removed his jacket and slung it over his shoulder, praying he wasn't ripe enough to smell.

They walked all the way into town and went into a small diner. Alice seemed to enjoy the small, homey places as much as he did. One more thing to love about her. They ordered pecan pie and coffee and sat stock-still to let the overhead fans do whatever they could do.

"Anything in Florida?"

Nick smiled. "Yeah. A kid. A sixteen-year-old kid, if you can believe that."

"What do you do about guys like that?"

"Try to keep tabs on them. Make sure they keep playing. Some kids peak early."

Their food was served, steam rising from the edges of the pie crust. "'Course, I may not be around to see it."

"Oh," she said seriously.

"I may want to get off the road. There's this girl, see."

She smiled. "She's got to you, huh?"

"She has."

"Maybe this girl would go wherever you go," she whispered.

Nick sipped his coffee. "You never know."

Nick took a shower, the water as cold as he could stand it. He felt as if the crust of the world had dug into his skin. He was toweling his hair when a knock came on the door. He was draped in a towel and the intrusion bugged him. No one about had any business with him. He kept drying his head as he walked.

"Who is it?"

"It's me, Nick. Kyle."

Puzzled, Nick let him in. Kyle stood aside rubbing the brim of his hat, looking out-of-place.

"What can I do for you?" he asked.

"Maybe nothing. I've been looking all over for Tim. Can't find him."

"What's wrong?"

Kyle took a breath. "It's Nate. He's all het up and I'm afraid something bad might happen."

Nick rubbed the back of his head with the towel a couple of times and tossed it on the bed. “What do you mean?”

“He’s half-drunk. Talking foolish. I told you he had a history with those people out there in the country.”

Nick felt a twinge of tension, a spur of apprehension. “What kind of history?”

“Goes way back. Nate’s daddy had some land out there. Not a lot. Maybe thirty acres. Nothing would grow. He might as well’ve thrown the money he spent on seed and fertilizer down the crapper. Useless. He took a couple of old-timers out there. Try to see what’s going on with the soil. While they were there that animal started making that awful noise. Old-timers about shit their pants. They all beat it out of there saying nothing would grow out there because the land was cursed.”

“That’s crazy.”

Kyle half-nodded, half-shrugged. “Crazy or not, he believed it. Few years later his Daddy hit a stump with his tractor and it fell over on him. Busted him up pretty bad. Was never right after that. Was going to sell the property. Nate said he wanted it. Took it over. Couldn’t grow nothing but bugs. Then his little girl got sick. They said it was lead poisoning. That was about, oh, twenty...twenty-five years ago.”

“Could’ve been bad plumbing.” Nick said, trying to move him along.

“Maybe. But Nate’s little girl never got well, either, and died before she finished school. Every time Nate has bad luck, he goes crazy, especially if he's been drinking. Goes out to that land ranting and raving like it was cursed and him along with it. You can still hear that monster's scream from that land."

"Had to be something else."

"It was. Some people from the county did a survey out there when there was talk about paving part of that road. There's a layer of salt not a foot under that land. Nearly all of it."

"Nate knows this?"

"Sure. But like I said, Nate can't take bad luck. He drinks. And he ain't right when he drinks. I was hoping to find Tim so we could head him off."

"Sounds like a good plan to me."

"Well, like I said, I can't find Tim." He paused, nervously. "Look. Nate's wife got sick day-before-yesterday. Found out she's got bad female something or other. Gonna have to operate on her and take out all her woman parts. It's a big deal. Nate went on a bender. I'm worried he might do something he won't be able to take back."

Nick's stomach did a loop. "You think he went out there?"

"Don't know. Said he was."

"Jeez, why didn't you say so!?" Nick gathered his clothes in a panic. "When?"

"Right before I came to you. Ten-fifteen minutes ago."

Nick unceremoniously pushed Kyle out of the room, the man with his mouth open ready to speak again. If Kyle was looking to ride second-fiddle out there, Nick wasn't interested. He moved quicker and made better decisions on his own. He dressed as if his life depended on it, taking little care. T-shirt. Underwear, pants, shirt, and shoes, no socks. Within five minutes he was headed downstairs.

Nick got into his sedan and sped off. He figured Nate had at least a twenty-minute head start. He rubbed his lips until they chapped. If Nate was soused maybe he would run himself into a ditch. Nick fretted that both parties had guns. A tragedy could be brewing, Even if he got there in time, he didn't know what he would do if they were shooting at each other. He sure as Hell didn't want to get in the way of buckshot.

He leadfooted the Ford beyond its familiarity until it fishtailed on the connecting road and he let off the gas. No point tearing his car up. The night was already deathly dark. City streets are ablaze. Neighborhoods have streetlights, and even if not, glows emanated from the porches and windows. Here, no lights, the houses few and far between, and even then were set too far back off the road for any light to matter. He made it to the crossroads and slid into the turn, skidding sideways toward the far berm but righted in time for him to floor it. He hadn't so much as seen a taillight.

He thought he heard a gunshot. He was still a half-mile from the old farmstead when he saw the headlights of a truck bearing down on him. And in a big hurry. He pulled to the right and slowed again. The truck flew past him throwing pebbles and dust in all directions. He couldn't tell if it was Nate, but he wasn't about to chase him down for a looksee.

It was the longest minute of his life. He roared into the driveway just enough to get clear of the road. He could see a lantern above the barn door, casting the area in an eerie glow. He ran, painful in dress shoes, panting as he crested the rise. He saw the old man kneeling down with his wife standing over him with the shotgun. They either hadn't heard him or didn't care. He wasn't about to take chances. He held his arms over his head and moved into the light as much as possible.

"Don't shoot."

The pair squinted in that direction and the gun remained lowered.

As Nick approached the pair the reality came down upon him heavy and hard. He hadn't put all the parts together. The monster goat was down. The old man knelt beside it stroking its neck. The old woman softly wept.

"Poor old Silas," the old man lamented. He seemed to notice Nick for the first time then. "Who are you?

"Nick Hirsch. I was just passing by and thought I heard a shot. What happened?"

"What you think happened?" the old woman said, spitting out the words. "Some fool shot him."

Nick knelt across from the old man and awkwardly held out his hand, the goat between them. The beast lay as still as the air. Not so threatening immobile, though Nick was sure to avoid touching it. The old man gave Nick the once over and finally shook his hand.

"Amos Johnson. This my wife, Flora.""

Suddenly the screech sounded from the barn. Nick fell over on his backside as the noise worked its way up his spine, poking nerves and rattling bone. Up and down, the siren wailed with no more than a second between. This went on for a good half-minute until something queerly bizarre happened. The shriek subsided just long enough to voice a single detectable utterance.

"Ma."

Nick thought he was imagining things but he noticed the growing look of worry on old couple's faces. Mrs. Johnson seemed close to desperation.

"What the Hell is that?" Nick blurted.

The couple sneaked a quick look at each other.

Amos shook his head, his hand still on the animal. "My Daddy was a slave," he began. "This here was just the backend of the property. Not good for much. Man Daddy worked for grew cotton. Daddy knew everything there was to know about cotton. Then he became a free man. Boss begged him to stay on and promised him a little plot if he did. Daddy didn't believe him but stayed for the cash money. Sure enough, when the bossman passed, this lot was in his will deeded to Daddy." He wiped sweat from his forehead with his shirt sleeve. "Hard for colored peoples to own land back in them days. Even harder if you surrounded by white farmers and they know you there but he made a little thing out of it. When Daddy went on this plot was mine. It was still hard. Nineteen hundred not much different than eighteen hundred. Nineteen forty-three ain't much better."

"They tried to run us off," Mrs. Johnson asserted.

"That they did," Amos said woefully. "They'd drive out here in the dark to scare us, shooting they guns off, throwing dead things in the yard. Writing mean things on the walls. We barely made a living as it was. She did washing. Tub was so big we had to keep it on the porch. I farmed a little. Used to fix cars, too, when they came in. Only colored people, though, and none of them had any money." He laughed to himself.

"We made do just fine," Mrs. Johnson said.

Nick listened intently but began to feel foolish, kneeling on the ground and talking over a dead goat. He also knew there was more to the story.

"What about that screaming?"

When Mr. Johnson raised his head, tears filled his eyes. "You a good man, Mr. Nick? Mind your business and nobody else's?"

"I don't know. I try to be. Don't go out of my way to hurt anybody. Keep my nose to myself most of the time.

"C'mon, then," Mr. Johnson said, rising to his feet.

"Amos," Flora said, a caution.

"Be alright," he replied. Then he shuffled toward the barn door and swung it open.

There were a few expected things in the barn—an old, broken-down tractor, tools, a small stack of boards in different sizes, paint and brushes and oil. A loft with a busted floor. Halfway down the right part a room had been built. No, more like a cage. The sides were sturdy planks but the front was a gate—a wide pasture gate—metal with horizontal bars. There wasn't any hay or feed or anything Hirsch could see, but he could hear movement. He stayed behind the old man.

"You ever heard of what they call perfound retarded?" Amos whispered over his shoulder.

"No," Nick whispered in reply.

That's when they reached the gate. Amos unlocked a lock and opened it. It was a room like a cell. It had a wooden floor, a bed without a head- or footboard, a wash basin, a chair, and a toilet. The toilet had no plumbing and must have emptied into a pit beneath the barn. There was no putrid shit smell, but an odor like sweat mixed with urine hovered over the area.

And when the thing shuffled into the doorway, Nick nearly added to the atmosphere.

Profoundly retarded wasn't all of it. A hulking, manlike figure, dressed in a plaid shirt and overalls shuffled forward. He had to be forty, maybe fifty. It was hard to tell on such a dark face. His spine was bent at a forty-five-degree angle just below the neck. He bore the mongoloid features of the retarded and his left eye sat askew, permanently looking down. His jaw was wedge-shaped and created a V of uneven teeth protruding from his mouth. And he was enormous. He must have been six-two and maybe two hundred-fifty pounds. His hands were giant paws, larger even than his size would dictate—the hands of a giant. His bare feet were also disproportionately large.

He opened his mouth and there came the siren squall. Amos immediately moved in and put his arms around the man, drawing him in.

"Pa," the man muttered. It was a horrible, harelip sound amplified a hundred times. Amos was a pretty big man himself, but the younger Johnson dwarfed him. Then Mrs. Johnson moved in and gave him a hug, too. The warped soul looked in Nick's direction and opened his mouth as if to unleash the shriek, but Amos got him calm and Nick slid out of his line-of-sight. Amos patted him again and .guided him back into the room.

"Go on now, boy. Lay down for a bit."

The behemoth stretched out upon the bed, punishing the springs.

Amos slowly closed the gate.

"We knew things would get a lot worse when the boy got too big for the house," he began. "People know about him they might hurt him. Man down near the bottom knew we was in a bad way. So he say he knows a man can fix all this. The man say he can scare everybody away. I say 'how?', and he shows me this mountain goat. Biggest thing I ever seen. Said he was just born that way. Never knew how he come by it. Said he took it all the way to Missoura to breed him. Ewe had twins. We bought one. Turned out bigger than his Pops."

"How come it's black?"

The old man's eyes twinkled. "Coal tar. Thin it out with some lard so it don't hurt the skin. A little salve in it too. It worked good.

Spread it on easy. Easy to add more on later. Needed to make him mean-looking."

"How did you know it would work?"

"We didn't," Mrs. Johnson said.

"But it did," Mr. Johnson continued. "We found some coloreds who worked for white folks in town and they spiced the stew. Said there was a thing out there was really bad. Kinda built on from that."

Nick nodded. "People think it's a demon."

"Jus' like we hoped. Got some lookers for a while but things got settled and folks left us be. He was so big and so dark, and the—"

"And the noise?"

"Um-hmm. We didn't figure on that right away. It just sort of fell in. Older the boy got, the louder he got. People thought it was the goat."

"How did you keep the goat alive so long?"

Amos flashed a rueful grin. "Now that was my idea. When the first goat started getting old, we asked the man to get us another one. Old Silas was number four. And he wasn't more than two or three. Had one or the other since the boy came along. Nobody saw the goats were different. They believed it was unnatural old."

"I guess you had a doctor look at your son."

Amos solemnly nodded and Mrs. Johnson began to tear up. "Once. When he was a baby. Long time ago. Said he wouldn't make it to ten. He was wrong."

Then Mrs. Johnson broke down and began to sob. Amos put his arm around her shoulders. "It's alright now," he said gently. "Shh. Shh."

"I'm sorry," Nick said.

Amos looked at Nick with the saddest eyes he'd ever seen, a man who had seen every kind of ugliness the world had to offer.

"Flo and me, we was older when he came along. But we was also blood kin. We had the same Daddy. Didn't know it at the time, o' course. I knew my Daddy got around a bit in them days, but we didn't find out until after the boy was born. Everybody shunned us when they find out. Even our own people."

Mrs. Johnson wept inconsolably.

"We live with it," he said simply.

"A judgement," Mrs. Johnson spat out between breaths."

"Now, now, Flo."

"I don't believe that at all," Nick offered, though he felt inept. "I can get the law."

Amos shook his head. "Leave it be. We'll get on like we always have. Just have to wait until we can get another goat."

Nick smiled with admiration. "Well, you made it all work. Ingenious, really." He dug his wallet out of his pocket. "Please, sir, ma'am. Let me help a little toward the new goat." He pulled out a ten and handed it to Amos.

Amos took it and nodded. "Why would you, a stranger, give us money for something you had no part in?"

Nick took a long breath.

"I'm as white as the rest of them, aren't I?":

Nick drove away and left them in peace. He'd offered to help bury old Silas but Amos said he was still tender enough to eat. He thought about that and didn't know whether to laugh or be sick. The twisted man-child made him sick. Half-brother and sister getting married and having a child without knowing what was what made him sick. People like Nate made him sick. Maybe someday colored people would be able to get out and about without ducking their faces. But not then. Not in 1943. If people knew about that poor, warped man, something bad could still happen.

It was nearly a year before the next goat appeared. Nick didn't think anybody noticed a void during that time. Only the curious came to look any more, usually after hearing the tale the first time. After that, they stayed away. Everyone stayed away. Those wretched cries had persisted non-stop, and some still believed there was devil-spawn in that barn. The ruse continued. The Johnsons lived their anonymous lives. Eventually colored people bought Nate's land and built on it. Ten families got their money together and made nice homesteads. One of them farmed the Johnson track as Amos was getting too old and made a go of it. The rest found ways to scrape enough together to survive.

Three years later, their misshapen son died from pneumonia. The current goat would be the last. Within the next few years Amos and Flora passed, eight months apart. A second cousin appeared to claim the old shack and property but sold it quick to a younger couple—also colored. Negroes had their part of the county and put down roots.

Even then, the legend lived on, long after all the evil in that place had returned to Lucifer. The tale of the goat man curled into dim and quiet nights. By 1950, legend would have to suffice.

Not long after that fateful day, Nick moved to Huntsville. He and Alice married the next year. They gave themselves a couple of years' quiet contentment, then began their family. They had two girls barely a year apart. He still did his job without fail, but the years on the road had compressed every bone in his body, and he was sore and sick of riding.

A few years after the war he got a call out of the blue from a small college in Georgia that was looking for a baseball coach. He took the job and moved his family.

Donnie never made it to the show. He spent four years in the minors, bouncing around the country. He joined the Air Force and became an officer and a fighter pilot. For the most part he was stationed in South Florida. He retired at forty-five and flew for Pan Am. He married fairly late and had three boys. He stayed in the sunshine paradise but came for frequent visits. He never complained about peaking in the minors and spent a good deal of time regaling Nick with tales from Podunk towns and back roads. Baseball, baseball. Once the pop of the glove is heard, or that unique sound of the crack of the bat—the smell of lime and pampered grass, the miasma of popcorn and boiled frankfurters, and the buzz of the crowd, often accented with solitary voices crying out from the stands as if all of life was fading—it stuck in the gut like mashed potatoes and moved through the blood like serum. More than a memory. A life once lived that had not been freely abandoned.

Nick's ultimate pride and eventual claim-to-fame was actually the delinquent kid from Mariana. He finished high school and spent parts of two summers in the minor leagues. At nineteen he led AA in hitting. At twenty he got called up late in the season and got some playing time when a starter went down. He hit .288 and had six home runs in eighty at-bats.

This was accompanied by nine put-outs from left field. He had such a quick release the ball was steaming through the air before anyone realized he had thrown. After three consecutive throws for outs at third, players thought twice about going first-to-third when they played the Tribe, even if the ball was down-the-line or near the gap.

He made his first mark—one of many—in the last game of his rookie season. The Indians were up by one but the Tigers had a man on second. The batter hit a rocket down the left field line. A sure double and tie game. Freddie Boggs backhanded ball, scooped it up, and fired toward home in a single motion, with the runner already past third. The ball blistered the air, and the catcher caught it on the fly, tagging the runner out a foot from the plate. End-of-game. He played in the Majors for seventeen years and retired a rich man. He later became a broadcaster when televised baseball became prominent.

Many years later, Nick had a chance encounter with him at an airport. Nick always tended to stay away from glad-handing any baseballer he didn't know personally, and he had not spoken to Fred Boggs since short-and-sweet congratulations when he got called up. Boggs probably wouldn't remember him and he didn't want to put him on the spot. The man saw Nick first, shouted at him, and embraced him in a monster hug. "Thank you for saving my life," he said at the time. Nick remembered that moment for the rest of his life.

A few years after Nick became a college coach, the school had grown into a university and decided to change their sports name and mascot. Nick had an idea that most seemed to like.

The Rams. And their mascot was the biggest mountain goat they could find, his coat dyed jet-black.

Five

The Widower

There's a running joke among the nurses who work the memory care wing. "We can show the same movie every day in the TV room. They won't know the difference."

Angie had overheard it a hundred times, as impenetrable now as the pervasive scent of cleaning products.

Dr. Neil Nordgren was a non-practicing GP, and the CEO of Morningside Senior Homes, a group of four large top-of-the-line, but end-of-the-road, facilities scattered throughout central Minnesota. He weighed two-hundred-fifty pounds, and at five-nine, looked like a bowling pin with a bad haircut.

Angie sat four feet away from Nordgren separated by a massive mahogany desk. His jowls splayed above his collar, his meaty fingers dancing at desk's edge, seeking an occupation. He leaned forward in his leather judge's chair, its springs signaling the strain. He jabbed his index finger on a thin file and inched it toward the center, carefully, as if infectious, though still close at hand.

"I have a situation," he said.

An involuntary wrinkle formed above her Pekinese nose. "Sir?"

"I need an assessment."

"Of course," she said, leaning to retrieve the file.

He waved her off. "It's a bit...delicate," he continued.. "More a favor for a friend type of thing."

"Okay," she said cautiously.

"Nothing cloak-and-dagger," he assured her. "This patient did not come to us through normal channels and I know how gossip gets around. Any records or observations are not to be shared with staff."

"No problem," she said, still perplexed. This is what she trained for. She wasn't some green kid.

Nordgren slid the file within her grasp and blew heavily. "You may find him...uncooperative."

She took the file. "I understand."

"Well, just do the best you can."

Angie puzzled over the encounter on the drive back to Bemidji, her home base. It was an odd day all around. The sun was bright, the temperature rising to the high fifties. A late snow had added a fresh layer of white to the grimy winter coat. Sometimes it would snow in December and grass wouldn't appear again until March. Now it was mid-April and the thaw would lumber forward.

When laid-in snow begins to melt it assumes a creamy appearance, like icing, and the reflecting sun creates swirls of rainbow colors at certain angles. Pretty in its own way, made more easily so by disappearing for the next two seasons. Summer didn't happen quickly in

Minnesota but two-stepped forward on hesitant toes. Angie loved the summer. Everyone in those parts did because it, too, was fleeting.

Back in Bemidji, Angie moved down the hallway toward her cubby of an office. She was short, trim and wiry, and by nature, not exercise. She had worn her dark hair long since high school, believing it made her look more serious-minded and less like a kid. She still looked like a kid, though at twenty-nine, was more of an adult than she'd ever wanted to be. She'd spent seven of the last ten years in some form of higher education, and was still subject to frequent upgrades, like a phone or computer, download and reboot.

She had graduated from the University of North Dakota, home of the Fighting Hawks—formerly the Sioux, until the tribes got all pissy. These days, she seemed to always be in energy deficit, though inherently good-natured and calm.

She had one failed engagement under her belt and dated when asked, though this was sporadic as she refused to date anyone in the medical profession and encountered few eligible men under the age of eighty.

Becoming a Nurse Practitioner required nearly as much time and coursework as becoming a doctor. Less blood-and-guts, more puke and shit. Becoming a Psychiatric Nurse Practitioner was at least as difficult as earning a PHD in psychology, but at times utilizing the same genteel posture, murmuring "Go on", in an overtly wise and understanding voice. As a nurse practitioner, she could prescribe meds, and as a psychiatric nurse practitioner, every resident who muttered "uh...uh..." more than twice in the same sentence was foisted upon her by doctors who had better things to do.

Nearly a third of the residents of Morningside et al had marked cognitive disorders. Many of these were on routine medications. Over a hundred were considered Mid-Stage, or Moderately Severe Cognitive Decline. Whatever the Hell that meant. Dementia was as tricky as a backache. Moderately Severe Decline could mean forgetting to brush one's teeth, to misplacing one's teeth, to playing with one's teeth, or even to hurling one's teeth in a fit of exasperation.

The simple fact was, everyone had teeth, real or manufactured, and it was part of her job to see they were used properly—or at least accounted for.

For the past three years, she had been the Psychiatric Nurse Practitioner for Morningside—her first solo professional post. It was a stressful job. Most of her patients were bound by the same affliction. Thoughts no longer moved smoothly downstream. They overran the banks in all directions, some dammed until they spurted through any slip of an opening, often with tears and the gnashing of teeth—and, as previously mentioned, many of these plastic instead of enamel.

Still, it was a good gig. Low six-figures and limited nights and weekends, as old people tended to go to bed early (or remain in bed under the influence of heavy-duty drugs). She answered questions from families. "How bad is he/she?" "How bad is it going to get?" And "How long does he/she have?" The answers could have been printed and handed out. "No worse than normal." "We'll have to see how things develop." And "No one knows, but he/she will be well taken care of." No one asks, "Will he/she ever get any better?", more than once.

Her suspicion already aroused, the file was two scant pages consisting of a name, date of confinement, and vital statistics. Nothing else of the life, medical or otherwise, of Leonard Morelli. Strange, he had been at Morningside-Bemidji for two months and she had not met him. Not even to ask, "How are you doing?" All she knew was that her cryptic meeting with Nordgren had been on this account, and that he had been diagnosed with final stage Alzheimer's.

Morelli was not on any medication. Last stage of anything usually meant strong sedation—the sleep until they croak approach. Certainly a cause for cynicism and reproach for the uninitiated but was instead an unavoidable warehousing, like the condemned on death row. Maintenance and routine care, like peonies.

She perused the pages again. He was eighty-seven years old and alone. What a life.

Leona Nilsen was a busy-body and gossip, an ace columniatrix. She had perfected the art of whispering to the point where every syllable was perfectly distinct, and yet unheard by anyone more than eighteen inches removed. She was also a suck-up and overly chummy, especially to anyone who might fuel the furnace with a tidbit of causerie for her repertoire. She was surprisingly soft-spoken for a woman of her bulk—consider the offspring had Louie Anderson serviced Rosie O'Donnell just before her biological clock donged for the last time—but was a good RN. Her upper-body strength was advantageous as well, shoving old lumps about their small beds.

She leaned into Angie, six inches above and adjacent to her ear. "Heard you drew the short straw on Old Man Morelli."

Angie looked up but didn't want to meet her eye-to-mouth. "I get nearly everybody eventually

"Hit me in the butt with a shoe."

"Wait. He's awake?"

"More than awake," she said with a grunt. "He's in the wing, right, like all the enders, y'know. Then a coupla weeks ago he just wakes up like Lazarus and starts ordering everybody around. Next thing I know, he's set up in there like the Sheik of Arabi."

"Hmm," was all Angie mustered, leaving Leona to ponder the clandestine on her own.

Morelli's room was indeed a surprise. Three of the four Morningside facilities had been community hospitals until the eighties when major players established large regional hospitals. This room had been the old doctors lounge, large and with a patio for smokers.

There had also been recent additions to the décor. On the left was a leather loveseat and a cocktail table, a widescreen TV on the wall. On the right was his bed, a nonstandard, adjustable queen with a dark wood nightstand. Adjacent was the bathroom, and in the far corner was a kitchenette, complete with refrigerator and microwave, again, unique. In the back, where the window would have been, a set of sliding glass doors lead to the patio. The patio faced Lake Bemidji, clearly visible as the trees had just begun to shrug out new leaves. And there sat Morelli, in a customized leather chair, thickly padded but narrow, four-wheeled, motorized, with power back adjustments and footrest.

He was pale, a muscular upper body, thin gray hair brushed back, and sharp features—a beak nose and small mouth. He wore a sweatshirt with a blanket across his knees, as it was chilly with a breeze, though sunny.

And he was in no way final stage anything.

She walked across the room and gently slid open the door as quietly as possible. Morelli was reading *The Woman in White*, by Wilkie Collins, a set of ear buds shoved into his ears, the end connected to a cellphone. He read and listened to music at the same time, soaking up stimuli like a junkie off a three-day itch.

"Mr. Morelli?" she called. She waved to get his attention.

He looked at her then, his eyes narrowing, his lips shrinking into a stern pucker. "Fine. No. Go away," he said tersely.

She stood in his line-of-sight but kept a distance. "Sir?"

"Your questions," he grunted. "How am I? Do I need anything? What can I do for you?"

She repressed a frown. "I'm Angela Dauwen, your Psychiatric Nurse Practitioner."

Eyes alight, a bemused smirk upon his lips, he said, "Good God! What happened to your legs?"

She quickly looked down and pulled the hem of her skirt away from her knees. She saw nothing. "What do you mean?"

"Oh. Sorry. You're just short. Does Santa know you sneaked off?"

"Mr. Morelli, I—"

"Jesus, you have hobbit feet. What do you wear, five-C?"

"B," she said seriously. "Can't find Cs."

"You could wear five-and-a-halfs to get the width."

"Or keep what I've spent a month's salary on already."

"Ouch. Scat, now. And close the door behind you."

"We need to have a chat," she said, a gentle firmness in her voice.

A fierce scowl. "That fat ass sent you to work me over, didn't he? Well, the only thing wrong with me is I'm old and still alive. Go tell him to leave me the fuck alone." The old man then swiveled his back to her.

Angie didn't move but tensed. She then understood some of Dr. Nordgren's warning.

She waited for a moment, then recognized the music through his earbuds, even muffled. "Springsteen," she said. "*Jungleland.* I love Clemons' tone."

Morelli sighed in exasperation and turned off his music. "Could you *please* take your high-school-cheerleader curiosity somewhere else before I have a stroke?"

"I was never a cheerleader," she said, "I wanted to play the sax. Got the clarinet instead."

"Yeah, that mouth of yours wouldn't make a good-sized dog's anus." She didn't bite, so he continued. "Wanted to be like Stan Getz. The Bird. Wait. I got it. Kenny G."

She smiled. "More like Clarence Clemons. Doc Kupka, maybe. You like Springsteen?"

Morelli's eyes widened a bit. "I was only forty in the mid-seventies, Missy. You weren't even born yet. Hell, your Mama was just a baby."

She inched a step closer. "Music is eternal."

He offered a grudging nod. "It is. Not much call for rock clarinet, though" he said.

She felt a rush of satisfaction. She'd broken the ice. "Well, I've taken enough of your time. Thank you for your patience."

"No problem," he said.

Memories are never really lost. They are like those tacky sweaters gifted by well-intentioned aunts, stored in plastic bins slid under the bed, especially those so waywardly colorful or patterned as to defy practical use. Then—and this is what astounds family and medical professionals alike—they can unexpectedly rise unbidden to flower and function, like a newly purchased mauve skirt that now seems perfectly attuned to that teal pullover with embroidered roses previously thought unwearable.

Both existed to fleetingly thwart the chill of premature winter, fashion be damned, then vanish like morning fog.

Set sat at her desk with the lights off and leaned back in her chair. Her instincts buzzed around her head like bees. She had an inkling and frowned. She was a quick study though she often wished otherwise. She was cautious, deliberate, even wary. Yet she *knew* and she hated that she knew, just as she knew her high school boyfriend had cheated on her. She'd second-guessed herself to the point of neurosis then and she would second-guess herself now, but in the end, the truth would bear out just as it had when she kneed the horny prick in the crotch.

Many Alzheimer's patients, like other terminals, have brief sparks or recovery, scant, short-lived, the bane of hopeful families looking for a miracle. These staccato returns to sentience can even be more demonstrable with patterns of recognition and lucidity long dormant, the brain mustering a final power surge.

Rarest of all are those whose sudden *resurrection* exceeded a few days. If Morelli had been so static for months and had indeed risen from oblivion, he was probably unaware. Worse still, he would eventually close his eyes and awaken not realizing his brain was now hibernating, and would remain so until his heart also surrendered.

Morelli was dying and didn't even know it.

Bemidji is in the northwest corner of Minnesota, east of Grand Forks, North Dakota. It is a small town, known for hockey, Lake Bemidji, and a large statue of Paul Bunyon that looks like it was carved by someone on a bender. In the old Ojibwe tongue, it means 'lake with crossing waters'. The average mean temperature is thirty-seven degrees, so the short summer is prematurely sought, overdone at times—if the ice has melted, the lake beckons. Many locals have native blood, and native issues insinuate themselves into every aspect of life.

Local tribes hold Pow-Wows and natives from all over come to attend. Regional TV stations send crews to cover it. They always film natives dancing and chanting as if that's all Indians ever did. Maybe cowboys would ride through whooping and firing off six-guns. Of all the stereotypes of every culture and subculture represented in those parts, nothing was worse than those pertaining to Native Americans. They drank. Some of them. No more disproportionately than any other segment. They made their money with casinos. True. Service industries employ more people per dollar earned than manufacturing. They were given a lot of land. They weren't *given* anything. They were confined within grassy prisons after the U.S. seized their lands, all by the will of God, of course. And rare was the land with intrinsic value, filled with treasure.

They simply wanted to *be* on their own terms. And until those terms were mainstream enough to satisfy the rest of us, they would continue to struggle.

One of America's greatest and impeachable ironies is that Natives were expected to assimilate when black people weren't allowed to assimilate, and none of the white European cultures were asked to assimilate into some absurd American ideal that no one could define and never really existed in the first place. Americans are sludge, the offal of a thousand breeds, and only Natives were plied with such vile and rapacious deceits simply because they already occupied lands the greedy self-righteous coveted.

Bemidji is otherwise sedate, even laconic, though curling matches, which are played with brooms and a large, round disk called a stone, have been known to invoke expletives such as *Uff da,* which is Norwegian slang for 'bite me'.

The late actress, Jane Russell, whose bust was made infamous by Howard Hughes, hailed from these parts, as does The Bemidji Pioneer, the local newspaper, which fishermen will tell you makes great wrap for walleye.

More, it was where she'd grown up. Bemidji borders the Chippewa National Forest and has four hundred lakes within thirty miles. There are soft hills and aster valleys, and once the snows melt, the whole world is green. Angie loved everything that went with it. Even agonizingly long winters had not discouraged her, though the first snow is not greeted with childlike delight as much as resignation, and when the wind chill is twenty-below zero, there is not enough clothing rent by human hand to stave off misery.

The other trio of homes Morningside owned were in Bagley, Walker, and Park Rapids, all small towns. Park Rapids is a very small town, but where the corporate offices were. It was also the farthest removed from the others, a fifty-mile jaunt down U.S. 71—an easy drive the first thirty—then twenty miles cross country on County Road 4, a two-lane blacktop which was always clogged with farm vehicles during the spring and summer, and snow plows during the winter. Winter driving was treacherous and an adventure even when the road was clear with impatient people determined to pass and patient people equally determined to mosey. Collisions were rare but adrenaline spikes were not. Drainage ditches separated the road from farm fields and occasionally the dim red glow of errant taillights peered from beneath a snow bank.

Angie didn't enjoy the two-hour round trip but loved that Nordgren and the other wonks were fifty miles away. The corporate office was attached to the facility in Park Rapids, but she didn't have to check in before making her rounds. She hoped any reports to Nordgren on Morelli could be handled by phone. She wasn't ready to tell him anything. Something rare and exciting had happened and she needed to understand it.

Nordgren had taken a personal interest in the old man, and Angie guessed it had to do with money, as illustrated by Morelli's apartment-cum-room, but she would find some way to stall.

Angie spent a lot of time on the road. She drove a six-year-old Dodge van with two hundred thousand miles, a gold number like a million other vans, inconspicuous, functional, and bland. It had been provided by the company, so she shouldn't complain, but she'd seen more pick-me-up in the walker races to the common room to see who could get to the TV remote first. The heater worked great, but the air conditioner blew like an asthmatic with COPD. Unless she could get a repair approved, summer travel would be sticky.

All-in-all, she was looking forward to a nice, leisurely summer, relatively uneventful, except in the likelihood a dozen-or-so patients would go bonkers. That, however strenuous, could happen in any season.

The next morning, she hadn't been on the road toward Walker five minutes before her phone rang. The van was equipped with digital display Caller ID and Bluetooth, allowing her to filter calls. It was Nordgren on his cell.

"Yes, sir?"

"Just checking in."

He never 'just checked in'. "On my way to Walker."

"You have a chance to see Mr. Morelli?"

"Stopped in briefly."

"How'd it go?"

At first, she didn't know how to respond. "As I expected."

"Oh? Better or worse."

"He's a handful, Sir. Just like you said."

"You in one piece?" Then he chuckled, a contrived stutter, like Elmer Fudd.

"I'll be fine, Sir."

"Well," he said, "just do the best you can."

Despite the reviews of disappointed tourists and smarmy locals regarding an interminable winter whose primary appeal lay in the oft-used pronouncement "It keeps the riffraff away", northwest Minnesota has four complete and distinct seasons. The overarching problem is that they can overlap and stretch far into the next, creating confusion and disorder. Memorial Day can be fifty degrees or eighty. Autumn leaves can be alight with color or white with hoar. Spring is a safe bet only for those who play longshots. Life is good, especially if one is at peace with the trickster who runs the universe. Another Minnesota aphorism states, "At least it ain't Canada."

Walker has Leech Lake as an eastern boundary, with Long Lake a sliver to the west. Twenty-seven rivers flow into Leech Lake. One wonders how Leech Lake became so popular, considering its moniker, but originally it was translated from the French *lac Sangsue*, which means Lake of Bloodsuckers. This could mean mosquitoes or other vampires, though originally the lake was a shallow bowl until the Army Corps of Engineers built the dam in 1882, absorbing every bit of standing water in those parts. It is believed the French adopted the name from the Ojibwe Ozagaskwaajimekaag-zaaga'igan, meaning lake full of bloodsuckers. Somehow bloodsuckers found its way in there from the get-go.

Outside the rain fell in thin sheets, gray abounding. Rain made deep pockets in the residual snow and thinned it into slurry. A dozen degrees cooler and it would have been snow. A dozen degrees warmer and it would have been a spring shower. Though infrequent, snow in April is not unusual. Winter's last hurrah, like a spinster in Vegas. Angie had seen spits of snow in May.

Thankfully, Walker was uneventful. She made her rounds and returned to Bemidji. She sat at her desk, considered making another run at Morelli, but talked herself out of it. Why risk spoiling a quiet day?

Nonetheless, the next morning Angie quick-stepped down the hall, unafraid, prepared for every contingency, and knocked. The rain had stopped but the day remained overcast. Like the denizens of Morningside, sometimes it took a while for the clouds to dissipate.

Morelli lay propped in bed with Family Feud on television.

"It's customary to await a response before entering," he said dryly. His voice sounded like sandpaper.

"Thought you might be outside. May I come in?"

"Most of you is already in," he grunted. "Too cold to sit out yet."

Angie moved to the foot of the bed, though at an angle so she wouldn't block his view. She sat on the loveseat.

"Good thing I wasn't watching *Barbarella* with my pistola out, all lubed and shiny. That Jane Fonda. What a minx."

She frowned at the vulgarity but said nothing. "I'll make this quick and easy. I just want to ask you a couple of questions."

Morelli grumbled and hit the remote with an agitated thumb, muting the television.

"Thank you," she began, "I see you're currently not taking much medication."

"I'm not sick."

"You've been prescribed—"

"Fuck that shit. I'm not sick."

"I thought you might be depressed."

"That's not an illness."

"No? What do you call it?"

"Darwinism."

"Are you in any pain?"

"I feel a headache coming on. I'm sure it will pass if you move your tiny ass out of here."

She sighed. "Now that's just plain rude." This came matter-of-factly, without real weight.

"Pay attention, Missy. I am not here to entertain you. I'm not here to help you further your career. Go drill into some other poor bastard's head. I told you already, I am the way I am because I am eighty-seven fucking years old. There's nothing you or anyone else can do to remedy that situation. If you have any questions, go ask that quack Nordgren."

"Dr. Nordgren assigned you to me specifically."

Morelli unleashed a caustic laugh. "That fat asshole." He raised the remote. "We're finished."

So much for 'off to a good start'.

Angie opted for a more assertive approach. She stood between the bed and the TV, blocking his view. "The quicker we do this, the quicker I'm gone."

She sat again and opened her notebook. Morelli erupted.

"No, God dammit! I may not be able to keep you from barging in here uninvited, but I am not going to let you fumble-fart around with some 'do you know where you are?' bullshit. I know where I am. I'm in Bemidji-fucking-Minnesota in a God-damned homeless shelter for dimwits!"

Though at least eight feet away, she involuntarily leaned back at the barrage. She softened. "Mr. Morelli..."

The old man fumed. "FDR, Truman, Ike, JFK, LBJ, Slick Dick, Ford, Carter, Reagan, Bush the puerile, Clinton, Bush the dipshit, Obama Rama Ding Dong, Chief Bad Hair, Obama light!"

"I'm sorry?"

"All the Presidents in my lifetime. Thought I'd save you the trouble."

Chastened, she closed her notebook, desperately seeking a different tack.

"What's Rama Ding Dong?"

Morelli scowled but lowered his voice. "Rama-lama-ding-dong is an obscure reference to music from fifties, early sixties."

"You know a lot about music."

"I've been around a long time."

"That your heyday?"

"What?"

"Late fifties, early sixties." Anything to get him talking.

He didn't bite, exactly. More a nip. "Some. I turned twenty-one in 1956. Good time for music."

She paused again, still trying to find a fingerhold. "How did you know my shoe size?"

Morelli smiled then. "I used to sell shoes a million years ago. I was eighteen. About your age."

She set the pad aside and looked at him squarely. "Tell me about that."

"What?"

"Selling shoes when you were young."

Morelli made a face like awakening to morning breath. "I was a freshman in college. I was lucky to go to college, and I needed money."

"Yeah? Where did you go to college?"

His smile was acidic. "Corinth Christian College. Near Lake Wales, Florida."

Surprised, she digested this. "When was this?"

"Nineteen-fifty-three," he said, without a beat.

"Good memory."

He did quick tilt of his head, and back. "I remember everything."

Arrogance and braggadocio were personality traits, not usually products of conditions.

"You're from Florida?"

"Moved there when I was five.. I was born in Ohio. My old man got a job with the old Seaboard Railroad."

"Are you still religious?"

He snickered.

"What?"

"You wonder why, if I went to a Christian school, I ended up a complete horse's ass." He said the word *Christian* as if he'd just swallowed a wad of phlegm.

"No. Just curious."

Morelli flicked on the TV. Someone had given a ridiculous answer and the Family Feud host was gurning for the audience.

"Enough," he muttered.

"Just a couple—"

"Nope," he said simply, and hit the volume on the television. The sound roared into prominence.

Angie got up and left without another word.

The facility in Bagley was drudgery. Bagley is a pretty town. Lake Lomond—this one unknown to Irish tenors—was inside the city limits. Bagley began as a logging camp in the late eighteen hundreds, and reminded her of the fictional Twin Peaks, though without the peaks. It was a short drive through woods and scattered farms, but she rarely managed to enjoy the scenery.

From the outside, the facility at Bagley was little different from the others, fewer landscape embellishments, perhaps, and outside recreational areas. Bagley was the dumping grounds for many of the needier patients. Most of the Morningsiders there were beholden to the government for food, shelter, and care. The Bagley home had the highest percentage of psychiatric and dementia patients—nearly sixty percent—and a dearth of hope.

Morningside-Bagley was a sad and lonely place, though the facilities were as modern and well-kept as the others. The mood always seemed dimmer, due in part to the whole lighting system being regulated downward for budgetary reasons except for the nurses' stations.

There were at least a couple of suicide attempts every winter, though some, like Alice Weathers, who tried to do herself in by dunking herself head-first in the toilet and flushing multiple times, would be comical had the situation not been so dire.

She was to interview a new patient today, and she dreaded it. Emily Blackfeather was an Ogala Sioux from the Pine Ridge Reservation in South Dakota. She was only seventy-one and far from home. She was a chronic alcoholic with early-onset Alzheimer's eating away at what her addiction hadn't already gobbled up. Coherent exchanges were doubtful, meaning limited talk therapy, and no opioids. The very same Alice Weathers, who had since moved on into the gilded night, rest her soul, had once locked herself in a closet when her Oxycodone had been withdrawn for fear of addiction.

"Who cares if I'm an addict," she'd shrieked. "I'm eighty-two years old!"

Angie entered the room with a nurse and found Emily asleep. Her relief was palpable and she felt guilty about it. Sometimes grace is embodied in the guise of procrastination. Emily had been dosed with benzodiazepine to combat insomnia and withdrawal. She was dark-skinned and dark-haired, now woefully emaciated, body and scalp, her hair strung thin like black corn silk. She had been found in her home unconscious, this a plain, masonry block hovel with a concrete floor and blankets covering broken windows. No one knew where her ex-husband was and her daughter had problems of her own. There wasn't anyone else. The government paid for her care now, small consolation for the thousands of square miles her great-grandparents had once roamed.

"Call me if you need me," Angie whispered, her eyes glued to the wraith before her. "I'll try to catch her awake next time."

The nurse nodded, and Angie continued her rounds amongst this hapless menagerie of derelicts. She sighed a lot at Bagley.

If Angie was becoming more jaded, she hadn't noticed, and certainly would have. She cared. She cared in the clinical sense, her emotions in tight-rein, her composure an automatic function. Her training had taught her that the human body was a machine, and if she failed as a mechanic, she never failed as Triple-A. But she also understood all too well that what might be considered a *natural* part of the aging process was a cruel deception—a pitiless requital for a well-lived life, as well as a cosmic comeuppance for any misspent years. This imbalance did not alter her faith. Her faith was rooted not in justice but in predictability.

Aging is terminal and chaotic, and joy-of-being invariably becomes the desire for relief. Once relief diminishes, death is made welcome, and this was a battle she fought frequently. She did not think it was her right to subdue the dark angel, but rather a function of salvage, just as a stunned survivor walks through the ashes of a house fire plucking charred mementos of a once-thriving life. She often wondered why the human condition, rife with eloquent design and execution, sputtered on so pointlessly instead of simply stopping.

As for the bellicose Mr. Morelli...all she knew to do was to keep him talking.

"Mind if I join you?" she asked pleasantly, peeking through the sliding glass doors.

Morelli scowled and closed his book. He was still working on the Collins.

"Reading is so good for you," she offered.

"Is that why your lips are in such good shape?" he snarled.

She smiled to herself.

May was off to an optimistic start. The snow was gone. The air was warm. A pair of chokeberry trees were beginning to birth white blossoms toward the lake, accenting the omnipresent pine and spruce. Red maples were thickening with green and the dull grass was finally rising without restraint. The day was bright, and the old man sat with the sun upon every part of his body but his head. It was mid-afternoon, near seventy, and no chill at all.

"Is this going to take long?" he grumped.

"Shouldn't."

"Pull the chair out here. Least then I won't have to look down at you."

"Funny," she said, and disappeared inside.

The chair was comfortable, and like nearly everything else in Morelli's room, not standard issue. It was chrome with fake leather and a short backrest.

"There aren't many short jokes I haven't heard. About being young, either. Maybe being short makes me look younger."

"Or being young makes you look shorter."

"Fair enough." She paused. She didn't know how long he'd been *away* or what he retained. "How did you spend last Christmas?"

He scowled. "I don't celebrate Christmas."

"Who was President in 1999?"

"Clinton. That pussy-hound. He'd probably rather screw a cantaloupe than that wife of his."

"Where were you in 1965?"

"San Francisco, California. And you're on the clock."

"Really?" she said. She paused momentarily. "I'll bet that's an interesting story."

"Tick-tock," he grumbled. "Next?"

"Okay. Tell me more about that school—Corinth."

He released a prolonged and exaggerated "No-o-o-o...."

"Then tell me how many times you've been married."

His eyes and mouth shrank again. His warning, as obvious as a snake's rattle or the tornado siren. "That has nothing to do with anything," he said flatly.

"Just trying to understand," she said. "Tell me anything. Lie if you want."

He nearly smiled. "Four," he said. "I've been married four times. All of them have passed away."

"I'm sorry. Your file is..."

"Decidedly incomplete. Vague. Suspicious, even."

"Not suspicious necessarily."

He nodded slowly. "Time's up, Sis. Maybe the next time you're passing by."

"That would be Thursday."

"If I'm not dead by then."

The next morning, Nordgren called again. She let it go to voicemail. During his lunch hour, when she knew he scarcely allowed himself to be disturbed, she called and left a voicemail of her own, stating that everything was going well and as planned.

She tried a new approach with Morelli. She had come empty-handed, as if to simply sit and chat.

She found him on his small patio and pulled the guest chair outside. He reclined the long back of his custom chair a few inches with the push of a button, and with a sense of purpose. Maybe he was going to feign sleep until she took the hint. At least he hadn't barked at her—yet. The wind made ribbons in her hair, but she didn't fuss with it.

Morelli still eyed her suspiciously. "Why'd they send you?"

"Everyone else is afraid of you."

He laughed at that. It still had hair. "Are you Doctor something?"

"No. Just Angie."

He was still working on the Collins novel and picked it up. She didn't want to lose grip.

"Tell me about Florida."

"No."

"Okay. Tell me about San Francisco."

He looked out toward the lake momentarily. A couple of solo fisherman sat motionless in their separate boats, a good hundred yards apart. "A long time ago," he said seriously. "What do you want to know?"

"How you ended up there."

He continued to sit silently.

"Take your time," she said.

His shaggy eyebrows dove inward. "It's not my memory, Sis."

"What, then?"

"I'm debating whether you're worth the effort."

She nodded. "Consider it part of my continuing education."

He muttered to himself but rose to his feet. "Let me get some coffee first and think about it."

He moved steadily, purposefully, his thin face and narrow chin aimed forward. He did not appear encumbered in any way. She wondered why he had wheels on the chair. When he returned, he sat, and took a sip.

"Why do you have a motorized wheelchair?" she asked.

"So I don't have to drag the damn thing in and out," he answered.

The moment settled.

"Okay, there's some background here." He slurped his coffee, loudly and purposely, as if to taunt her. "It all started with a song."

"I like it already."

"I was living in Tampa. I had this song, see. Called *Walkin' the Sax.* It was kind of a novelty tune, except it was really about getting laid."

She paused, as if catching up. "You wrote the song?"

"I just said that."

"Okay. Okay. Sorry."

"It was about a guy whose girl wouldn't put out so all he had was pounding the pud."

"Masturbation."

"Jesus, aren't you quick."

"You can save the sarcasm, Mr. Morelli. Go on."

"I called yankin' the wank, walkin' the sax. Only problem was, I couldn't play the sax. I couldn't play anything. Well, one day—guess it was fifty-eight or so—this Revue came to Tampa. Some shows worked that way. You had three-four singers travel together and use the same backup band. They called them Revues. I went to the show."

"I get it."

"You ever hear of Smiley Horton?"

"I don't think so."

"Sax player. Played on some of the greaser hits. Ended up in Motown."

"Gotcha."

"Anyway, after the show I seek out Smiley. See, all the saps hung around for the stars. Nobody cared about the band. So there wasn't anyone around. I approached Smiley and told him I had this song and needed help with it. He thought I was nuts, of course. I hummed the sax riff and sang a little of the chorus. '*My baby sent me away, said save it for another day, now I'm just lying on my back, walkin' the sax*'."

Angie stifled a smirk.

Morelli continued. "He liked it. He was living in Atlanta at the time. Said if I could come up with the dough he'd help me record it, after he finished the tour."

"How much money?"

"Five hundred bucks. That was a fortune in those days. Might as well have been a million. It took me six months. I was dead busted. Took a bus to Atlanta."

"He take the money and run?"

"No, Sister. He was on the up-and-up. Put together a little combo for me. Bass, drums, guitar, and Smiley on sax. Backup girls. I sang."

"You're kidding."

Morelli grinned genuinely. "Yeah, I know. Pimply kid with a drawl and four colored guys. Well, black guys. You know what I mean. Anyway, we made the record."

"Sorry. How's that tie-in to San Francisco?"

"It was a hit." he said smartly, then gulped his coffee.

"Wait. You had a hit record?"

"You bet your nubile pubiles. You think I'm lying?"

"No. It's just—"

"I know. I know. I'm just a crusty old fart who never accomplished anything, right."

"Sorry. Please go on."

He gathered his thoughts. He seemed bewildered for a moment, as if surprised by the memory, like finding an old photograph long-since lost.

"Anyway, Smiley knew a DJ at this black radio station. Black people were a lot hipper than the white kids. They caught on right away. People started asking for it. Big station in Chicago played it. It hit the charts. We got on a tour. Had to add a couple more songs, but Smiley had one and we did an updated version of an old blues song *Rock It For Me,* written by a guy named Chick Webb with Ella Fitzgerald singing back in 1938. So we had a three-song set and were openers on this tour. Bill Haley was the headliner. He'd had it by then, but still drew a crowd. More stations started playing it. It cracked the Top 40."

"That's amazing."

Morelli was on a roll. "Got an offer to do an album. Albums weren't much in those days. Most kids liked the forty-fives. We had to do a lot of covers, reworked some more old blues tunes, but we got nine more songs down in two weeks. *Sax* hit the Top Twenty. Got our own tour—small jobs—but nobody behind us. We played gyms, clubs in Dixie where I was the only white face in the joint, street dances standing on top of a flatbed truck. But the record kept selling. And the album started selling. All of a sudden, I'm pulling down nearly a grand a week, instead of selling shoes for six months for the same dough. We milked that gig for two solid years. Had fifty grand in the bank by the time it all played out." He paused, then added, "God, I haven't thought about that stuff in a million years."

"Why didn't you go on?"

Morelli shrugged and settled back. "We were tired of it. We were never buddies or anything. Guys wanted to move on. Burned out on playing behind a goofy paleface who couldn't sing. Like I said, Smiley landed in Motown playing backup on all those hits."

"Why didn't you get another band and keep going?"

He smiled again, a smile impossible to interpret, like a stargazing shark. "Zelda," he said simply. "And that's all for today."

Angie Googled *Walkin' the Sax* and was surprised to find a full Wikipedia entry. She read it with a certain delight, like a teenager with a secret no one else knew. Everything he told her had been true. The name of the band was Len and the Royal Flush, which he hadn't mentioned at all. There was even a picture, a pale man standing before four blacks, their arms and hands extended as if ready to snap their fingers. Morelli looked fit, muscular even, but with the same thin face and high forehead, making it appear as if his hairline was already receding, though his hair was dark and brushed back into a full pompadour, the same as the rest of the band. The picture was black and white but he had that same smart-ass smirk telling the world he knew far more than he was saying.

Earl Hogue was an escape artist, and masterful, especially considering he was eighty-five years old. He was thin and broad shouldered like a lightweight boxer. Like many others, Earl's dementia was arbitrary and defied strict diagnosis. His memory was sporadic. He knew who the President was in 1964 but not the year he got married.

He also liked to roam. Despite the fact that there were cameras everywhere, he managed to avoid detection and sneak out. He was already on a short leash. He'd recently stowed away in the SUV of a couple who had come to visit the wife's mother. Earl didn't even know the family. They didn't discover they had a passenger until the husband had to hit the brakes for a hay-baler crossing the road and heard the thump-thump-thump of old Earl tumbling in the back, followed by a loud, "Criminey!" The general consensus among the nurses and the attendants was to either lock Earl in his room, which was illegal, or attach a GPS to him, which was still under consideration.

For the time being, security was to monitor his whereabouts every fifteen minutes. This should have sufficed. It didn't. He seemed to know instinctively when the coast was clear, like antelopes on the Serengeti. Naturally, many of his escapes were timed when the more mobile residents were ambulatory and drew most of the attention.

Angie got the call while she was in already in Walker. Naturally, no one knew how Earl had slipped away again, but a complete search of the facility yielded neither Earl nor the means of escape, though the first thing Angie noticed upon entering his room was his clothes draped across the bed.

She darted to the parking lot, into her van, and off to the races. The home in Walker was a quarter mile to the next intersection. There, nearing the intersection, was a figure in a large dress ambling along. The house slippers provided a hint, but the worn fishing cap—and razor-cut hair beneath—was a giveaway. She passed the old man and pulled onto the berm. She opened the passenger door and Earl got in without a word.

"Nice dress," she said as she swept a U-turn.

"Too big," Earl complained. "If it'd fit, you'd never have known it was me."

"What about the hat?"

"Oh," he said. "Yeah. Forgot about the hat."

Angie sighed in exasperation. "Where are you trying to go when you wander off like that?"

"Hadn't given it much thought," he said.

"Then, why do it?"

"Man needs a hobby."

Earl promised to behave himself, the staff promised to be more diligent, and some of the women in the senior Weight Watchers program signed a petition to make sure Earl stopped prowling through their closets.

Things calmed and resettled into normalcy, until a few weeks later, a high-school kid working with the lawn maintenance crew reported his riding lawnmower missing.

She'd brought coffee for them both, black for him, a half-caf vanilla latte with double milk for herself. Morelli seemed pleased by the gesture and took a sip. "This isn't one of those things where some weasel shits out the beans, is it?"

"A bear eats the weasel first. *Then,* they pluck the beans from bear crap."

"Bet they're hard to sneak up on."

"Harvested by people dying to know the answer to that timeless question, 'does a bear shit in the woods?'"

He nodded. "So what form of nonsense do you have for me today?"

"Zelda. San Francisco."

Again, that odd smile, part-delight, part-B movie villain. "Well, let me see." He sipped and sipped again, though neatly now, almost delicately, never making a sound. The din of a boat motor echoed distantly from the lake, the noise trailing the boat, an illusion created by the speed of sound vs. the speed of light.

Finally— "We played Vegas toward the end of our run."

"Len and the Royal Flush."

He was surprised. "You've been snooping."

"Part of the job."

"Well, don't get too cute."

"Promise."

He paused again. "Vegas was a lot different then. Lot of dumps. Wasn't wall-to-wall glitz like now. We were playing this lounge—something ridiculous—the Blue Lizard or something and Zelda was a cocktail waitress. Wore this goofy blonde wig. Her real hair was black. Black as a crow. Kept it cut short in what they used to call a pageboy. She was a beatnik. Was into Ginsberg, people like that. Dressed in black all the time. Pale like a vampire."

"Okay."

"We had a couple of more months on the road before we shut the band down for good. Then I went back to Vegas. Started hanging out with her and her beatnik friends. Listened to a lot of bad poetry. Drank a lot of bad coffee. Got turned on to reefer, though. That was nice. And God, could she hump."

Angie shifted instinctively. "There are ways to describe things without being coarse," she said plainly.

Morelli laughed. "You shy?"

"You don't have test me to have my attention, you know."

He eyed her for a moment. "Maybe not. Anyway, I learned everything I ever needed to know about pork— making love—from her."

"You fell in love?"

"I don't know about love. We were monogamous. She had a place and dope, and I had bread. And we stuck. Couldn't stand her friends. Fake-ass shits. But when it was just the two of us, it was nice."

"If you didn't like that scene, why did you stay with her? Sex?"

"Scene. I love that. Please. If you try to relate it'll just piss me off."

"Sorry. So why did you stay with her?"

Morelli exhaled long through his nose. "She was different. She could see all sides of things. Kennedy was President and everybody thought something new was coming. We talked about a lot of stuff. She didn't treat me like a rube. Folk was hitting it big in New York, Dylan, Peter, Paul and Mary, so we talked about moving there to be a part of it. I even bought an old flat box guitar from a hock shop and tried to learn to play it. Could make my way through a handful of chords. Just enough to suck."

"But you didn't go to New York."

He shook his head. "Kennedy got wasted at the end of sixty-three. Everything was down-down-down. Ginsberg had been in San Francisco since the mid-fifties. But he went to Europe about this time. But things were still happening in San Francisco. Kerouac and Cassady and Kesey. Music was starting to change, too."

"So you went to San Francisco."

He nodded and a small, wistful smile crept upon his lips. "We did. 1964. Moved to the Mission. It was cheap. That's where all the Latinos lived, but was being taken over by the fruits, the beatniks, and anyone else with a fucking cause."

"Hippies."

"The real ones, yeah. Still a lot of bad coffee, bad poetry, and bad folk songs. Hunter Thompson started writing about how San Francisco was becoming the new center of the universe. You could live cheap on what I had. We could go into any place in the city, do just about anything we wanted, and have a stash of the best dope around for five hundred a month."

"No kidding."

"And not sweat it. So that's what we did. Saw every band around. Most didn't last. Some became legends. Haight-Ashbury started happening. Sitting in the park. Playing tunes. Smoking dope in the open. You could screw somebody new every day if you wanted."

"Did you?"

He grinned at her. "Nah, I was hooked. I was trying to get Zelda to marry me. She always said it wasn't necessary. She was right. Everybody knew we were together. She'd tease me and call me square-boy. I mean, I still wore my hair short, liked regular clothes—no beads or sandals or any of that shit—and I liked to take regular showers."

"You didn't get married."

"We did, finally. Spring of sixty-seven, it must have been. She grabs me by the elbow and we go to the courthouse and do it up the straight way."

"What changed her mind?"

"She was pregnant," he said lowly. "We were both cool with it. I mean, I was past thirty by then. Ready, I guess, if there is such a thing. We still didn't have to get married. But suddenly...she wanted it all legal and done."

Then, a melancholy look slowly spread across his face like a cloud over the lake. Angie wondered if he was phasing out again. She knew she was testing her welcome, but asked, "This was sixty-seven?"

"The *summer of love*," he said. There was an edge to his voice, a self-deprecating sarcasm, a damning judgment.

"I've heard of it, of course," she said.

His scrutiny was taunting, condescending. "Of course. The summer we all became hippies. Funny thing. It was all tourists by then. The real hippies had fled. No more beatniks, either. No more hep cats. No more finger snapping. Still bad coffee and bad poetry, but now it was all set to music. But San Francisco became...dismal. Fake."

"Sounds sad."

"Yeah. I suppose it was." He took a breath and then he was gone again, lost to her in a nebula only he could see.

She drove unaware, the day exquisite and perfect, little wind or clouds, the sky the shade of blue jay wing, May alive with latent blossoms. Milkweed and wild onion. Red baneberry and bog rosemary. The porches of the homes bore hanging baskets of periwinkle and licorice, and prairie rose shrubs. The maple and ash were becoming full, giving even the populated areas a forested appearance. The day gets a running start. The morning clears faster, the swirl low upon the lake fading into the wrinkle of the sun. Warmth comes earlier, though ambient heat is slow waking. If the high is going to seventy-five, it's a daylong process, and the temperature may not reach its peak until evening.

Morelli was going back and she was letting him. She wasn't sure this was the best possible outcome but he was most alert when skating the past. Whatever was to be discovered, whatever unkempt rooms they would enter, if there was to be any healing at all for him, it was to be found among the dried and discarded fragments of the life long forgotten.

Then, disaster, of such haste and bewilderment she still couldn't grasp it right away.

"Who's Betsy?" she asked. Harmlessly.

He looked at her quickly, harshly. "What?"

"You called me Betsy, Mr. Morelli. Is it slang for something—like chick?"

And then, for the first time, he looked genuinely mortified, a visage she recognized, a sad, hollow despair of untold grief. Not weeping, wailing, or any other manageable expression loosed by profound weariness, but an ungovernable horror only the aged cast, and only those who watch consistently can fathom. She'd seen the look countless times. Yet this was different, more dramatic—traumatic. Death in every square millimeter of countenance.

"Mr. Morelli?"

"Leave me alone," he said mournfully, left his chair, went into the bathroom and closed the door.

Angie was assigned a new RN candidate working a psychiatric practicum. Her name was Chrissy. This should have given her a clue.

Chrissy was tall, blonde, and giggly, and had a face as empty as a cheap motel. She would be there for six weeks. She would still do coursework but would travel with Angie two days a week. This put her in an irritable mood. She was not a babysitter. And the fact that the youngling was statuesque, svelte, and beautiful only salted the wound.

"Why psychiatry?" Angie asked. They were on their way to Bagley, the foyer to Hell.

"I don't know. Thought I could get into it," Chrissy answered.

"You must not get depressed easily."

"Oh no. I'm up all the time."

"Because you're dealing with troubled, elderly people, and it can weigh on you."

"Except when Jack died."

"I'm sorry?"

"He was a shoodle. Sweetest little guy."

"You lost me."

"Jack. My dog. Half Shih Tzu, half poodle." She drew a long breath. "He died. That was depressing."

"Well, you're going to see a lot of depressed people the next six weeks."

"I can take it. Besides, I don't plan on working with depressed people anyway."

Angie opened her mouth, but nothing came out for a minute. "Thought you wanted to work in psychiatry."

"I do," she chirped. "But not with the *really* depressed people. Just those that need a little pick-me-up."

Angie nearly swallowed her tongue.

Angie headed toward Park Rapids with the same sense of apprehension as when she had a mammogram. She wanted to avoid Nordgren, if possible, and she had Chrissy in tow, who had jabbered non-stop about her weekend with her boyfriend, Greg, an aspiring musician, who played in a punk band called The Groin. Angie had decided to just let her tramp the halls on her own. Maybe she would do something really stupid—get *caught* doing something really stupid—and they'd shitcan her practicum.

Park Rapids is a small and quaint. Oddly, however, having been named for the rapids on the Fishhook River, it doesn't have the rapids any more. The river was dammed around 1930, though they left the name intact. It does claim to be the headwaters of the mighty Mississippi River, its humble beginnings decidedly creek-ish. They also have Jasper's Jubilee Theater, a hit with upper Midwesterners too cheap to go to Branson. This summer it advertised 'clean comedy'. What's the fun in that?

Once past the charmingly small downtown, the area, like most of this part of Minnesota, is rural. It doesn't take long to be in the country in any direction. More, this is still the Plains in nearly every sense, though bison no longer roam free. Occasionally, however, a stray moose wanders in and clogs traffic, such as it is.

There is an inherent sweetness in the temper of such places. No one seems to long for bustle and elbows, and even minor and infrequent urges are placated by semi-annual excursions to the Mall of America in Minneapolis. Kids yearn to shed these bucolic environs, but most return after a good dose of hubbub. Successes are held gripped in weathered hands and shoved deeply into pockets, rarely seen and never spoken of.

Farming is reliant upon prices as much as any other endeavor, though the keepers of the land would be loath to delight in the misfortune of others to drive prices upward, unless, of course, the unfortunate individual was a Packers fan, and even then, his recovery would be prayed for during Sunday services.

At her desk, Angie worked the internet. Corinth Christian had indeed been a small, coed college in central Florida, specializing in 'A Bible-based education to prepare young people to combat the evils in the world'. Morelli must have been a naïve young man then. The college didn't exist any longer. It hadn't lasted much past the fifties.

She didn't see Morelli for several days. Her time was consumed by old patients having breakdowns and new patients working up to breakdowns. One of her Walker patients had had enough, screamed at the top of her lungs she was going to wait until the first semi came by and jump out in front of it. Seventy-two hours observation in the hospital.

The cascade into madness is nearly always accompanied by preter-natural strength. Two attendants were trying to subdue her at even odds. Not to mention that she could've died of old age waiting for a semi to come by in Walker. The town of Walker has fewer than a thousand residents, though it also has the Northern Lights Casino, operated by the Leech Lake Band of Minnesota Chippewa. A Prince tribute band was currently headlining. It was a good time to be a Chippewa.

And Chrissy speaking to the poor, distraught woman as she would to an errant puppy who peed on the floor. "Now, now, now. Behave yourself."

As she approached the door to his room, she heard a commotion, a voice raised in anger—Morelli's, followed by a shriek of surprise—a nurse's, followed by a hard wham! against the door, and the nurse's hasty exit. Leona barreled out as fast as her chubby legs would carry her, her face an amalgam of anger and fear. She nodded when she saw Angie but didn't slow.

"That man's an asshole," she said, and retreated up the hall.

Angie slowly pushed open the door. The first thing she saw was Morelli's stainless-steel Yeti mug, its contents splattered on the wall and floor. Fortunately, it had been nearly empty. After a moment, Morelli exited the bathroom with a hand towel. His face was red with rage.

"Here," she said. "Please."

Without a change of expression, he tossed her the towel. She wiped up the mess in a few seconds.

"There," she said. "I take it you would rather be alone."

"I was going to sit out," he said, non-committally. "You can stay for a minute." He muttered, "Fucking cow." Then he mounted his chair and rode through the outer doorway.

This time she brought Guatemalan coffee, milder, not so harsh. Morelli nodded per his custom after the first sip but made no comment. He eyed her with the same grim expression, but said mischievously, "If you really want to be a pal, bring me a McDonald's milkshake. Vanilla."

She paused. "Technically that would be food. And I'm not allowed."

"Thought you ran this place," he said meanly.

"Let me see what I can do, okay?"

He did not respond.

"Want to tell me what that was all about?"

"Every fucking day it's the same fucking shit. Take my temperature. Take my blood pressure. 'When was your last bowel movement'?" He said the last of this in a snide, mocking voice.

"Sorry. But that's her job. You know that. She doesn't make the rules."

"I was just waking up from a nap. Told the fat ass to come back later. She ignored me."

"Sorry," she repeated. "Protocol. Guess we're all locked into a routine. That's it?"

He glared at her. "She asked me what day it was. Same as every other fucking day."

"That's just to make sure your brain is awake."

"So what? Look, I'm not stupid. I know why I'm here. You know why I'm here. I don't need a reminder, and what the fuck difference does 'what day it is' make anyway? They're all the same."

"Okay. I get that."

"Then she did her 'When was your last bowel movement' shtick, and I told her more recently than she'd gotten laid."

Angie stifled a snicker. "That was pretty insensitive."

"Tired of that old porker. Never could abide a woman with fat big toes."

Feet again. Was he some kind of fetishist? "Any way you could bear it for two minutes a day if I make sure she doesn't ask you what day it is?"

"Maybe," he grunted. "If I'm not asleep."

"Fair enough." She took a beat. "So what day is it?"

Morelli snapped his head toward her and caught her grinning like a spaniel. She began to laugh. He shook his head and chuckled low under his breath.

"If it's Wednesday it must be tater tot casserole," she giggled.

"Mm-mm," he said facetiously. "Can't wait." .

Angie changed his orders with Leona huffing and puffing, as if this was the worst indignity she'd ever suffered. "Why do you coddle that old fart?" she demanded

Angie lowered her voice to a whisper. "I'm thinking he must have something on Nordgren."

"Really?" The bulky woman was all ears now.

"That big space, y'know. I think I'm getting close."

"You'll tell me, won't you?"

"You'll be the first."

Leona nodded, then winked.

Chrissy got her first write-up and sat with her lips pooched out enough to hold rain. Angie was growing wearier and less patient by the day. The girl was like a toddler with a broken cookie.

"Look, this isn't personal. We have to keep these records for the state. They hear about a complaint that's not written up and in a file, they get crabby."

"I didn't do anything wrong," she whimpered.

"No. Your intentions were good. Certain things require a little...diplomacy."

"All I did was try to explain she had options that would help everyone involved."

"Chrissy," Angie began, "You just don't tell an eighty-year-old woman she needs to start wearing diapers instead of peeing the bed. Or that they come in her size now. Or that they've improved a lot since she was a baby."

She was returning to Bemidji from another day at Walker when her phone rang. And it had been such a relaxing drive, too, even with Chrissy prattling on. She didn't answer. She'd wait until lunch again and leave another voicemail. Maybe something like, "If you don't leave me alone and let me do my job, I'm going to spit in your eggs."

"Why didn't you answer?" Chrissy asked.

"Wrong number," Angie said.

"How do you know?"

"Caller ID on the screen there."

"Oh, I thought I saw a name. Mine only shows a name if they're on my contact list."

"Mine too. Unless it's a wrong number. Then it says, 'wrong number'.

Chrissy nodded. "Smart."

She held out the milkshake. He took the milkshake with a simple, "McDonald's may be shit, but they still make the best vanilla shakes."

"May still need to melt some."

He nodded, and sucked, and got about a half strawful. "Damn, that's good."

She extended her legs and crossed them. "Tell me about Florida."

He soured. "Not much to tell. Left when I was a kid."

"You went to school there."

"It was close, it was cheap, and you could still get a teaching certificate."

She smiled. "You wanted to teach?"

"Hell, I didn't know what I wanted to do. Never did, really."

"You wrote a song. Made music."

"Yeah, but I got lucky. Wasn't driven."

"You mean like finding a passion?"

"Maybe."

"Was once engaged to a guy like that."

"Your pooh bear?"

She laughed. "He'd have died if I'd ever called him that."

"He was a bum, a ne'er-do-well, 'a rambler and a gambler and a sweet-talkin' ladies' man'?"

"I know that from somewhere."

"Joni Mitchell."

"Yeah, okay."

"Met her first husband once, back in the old days. Chad Mitchell. Folkie. Had a trio."

It was mid-morning. Summer glowed. She took a turn watching the lake. A score of geese rose from the surface as a boat passed. The sun danced synchronously upon the water like elfin ballerinas, wavering as if intangible.

A couple held hands as they walked in the grass across the rear grounds, probably taking a shortcut to the coffee shop. They were overdressed, him with a white long-sleeved shirt and trousers, her with a floral-patterned blouse and pale skirt. Too old for students. Probably instructors who drew the short straw for summer school. They laughed together at something unheard and rubbed shoulders, their steps seeming lighter than air. They did not look toward the facility at all, nor the lake. Their eyes found only each other. Angie sighed.

"Finding a passion is not as easy as you think," she said.

"Maybe. I regret not choosing a profession. Being totally involved in something."

"But you were successful."

"Yeah, but I didn't care. Hell, maybe that's why I was successful. Like music. Never had the discipline to really pursue it." He paused and looked at her earnestly. "Satisfaction has to come from somewhere. Like you. I never had that. I never really cared that much about anything. And I missed that."

She was surprised by his candor. It made him seem almost—human. She met his gaze. "You cared about Zelda."

Again, his face grew long. "That I did. But it wasn't enough."

It was the first really hot day of the year and still a few days shy of the Memorial Day weekend. This far north, the humidity rarely comes from swirling storm systems. It comes from Minnesota being covered with water. Water evaporates and hangs in the air like a wet sock. Dripping-from-your-drawers humidity is as uncommon as a Presbyterian.

The water temperature was still too cold to swim, but that didn't stop pleasure boaters nicked with spray, the wind abating the sun, wakes rising into brisk amber mists. Traffic was busy, too. It was a weekday, a workday, and the lunch hour, though the citizenry seemed compelled to be out and about—and motorized—as if they were afraid they'd miss something.

Things were relatively calm at Morningside-Bemidji. Patients and guests could go outside, or at least, those who were able. A short row of wheelchairs was lined beneath the eaves, their inhabitants looking like some avant-garde performance art piece of gargoyles dressed from yard sales. Even so, the warmth seemed to pacify those of faltering bone and diminishing mind. None were whole, yet many were rich in spirit, absorbing, then reflecting, some rare element of grace known only to those who had visited the world for such a long time. Or else, their morning meds were just kicking in.

Those who'd had an effortless whiz were doubly blessed.

Leona informed Angie that Morelli hadn't been sleeping, and had been more ornery than usual.

Angie found him in bed, sipping his own coffee, staring at a blank TV, as if finding some hidden play in the dark screen.

"Sorry, I didn't have time to swing by McDonald's," she said.

Morelli simply shrugged.

She moved toward the chair but continued to stand. She wondered if dredging up the past was draining his batteries when most of their potency had already diminished. She felt guilty, responsible, though she told herself process was non-threatening, even therapeutic.

"Sit, if you're staying," he grumbled. You make me nervous hovering around like a gonad."

She sat. "You want to tell me what's bothering you?"

He wagged his head. "Nightmares," he muttered.

"You want to tell me about them?"

"No. They come and go."

"Do you think you're overstimulated?"

He glared at her. "Save the psychobabble for the crips and the crazies."

"Sor-ry."

He snorted abrasively. "You are one relentless munchkin."

She spoke in a terrible falsetto. "Just following the Yellow Brick Road."

"Take the left at the scarecrow this time. Might be surprised where it leads."

"Tell me more about San Francisco or is that what's bothering you."

He seemed confused for a moment. Then. "Where did I leave off?"

"You and Zelda. Parenthood."

His aspect morphed into that troubled look again. His eyes moved to the outer door. He scanned the area longingly, as if the sun might cleanse the brume and return hue and tone to his flesh. Yet he remained unmoved.

He raised his bed some, shoving his pillows behind his shoulders. He began, though fragmented at first. "That summer ruined everything. Too many people. Too many posers. Some things were still cool. In June was the Monterey Pop Festival. Hendrix, Joplin, and a lot of everybody. This is two years before Woodstock."

"Were you there?"

"Monterey? No. I was into being married, and the baby. Lotta good jams, though. More good music than bad."

"Good times."

"Yeah." He stopped, as if reliving the memory before continuing. "Zelda was due late September—early October. By the summer she was showing pretty good. She cut out smoking dope, drinking, a regular Suzy Homemaker. I'm sure she got a few second-hand buzzes when we took our walks, because the shit was everywhere. L.A. may have had smog, but we had weed fog." He drifted for a moment.

"So was it a boy or a girl?"

"Huh?"

"The baby."

Again, that look of disbelief-cum-incomprehension-cum-despair. "Boy. She went into labor in August. Too soon. I was in a panic trying to get her to a hospital."

Angie waited for the punch.

"The baby was stillborn."

"Oh God. I'm so sorry."

"So was I. But nobody was sorrier than Zelda."

"That had to be impossible for her."

"Yeah. Zelda took it hard. Really hard. If she hadn't had to go through delivery and all that, it would've been better. But she pushed out a dead baby and that did something to her."

Angie held her tongue and waited. He went on, though his voice slowed and his words were bare of inflection, his eyes sagging so the red flesh inside the lower lids looked like wounds.

"She clung to me like she was scared I'd just disappear. And we still did stuff. But she was like a robot or something. One night she was lying on the bed on top of the covers. Just staring at the ceiling. That's when I noticed her feet. Bruises."

Feet. Again.

"What about the bruises?"

"She was shooting up between her toes. Trying to keep me from finding out."

"God," Angie murmured.

"Junk," he said. "I didn't know anything about heroin. But I was afraid if I braced her about it, she'd fold."

Again, she waited. Now he was watching her, the same sad eyes, but narrowed as if inspecting her for duplicity, or some pitying judgment, any invitation to lash out. Finding none, he resumed.

"We usually took a walk around dusk. It was late September, but still warm. It had been a sunny day and dusk was perfect. She bailed on me. Said she just wanted to rest, but for me to go on. And she smiled at me. She actually smiled to let me know that things were getting better. And I felt better."

He paused again and closed his eyes as if to sleep.

"I went on. She was in bed when I got home. And she was dead. She had ODed. I never knew if she'd done it deliberately, but I always suspected she had."

"Oh Mr. Morelli." she said softly.

His eyes were rheumy when he reopened them. "She'd shot up in the arm this time. The works were lying right by her elbow. She wasn't even trying to hide it from me."

"I'm so sorry," she whispered.

"All out for Lotus Land," he said gently. Then he looked away and vanished.

At Walker, Chrissy followed her like an Afghan hound on a short lease. The girl was a long-legged menace anyway—a threat to the civilized world. Maybe she would grow up...by the time she was fifty. She didn't belong in nursing. She belonged on a cruise ship, maybe teaching an exercise class.

The duty nurse said, "Mr. Hankinson flushed his hearing aids. Wanted to make sure the toilet had enough power before he took a dump. Remember, the last time, he went nutso because there was a floater that wouldn't go down? "

"Christ," she barked. "Before you make this a psychiatric issue, why not have Maintenance look at his toilet first, huh?"

Wounded, the nurse edged away.

Angie reached down and realized she'd forgotten her satchel. "Damn, my briefcase."

"I'll get it," Chrissy chirped.

"Thanks."

Claire Abernathy was a ninety-year-old widow whose family was far-flung and out-of-touch except for a weekly phone call. The woman sat up in her bed, staring at her dining tray, weeping and wringing her hands.

"What's the matter, Mrs. Abernathy?"

"There's bugs in my jello."

Angie moved closer. "Those are little carrot slivers. Good for your eyes."

She squinted hard at the jiggling square on her plate but stopped crying. "Oh," she said. "Doesn't seem to be doing much good, does it?"

The door swung open and Chrissy bounded in. Then Angie noticed she was empty-handed.

"Did you get my satchel?"

She shook her head. "Guy said he would get it for you, so I wouldn't miss anything. Very nice old man."

Angie nodded absently. Then her face swelled in all directions at the same time. "Earl!" she shouted.

She ran down the hall as fast as her legs would carry her, Chrissy on her heels.

"Why did you give him the keys to my car?" she angrily demanded.

"I thought he was like the valet or something," she said.

Angie burst through the front door. "Didn't you notice the pajamas?"

Chrissy protested. "I thought it was a uniform!"

There went Earl Hogue in her van, out of the parking lot, the back of his head barely visible above the seat, the flashers blinking with abandon.

The police had no trouble tracking him down. He was driving twenty miles-an-hour on the two-lane highway with a speed limit of fifty-five, at least six cars lined behind him, a cacophony of horns and curses polluting the air. A farmer on a tractor parallel to the road passed them all.

Chrissy was written-up again, pouting at the injustice of it all.

"I swear I thought it was a uniform," she muttered.

"Just so you know, there were five cars ahead of me in the drive-thru," she said.

Morelli stuck the straw into his cup and stirred.

"You said you wanted it thick," Angie said.

He pulled the straw from the cup and licked the ice cream mixture clean. "So I did." He put the cup in the cup holder in the arm of his chair. "Needs to sit for a bit."

They remained indoors. Outside, the day looked pristine until you noticed the treetops, bending and waving like one of those goofy advertising windsocks. The bluster was all bark, but unpleasant. Even the small bass boats couldn't tame the wind. They would spin in super slow-motion, like the eddy of a clogged drain.

Morelli sat in his chair, pensive, staring out the glass doors to the patio like a restless kid longing to be outside. Angie sat at the end of the small loveseat facing him.

"Did you stay in San Francisco?" she asked.

"What?" he asked.

"After the fall of sixty-seven," she said delicately.

"Oh, I moved to a farmhouse outside Sunol, California. It wasn't really a farm. Five acres. But it was quiet and remote."

“Close to San Francisco?”

“Yeah. Not far. Alameda County.”

“Sounds nice.”

“Yeah. I wanted to be in touch with the city. I just didn’t want to be there every day. I liked the quiet.”

“Any new adventures?”

`“Huh? Oh. I guess the next thing would be Paul Clennan.”

“Paul Clennan?”

“One of the guys I knew from the old days was Dude Clennan. He called everybody ‘Dude’, so people hung that on him. He was a kind of apocalyptic hippie. Talked about the end of the world and shit like that. Anyway, I go to Dude’s one day and in there with him is this guy who looks like a narc. Buzz-cut, clean as a nun’s undies, shiny black lace-up shoes. He was Dude’s brother and had spent six years in the Army. Lucky bastard was stationed in Korea the whole time. Viet Nam was a few miles across the water and the only way he’s going get shot at in Korea is if he doodles somebody else’s wife.”

“I thought the war was all but over by then.”

Morelli shook his head. “Should’ve been. Didn’t really start drawing down until seventy-three. Nixon,” he sneered. “What a tool.”

“This Clennan fellow stay out?”

“Yep. He bids adios to Uncle Sam and comes to hang with big brother until he can find a job.”

“What’d he do?”

"He was a mechanic in the Army. A wizard with cars and trucks. I see he's driving a sixty-five Bel Air and it's immaculate. Then he says, "Guess what I paid for it?" New cars were twenty-five hundred or more. So I guess eight hundred, maybe a thousand. He grins—he had these buck teeth like a horse—and shakes his head. Says two hundred. I say he's full of shit and then he shows me the odometer. Got over two hundred thousand miles on it. Then he lays it out for me."

He stopped and drew on the straw again. The shake had softened and the thick liquid rose up like a cartoon thermometer. Morelli paused after a long slurp and squinted until the brain freeze subsided. He looked comical—like a kid.

"He tells me he got this car at an auction. Looks like crap but the guts are still solid, even with high miles. He painted it for fifty bucks. The rental company kept it on the road for five years and then retired it. They figure it's worn out. Who wants to rent a five-year-old car anyway? Tells me he put less than a hundred bucks in it. Cleaned it inside and out. Made sure nothing major was busted, tightened it all up, tires, battery, everything. Then...I start thinking."

"I'll just bet."

Morelli smiled mischievously. "I look around at used cars and I notice a couple of things. First, they're asking a lot for five-year-old cars, and second, all the people doing that kind of business are sleazy."

"Ah."

"I go to one of these auctions with him. He's right. Lot of old cars that look run to death. But I make him an offer. I buy five cars cheap and he fixes them up. Split the profit. We sell them through the paper. We do this and sell the cars in two weeks. Am I boring you?"

Angie had stifled a yawn. "No, sir. Sorry. Couple of restless nights. Job stuff."

He grins like a cat. "Old farts getting to you?"

"Only the really stubborn ones."

Then he laughed, a short, unpleasant sound. "We done?"

"No, go ahead."

"Obviously, I see a potential. A few things I need to know first. Is there a steady supply, one, and will he stick with it and not fag out. He says he's in all the way. So, I rent this space that used to be a gas station. Room for maybe thirty-forty cars. I also do a couple of things I figure will help. First, I call it 'No Car Over Five Hundred Dollars'. Second, I offer a six-month, six-thousand-mile warranty."

"Wasn't that risky on old junkers?"

"See, that's the thing. They weren't junkers. Just driven a lot. Warranties are bullshit anyway. All the heavy parts are made for use. It's cosmetic damage, cleaning the interior, and things like that. Maybe a little paint touch-up. We open with like twenty-five cars. We do a little advertising. We sell out in a month. Next thing you know, we lease this big space used to be a restaurant. Parking enough for a hundred cars. We keep going to auctions, buy up rental cars, ex-cop cars, company cars, things like that. By our third year we were selling twelve hundred cars a year. Clearing about a hundred-fifty bucks per. We expand but we never get greedy. And we honor our warranty even if the owner has done something stupid like bang into a curb and knock the front-end out-of-whack or blow out a fuel pump hot-rodding the damn thing. That gives us a good reputation. By nineteen seventy-five we have ten locations, selling ten thousand cars a year."

Angie paused. "Wow. You got rich."

"Well, I was putting most of it away. And Paul owned a piece. And we tried to pay everyone decent. I stayed in the little house near Sunol. By the time we capped out I had a couple of million in the bank."

"And you were what—forty?"

He poked a shoulder skyward and took a sip of melted milkshake. "The business was going great. But I was still..."

"Hurting."

"Yeah, okay. Lonely, for sure. Wondering if things were, you know...remember that old song *Is That All There Is*. No, you wouldn't remember it. Way before your time."

"Peggy Lee."

"So you heard of it?"

"She's from North Dakota."

"That's right. I keep forgetting we're so close to there. I've only been around here since I moved into this shitpile."

"So what happened?"

"Beverly," he said simply.

Chrissy had the attention span of a bumblebee. On the drive to Park Rapids she had rattled on about some reality star-turned-aspiring model, the girl first having birthed a child at a very young age, then onto to some show where they crammed a bunch of people together and filmed it, purportedly 'unscripted' but with peevishness and teeming with clenched-faced emoting, and now as the guest-panelist of some second-rate talent show featuring unpleasant-looking people performing equally unpleasant acts. The sum of such accomplishment made Angie make a mental note to send some money to Planned Parenthood.

"Now I hear Playboy is paying her big bucks to pose for them," Chrissy said excitedly.

"A dream come true," Angie said drolly.

"I know, right? I also hear that she's on the list for *Dancing with the Stars.*"

"I hope she's saving her money."

"Oh, she makes tons, I'm sure. She already has a fragrance coming out. Devil Me, or something like that. Oh, and she was dating this hip-hopper. But he's a wannabe. Doesn't even have a record deal."

"So sad for him."

"Yeah. I saw his youtube video. He's like a cross between Chance the Rapper and Justin Bieber, except he doesn't sing. He raps about how much it sucks to live in America, while these three hos sing *America the Beautiful* in the background. It's outrageous."

"I'll bet."

"No kidding!"

"Well, if her career stalls out she can always crank out another kid."

"Don't you know it. She's got it going on."

"Then maybe she can be on one of those rehab shows."

"Hey, I never thought of that. But once she finishes her plastic surgery she'll be a supermodel for sure."

"For sure."

Maybe the RN curriculum had gotten a tad too easy.

It was later in the day, but the sun was still bright, shining at an angle that skimmed the treetops. Stray dandelion seeds flitted in the air like mini-paratroopers on a mission. Sounds were intrusive, cars in route to wherever and car doors slamming in the shopping center parking lot, followed by muffled voices, the tone of which dependent upon whichever business they'd come to visit. The voices entering the hearing aid store were always louder. A small plane flew overhead. Summer is also the time to tempt fate in every extreme.

There was ample shade on the patio, but the shadows seemed to move first one way then reverse course. Morelli had situated himself with the sun in profile, warming his face but avoiding his eyes. Angie sat with the sun to her back, feeling it at the crown of her head.

"Can I ask you question?"

Morelli slurped happily, then looked at her. "It's not one of those 'how many nickels are in three quarters', is it?"

She made a little sound through her nose. "No. Why do you want your milkshakes extra thick if you have to wait for them to melt, anyway?"

"Why get hot coffee if you have to wait for it to cool before you drink it?"

"I don't know. That's the way it's made."

"Hot water brings out the flavor. Thicker means more ice cream and less milk."

"That makes sense."

"Pretty good for a senile old fart."

"Pretty good for anyone."

He nodded. "Fifteen." Then he sucked hard, rendering a sound from his cup like a worn transmission.

Angie was confused. "Fifteen what?"

"Nickels in three quarters," he said.

The wind roused again, but Angie was comfortable and didn't move, watching the thin tops of the trees dance the hula. The wind wouldn't last this time. She didn't know how she knew. She just did. In the distance kids threw Frisbees near the park by the lake. Moms pushed strollers or jogged behind them. It was a weekday, but the lake was still relatively crowded. She wanted to be elsewhere, taking better advantage before it was all gone again but she was where she was supposed to be, damn the warmth, damn the light, dammit all. She sighed.

"Beverly," she offered.

Morelli's eyes brightened and he set his cup aside to allow the remaining contents to soften further.

"Beverly was a lady. I don't mean she was naïve or would allow herself to be walked on or anything, but she loved being female and wanted to be a wife and mother."

"My best friend is that way."

"Well, I'd never met anyone like her. I mean, she was like Donna fricking Reed. She didn't run the vacuum in a cocktail dress and pearls, but she was always neat and put together."

"How did you meet her?"

"Our second location was in San Jose. Decent-sized town and a good market for us. This was way before all that Silicon Valley shit. The lot was next door to a bank, and she worked as a teller."

"I thought she was a homemaker."

"Well, she wanted to be a homemaker. She was divorced and had a six-year-old kid."

"So you started spending more time in San Jose, I take it."

"Yes I did. And we hit it off. Tell you the truth, I just liked having her around. She was a good listener. I told her about music and my life in San Francisco. She'd lived in the area forever, but all my stuff was alien to her. Of course, my life was tame by sixties' standards, but we'd led very different lives."

"You tell her about Zelda?" she asked softly.

"Eventually, yeah. Everything."

"You got along with her son?"

"I knew absolutely nothing about kids. Tried, though. I was a few years older than Beverly. I was forty and a young forty but didn't know how to relate to a six-year-old."

"But you didn't want to walk away."

"No. It was a real courtship, too. Old-fashioned. Real dates. Took me forever to get into her pants."

"Yuck."

"Please, Princess. You ain't no virgin."

"She wanted to make sure you loved her for who she was?"

He grunted. "Let me tell you something. No one ever loves someone for who they are. They love them for who they can be to them."

"What did you love about her?"

"I guess she taught me the value of self-respect in a way."

"Intrinsic value."

"Glad to see all that tuition paid off."

"Good for something, right?"

"Well, I never considered what kind of a person I was but Beverly talked about goodness as if it was a tangible thing."

"What was it?"

"Trying to think of an example. Oh. We were doing something with the kid. A minor league ballgame or something. And I had to make a quick stop at the store. Rolaids or whatever. Had acid reflux before anybody talked about it."

"It's in my secret file."

"What? Oh, you're a real scream, Sis."

"Out with Beverly and the kid at the store."

"Yeah. There was this guy in a wheelchair parked outside. He had a sign that said, 'please help a veteran' or something like that. Young guy. Long hair and fuzz on his face like a lot of Viet Nam vets those days. He was a double amputee. I get back in the car and we're driving away and Beverly asks, "Did you give that soldier money?" I didn't know what her beef was, so I said, "a little." She says, "Why? Doesn't he get help from the government?" And I said, "Maybe. But no amount of money is going to make up for losing both legs." She says, "What did you say to him?" And I said, "I apologized for all the people who treated him like shit. Like being a soldier was a bad thing."

"It was a very unpopular war."

"So what? You'd rather have guys refusing to fight and getting a lot of people killed just because of politics? Guys on the line don't care about politics. They just want to live through it. Soldiers are asked to do things regular people couldn't understand in a million years."

"There's no higher level of nobility?"

"Not for a soldier. Save fucking nobility for the guys not getting shot at."

"What did she say?"

"She scrunches up beside me and whispers that I'm wonderful. She says she watches twenty people walk past that guy and I'm the only one who stopped. Later, she tells me that helping people without questioning anyone's motives—or whatever—is an act of goodness."

"Fundamental decency."

"I don't know. All I'm thinking is that I'm going to get into some serious flesh."

"Of course you did."

He grabbed his cup again and slurped. The shake had melted and that familiar sucking sound broke the mood. "Damn. Don't they make these things any bigger?"

No sooner had Angie arrived at Bagley when her pager went off, a 9-1-1 and a room number. Angie fled the darkened room into the harsh hallway lights.

The room number was Emily Blackfeather's, and the only nurse present had her hands full. Emily was thrashing, and had pulled her G-tube free as milky liquid spread into a large oily spot on the front her gown. As the nurse fought to hold her down, Angie grabbed the other reedy arm, still strong enough to repel them. The Indian grunted and swung her head from side-to-side shouting, "Thipi! Thipi!" *Home! Home!* in the old language.

"Chrissy come here and help me!" Angie ordered.

Chrissy shuffled near. "What do I do."

"Hold her arm until I can get a hypo ready!"

Chrissy obeyed, but faltered and fumbled as the woman glared at her with maniacal black eyes. Angie tried to wedge herself between them with a hypodermic hovering above the old woman's arm like a snake ready to strike.

"Pin her arm down!" Angie shouted.

Chrissy finally got the arm still enough for Angie to move in. She found the spot and plunged.

The effect was not instantaneous. Blackfeather's system wouldn't tolerate much of a sedative. Soon, however, she relaxed, her dark eyes still open wide and shining with displeasure.

She looked at Chrissy and spat, "Ipa! Ipa!"

Then she became silent and still. Angie stood back, pulled herself together, and issued orders.

"What'd she say?" Chrissy asked, trembling from the ordeal.

"I don't know," Angie said. "Something in Sioux, I think."

The nurse who had managed to keep Blackfeather in bed, straightened her smock and smiled. She looked at Chrissy. "She said you were an ugly witch."

The next day Angie got a note from Chrissy who said she wouldn't be returning. Angie didn't mind. It was the note itself that drew a dry smile. She thought about framing it and putting it on her office wall.

Part of it read, "I like being a nurse. Not sure I want to work with such sick people, though."

She brought an extra-large milkshake with her this time to insure her welcome, such as it was.

"This is as big as the come," she said.

"Well, you can't have everything."

Again, the weather had turned mild, overcast. The sun played hide-and-seek with the clouds, and the sound of jet skis echoed across the water, accompanied by the gleeful shouts from unencumbered kids. She almost envied them, their relative abandon, their sheer lack of responsibility. But another part of her looked there and thought, "Just you wait. Are you in for it."

A mosquito buzzed her ear and she swatted at the sound. There is nothing more seditious in nature than that high-pitched zzzz ramping off the tympanic membrane. It's a cosmic preamble, like the odor of a fart. No one from other regions would believe the preponderance of mosquitoes in the upper Midwest. The winters don't kill them as would seem rational. Eggs are laid in the fall in damp soil. They sleep but don't die. Once the sun hits them in the spring, they submerge, then hatch. Thousands of larvae can flourish in the water contained within an upturned leaf, and Minnesota has enough water to turn the Mojave into a swamp.

"You married Beverly."

"Seventy-six, I think it was. Found this great house on the cliffs in Carmel and we moved."

"Things were good."

"Yeah. Great, even. Got the kid into a good school. We'd socialize a little. We got bicycles and tooled around. Spent nearly all our evenings and weekends together. The business was doing well but my head was with Beverly."

"She'd brought peace into your life."

He took a moment. "I didn't think about it in those terms, but yeah, that's the way it was. She was a nurturer. I didn't realize how much crap I was carrying around until I saw the other side."

"Can you tell me about it?"

"Well, you know. Zelda, for one."

"Lot of baggage there, I imagine."

"If you want to call it that."

"What about earlier. In Florida?"

Again, he eyed her, now with eyes sharp and hostile. A switch had flipped, undeniably so, and bared its teeth. "No, no, no. Florida was nothing. Stupid kid's stuff."

"You grew up there. You spent your formative years there."

He waved his hand dismissively. "It was nothing."

"You went to a Christian college. But you never talk about religion, or faith."

"What the fuck is this? You wanted to hear the story. If you want to root around like some psychology fuck, do it somewhere else!"

"But I am a psychology fuck, Mr. Morelli. I don't mean any harm."

"Yeah, yeah, yeah."

She let it drop. "I'm sorry. I didn't mean to make you angry."

He seemed appeased, and the blush faded from his face.

"I haven't heard a 'happily ever after' yet."

Morelli half-grimaced a smile, more the relief of a survivor after a close call than genuine pleasure. Then, he sighed deeply. "Well, I got stupid."

Then, just as quickly, a dull lifelessness settled upon his face, like the moment before surgery and the anesthetist says to count backward from a hundred. *Ninety-eight...Ninety-seven...*

"Tell me how you were stupid."

Morelli gave her a quizzical look.

"Beverly. You said you got stupid."

"Oh. Yeah. I did. Well, I didn't think it was stupid at the time. In fact, I thought it was great."

"What?"

"I sold the company."

"The car company?"

"Yep. Guy from L.A. offered me four million dollars. That was a ton back then. Of course, it wasn't all mine. Paul got a million of that. He had to agree to stay on, though. Buy and see the cars got fixed. Uncle Sam got a piece. Bought some stock. But...I still had most of my savings."

"High-on-the-hog money."

"Indeed."

"So why did it turn out wrong?"

Morelli seemed to dwell on this, as if he wasn't sure how to explain it. "Because I didn't know what to do with myself," he said finally. "I thought spending more time with Beverly would make everything that much better."

"Too much of a good thing?"

"I got restless. I was pretty grouchy for a year-or-so there."

“Hard to imagine.”

“I know, right.” He smirked then resettled. “I wasn’t smart about it. Started picking silly fights with Beverly just because I didn’t know what to do.”

“So you had to find another diversion.”

“Well, the diversion turned out to be picking on the kid.”

“Hard being a step-parent.”

Again he seemed absent at first, then began as if someone had undone a pause button.

“The kid had always been a Mama’s boy. He was a teenager by then. Didn’t have a crew to hang out with. Watched TV all the time. Hardly ever said two words to me.”

“Not unusual with an only child.”

“I know. Child psychology was not my forte. But this kid was as hopeless as a fat girl on prom night.”

“No direction.”

Morelli craned his neck as if stiff and groaned. “It was a big house. Had his own TV. The big TV was in the den. He was watching some silly-assed movie and I wanted to watch the Space Shuttle. So I told him if he wanted to watch the movie, go into his room.”

“A common disagreement, I imagine.”

“Yeah. Except he decided then it was time to rebel. He came at me. Said he hated me, and he wished his mother had never met me, and on-and-on. I grabbed him by his belt loops and shoved him toward his bedroom—him squawking all the way. He swung his hands and hit me a couple of times, but not hard enough to hurt. Beverly came running and pulled at me to let him go. I...must've shoved her or something. As a reflex. And she fell and hit her head against the wall. Then all Hell broke loose. More crying than an Italian funeral. We separated after that."

"Oh, man."

"I was okay for a week or so. Stayed in a hotel. We talked on the phone. Both of us apologized, but I was still steamed. Told her we ought to send the kid to military school to make a man out of him. She got hysterical about that."

"So you didn't reconcile."

"No. She pulled the plug."

Occasionally there are days when everything fits perfectly and falls into place, reminding us of far-reaching possibilities, and also—perhaps ponderously, that such days are all too infrequent. These are days when the law of averages fails in one's favor and are not part of human construct—like traversing a three-mile city street and hitting every green light. Days when the heavens are aligned in perfect synchronicity and say "you betcha" to the whole sublunary world.

Angie believed God was smiling down upon all the fair denizens of the wild north, including her.

The next day an arctic cold front moved in from Canada and there were a couple of days where gray completely covered the world and the highs were in the upper fifties. This is not completely unheard of in late summer, but unusual. It would pass and people would forget once the sun bumped the temperature twenty degrees, but it made for the short-term blahs. Cheerful people shut down for the duration, waiting for the change. Grumpy people became grumpier, even after realizing a change would soon come. Depressed people howled at the moon just because it was there.

Morelli still insisted on sitting out, though now wearing a heavy coat and toboggan cap. He looked like a hermit crab, and the blanket made him appear an invalid. His mien never changed, which made discerning his genuine disposition all the more murky.

Angie humored him but was underdressed. She had worn long sleeves, and her blood was not as thin as his, but she didn't have a sweater or jacket, and her legs were bare except for hose. She could feel the chill on her face and hands. The skin on Morelli's hands was so thin, purpura bruising had created asymmetrical blotches that looked leprous.

Anomia is a technical term for failure to remember the name of a common object, a likewise common occurrence. Of course, it could also mean a respiratory infection to West Virginians, but when Morelli asked her to fetch his...as he snapped his fingers three times, she knew he meant his coffee mug.

"Think about leaving the west coast?"

He shook his head. "No, I wanted to stay in California."

"You think that had anything to do with Beverly?"

"Well, I moved to L.A. and Carmel was three hundred miles away. It's not like I was living in her back yard."

"Okay."

He looked at his hands, extending his fingers as if inspecting his nails. He stared for several seconds with no additional motion or comment. It didn't matter. His purview was elsewhere.

Angie waited. Usually, he soon provided a clue.

"You never forget the taste of lipstick," he said.

"No. I suppose not."

"Things were changing. Reagan, people feeling good again about being insurance salesmen and Tupperware ladies. Like the fucking fifties. I started realizing that I was out of my time, too."

"You weren't that old."

"No, in 1985, I turned fifty. Still plenty of life left. But I started thinking way too much about too many things I couldn't control. I knew about depression. But no one was talking about it, at least like they do now."

"You'd been through a tumbler."

He sighed. "Whatever it was, I'd had enough. I didn't know what to do. I tried going out more, being around people. But it didn't help. I even thought about starting another business but couldn't find anything that made me feel it was worth it."

"Were you suicidal?"

"In a way, I was. Not to kill my body. But I wanted to kill everything else around me."

"What did you do?"

"I pissed all my money away."

"No. How?"

"I gambled in the stock market. I bought long-shot stocks that deep inside, I thought would probably tank."

"Why didn't you give it to charity."

Another long silence. "I didn't want to atone."

Angie sighed for them both. "You wanted to fail."

"Well, I hit rock bottom for sure. Got so desperate I even asked God to show me a sign."

"What happened?"

A queer smile dimpled his drawn cheeks. "One of the stocks I took a flier on was an IPO. The company had been in business for a few years already, and was doing well, but I thought eventually it would crap out. This was 1986, I think. I didn't know anything about computers."

"How much did you invest?"

"Half-a-million dollars."

"Good Lord."

He looked at her and his eyes sparkled, an abashed smirk that still reeked of victory. "It was Microsoft," he said.

Angie was on her laptop on the sofa. Suddenly, she looked up. "Holy crap!"

Five-hundred-thousand dollars of Microsoft stock in 1986 would be worth three hundred million dollars today. She knew, of course, that no one would likely leave it untouched for thirty-five years—everyone would naturally dip into it, especially earlier on when it first blossomed and luxuries could be afforded. That part wouldn't compound, obviously, but it could still be worth a hundred million or more.

"Ho-ly crap." She repeated.

Summer rebounded in earnest. Angie broke a sweat nearly every jaunt those days, as the temperature rose into the mid-eighties, and the A/C in the van was as weak as an octogenarian blowing out his birthday candles. There was not much she could do. She wore light, summer clothes, washed her face and underarms at every stop, and kept deodorant in her case. Sometimes, she would find a vacant room and sit on the A/C vent for a few minutes.

She was in the restroom in Park Rapids when the call came that Earl Hogue was missing.

"I knew I shouldn't have let them watch *Escape from Alcatraz* last night," the nurse said.

Walker was less than thirty miles away, and Angie was in her van and on the move within ninety seconds. Within two minutes, she was sweating again. Her phone was on hands-free.

"Why wasn't somebody watching him?" she asked, exasperated.

"He was. He's watched in the common room, in the hall, especially when he's outside. There's somebody on him nearly twenty-four seven."

"You check everybody coming in and out?"

"Yes. Every visitor. I see maybe he could get outside somehow, but I don't see how one of the cameras wouldn't pick him up."

Angie flicked at the steering wheel as she worked her brain. "Any deliveries?"

"Just UPS. Like always."

"Front or back?"

A pause came on the line. "He couldn't get out through the warehouse. There's a camera back there."

"He could if he was in the back of the truck."

"Oh, Lord."

"Okay. Call UPS. See where the driver's been after he left there."

"Gotcha. How could he hide in all those little boxes?"

"That man could hide in a fishbowl."

Ten minutes later they found him wandering in Reeds Family Outdoor Center, a local sporting goods store. He was dressed in camouflage off their racks, presumably for...camouflage.

One of the managers had Earl by the elbow, waiting on the back dock, when Angie pulled up. After greetings and an apology, Angie got Earl situated and buckled.

"I need a pair of handcuffs," she grumbled, though the old man appeared contrite. They were just about to pull away when the manager came dashing out again.

"The hat!" he called. Angie was confused, and the man then pointed at Earl's head. She looked again and Earl was wearing a camouflage hat with ear flaps, the tag still dangling. She snatched the cap off his head and handed it to the manager through the window. Then, they headed toward Morningside.

"Good Lord, Mr. Hogue, what is it with you? Is this something like mountain climbing? You do it because you can?"

The old man said nothing. His shirt was too big and his head ducked down inside the collar like a turtle, a few stray, unruly tufts of hair sticking out.

She was fuming. "You have no idea what you put us through when you do this. Not to mention the danger to yourself. Hit by a car. You could've gotten mugged!"

A tiny smile pursed his lips, and in a very small voice— "In Minnesota?"

"Hey, there're bullies everywhere nowadays. Plus, you put on their clothes. They could have pressed charges for shoplifting and what a mess that would've been. They might've even hauled you to jail. Come to think about it, maybe that's just the place—"

"Do you know who I was?" came a whisper.

Angie stopped, unsure of what she heard, or if she heard anything. "What?"

"Do you know who I was?" he repeated, as softly as before, but crystal clear.

Angie lowered her voice. "No, sir. Not really."

He turned and looked at her, stoic and still. "I taught high school algebra for twenty years. Became assistant-principal, then principal at a middle school near the Cities."

"I'm sorry. I didn't know that."

"It was the rule of eighty-two then. I was fifty-two when I retired."

"Twenty-two when you started. Plus thirty years' service. Eighty-two."

"I thought I had the bird by the tail. Margie and I would have grand ol' times."

"That doesn't sound so bad."

"It wasn't. For the first five years. Then I got tired of it. Tired of going places I thought I should see. Tired of doing things I thought I should do. Tired of being around the kids and grandkids when it wasn't a treat any more. For them, either. Even tired of being around Margie twenty-four hours a day."

"What happened?"

"Nothing happened. For fifteen years nothing happened. That's the point. Margie and I just wasted away. Her candle just burned out first."

"I know. I'm sorry."

"I'll bet you've heard the same story a hundred times."

"It's never the same story, sir."

"Well, maybe that's just you. I've watched you. I know you care. A couple of the boys on night shift care, too. Nice to see."

Angie sighed deeply. "Maybe we should have talked more before now. I owe you an apology. I should've paid closer attention. I should've seen—"

"Not your fault. Back then I knew who I was."

"Yeah."

"So who am I now?"

They pulled into the lot and parked just outside the front door. Angie headed for the door. Once there, she realized Earl hadn't followed. He stood before the car unbuttoning his shirt. There was another shirt beneath it. As he approached the doorway, he tossed the over-shirt to Angie.

"Better return this shirt, too," he said. "Doesn't fit, anyway."

They were in the sixth day of a late-summer heat wave. Everything was sere. The green was drying into an ugly brown. Farmers were harvesting their crops at breakneck speed. Even the lake had grown tepid, though still refreshing. The public beach looked like an albino bacchanal. The grunts from the BSU practice field seemed more debilitating. None of the Morningside residents wanted to go outside. The halls bore the odor of Lysol and old people b.o., an alien pungency rare in the outside world, but thus compressed, was as redolent as roadkill.

Angie was chafing inside and out, and feeling mean.

"So your gamble paid off and you were even richer than before."

He smiled, though with the faintest hint of guilt. "Stock started splitting right away. Before I could even react. Soon, it was worth ten times what I'd invested."

"Spoiled your plans to blow it all, didn't it?"

He eyed her carefully. "I know what you're thinking. This mean old prick had it coming to him and came out smelling like a rose."

She shook her head, though her senses were jumbled. "I don't know. I'm sorry."

"I do. I should've gotten my just deserts and didn't. And I'd love to be able to tell you that I became a better man but I was still a mess. Maybe even more than before. Confused, for sure."

"You still felt stuck."

"Still needed something to do. I started thinking about what I was good at. I knew I'd been lucky, but I'd also had some skills. Took some time but I realized that I was good with concepts."

"An idea man."

"More like, take a good idea and expand on it. Like with the cars. It had been my idea to set a price limit and offer a warranty. It had been my idea to expand when and where we did. I thought maybe I could apply that to other things."

"You started a new business."

"No. I bought minority stakes in businesses I thought had good growth potential. Good-sized stakes, but still a minority. I didn't want to run things. I wanted the people who'd put their guts into something to run it. I bought into an industrial hose company. Financed a sales force so they could cover the country. Bought into a medical claim service company. Hired more people so they had the time to really scour bills. No five-dollar aspirin, no twenty IVs a day. No two hours for a doctor who'd spent ten minutes with a patient. Saved insurance companies a ton. They loved us. Bought into a payroll processing software company that could do complicated payrolls, like union contracts and that kind of thing. A couple of other things. Then, the internet came along."

"Lot of people got rich then."

"Lot of people lost their asses, too. People thought every web idea was a good idea. I was very picky about that. Invested in a couple of things that went belly-up. But, I also invested in a web design company that was one of the first to have do-it-yourself website packages. It did really well."

"Amazing."

"More than the money, it gave me a purpose. I could make the rounds. Look at the financials. Have meetings to see where needs were—what I might be able to do. I still got on people's nerves, but I was generally seen as someone who earned his keep. Learned how to make suggestions without hammering on people."

"Did that translate to your personal life?"

"It made an impact. Suddenly I was pushing sixty. And I wasn't happy about it."

"Paradox."

"Didn't find anyone I could talk to."

"A conundrum."

"A fucking mare's nest. I could've had a relationship and just kept it casual, and I even tried it a couple of times, but—I was to the point where I wanted something a little deeper."

"What did you do?"

He paused. "I went to see Beverly. The kid was in college by then. We shook hands and made nice. Bev and I reconciled."

The lake had a couple of small sailboats trying to hold a flighty wind. She listened to him breathe. He had been huffing before, but now his breath had settled into an easy rhythm.

"How were things with you and Beverly?"

"Well, we still took it slow. Remember, we lived pretty far apart then. But gradually, yeah, we got it together."

"Was it hard to talk and not bring up the past?"

"Yes. And I was nervous, I'll admit. Played it casual, but those days were knee-knockers."

"Why?"

"Because if you really love someone there's always something at stake. If there isn't some heavy emotional turmoil when things go wrong, then you really didn't have much at stake, which is another way of saying you didn't give a shit."

"You were both older, too."

"Yeah, maybe."

"So you got remarried?"

"Not right away. I don't think it was that important. We had a history, even if it did go south, and we felt we were okay even if we didn't do the formalities right away."

Angie lost her shoe but let it be.

"You move back to Carmel?"

"No. I wanted a new start. A real new start. I had bought that house. We shared it for what, seven-eight years. But I didn't want to go back there. I wanted to be somewhere where neither of us had been before. She agreed."

"Where did you go?"

"La Jolla. Way down south. Another great house on the ocean, but new to both of us. She was worried if we were underfoot all the time, things might get tense again, so she volunteered a couple of places. It was like a full-time job, and I was gone a couple days-a-week, too, but neither of us was ready to retire. If we wanted an extra day, we took it. If we wanted an excursion, we went."

"You slowed down."

"I let some things go. Did a lot of things on the phone. I was still very active. Even invested in a few new ventures."

"What about her?"

"Beverly would find causes she believed in. Philanthropy became important to her. I enjoyed watching her. She felt so good when she could contribute. Some group needed fifty grand and I would pop for the whole thing. Should've seen her glow."

"Bet that hurt, though."

He offered that junkyard dog grin. "Like a bitch."

Angie rubbed a sore foot. "I spend too much time running around," she said.

"Well, part of the problem is your shoes. Those things are disasters."

Feet redux. She was wearing low-heeled pumps. "Yeah, but I'm stylin'. No old lady shoes for me."

He snorted. "I can hear your footsteps coming a mile away."

"Yeah?"

"Like a poodle with tap shoes."

"Early warning signal."

Again, he grunted. "So. Are we done tripping the past fantastic?"

She looked at him, feeling a sudden sense of loss. "Are we?"

Late August disappointed in the way only people who anticipate the renewal provided by too-brief summers would understand. The hot days were oppressively hot, and too windy to enjoy. These were invariably followed by thunderstorms that caused flash flooding because the ground had baked into brick with standing water in the streets because the drainage systems couldn't handle the flow. And every time it rained, it was a deluge—no softly fingering showers, no sitting on the porch watching it plop off daisy petals. There was never a long, soaking summer rain that cooled the night air. It howled like a banshee or breathed fire like a dragon. Everyone was ill-tempered and impatient, and the full moon brought added dissonance among the patients.

Angie spent the last week of August on her toes, sprinting from one emergency to the next, always accompanied by the wails of the misbegotten, temper tantrums and spoilage. Irrationality permeated the world she inhabited, as if some viral form of distemper had settled in without antidote. She was exasperated and exhausted, spent from sunrise to sunset, even to the next sunrise at times. She was called from her bed at least a half-dozen times, without relief, yet expected to provide this very balm to her charges.

Labor Day weekend brought the break in the weather, warm and still and fluid. Everyone grasped the irony, of course, as afterward, boats would be stored, patio furniture withdrawn, vacations ending with the advent of school, and a resettling of the norm. People flocked to the lake that weekend, and the students returning to Bemidji State took full advantage of the waning of the season.

One thing that elevated her mood was her annual review. She had dreaded these in the past, as Nordgren seemed duty-bound to enumerate her weaknesses, some, she suspected, as a means to justify only a minute raise in salary. This time, as she sat across from his massive desk, trying hard not to stare at a gap between two buttons of his shirt that revealed part of a hairy navel, she was stunned by both the brevity and the outcome of their meeting.

"Your work has been excellent this past year. Superb, really. I'm going to recommend a ten-percent raise and a new company vehicle."

She left befuddled, numb, gradually elated.

Angie got a call while on her way to Walker. Mr. Morelli was sick. Not an itty-bitty boo-boo sick, and not the black plague, but ill. He had the croup, and normally, that would be as threatening as a stye, but at eighty-seven years, minor conditions can leap into danger. He was running a fever of one-o-one, not life-threatening, but serious. Dehydration was a big problem, as well as additional brain cells taking the party bus to Woodstock. The doctor had given him antibiotics and vitamins. He had also thrown in a sedative for good measure, aware of Morelli's penchant for complaint.

He lay very still, his face a dark red mask, his eyes squinting into unseen reaches, his brow dappled with sweat. They had put a sterile skullcap on his head to rein in his fever. He was covered to his chin and breathed through his mouth.

Angie stood to one side as the nurse checked his IV. Her first thought, not so much an epiphany, but an awakening to an obvious but ignored confirmation, was that Morelli looked every bit an old man, weathered by open roads, spent from the journey, dying in that indisputable way of wrinkles and mottled skin and uneven breaths. No amount of bluster or vitality or wit could subjugate the presence of counted hours.

She felt sympathy for the lost soul, the same as every other lost soul who stood at the threshold of expiration, regardless of how a life of bumps and bruises, joys and treasured moments, had played out. Even those who had reveled in the brightness of days and smiled at the crossroads, viewed the beyond through tears. And even those who relished the coming end, brought about by toil and strife, stalled at the door to the outlands of a new world.

He looked at her then and she gave him a slight smile.

"Just checking in on you. I'll let you rest."

He looked at her with a beseeching cast. And took her hand. "I need you to find her."

"Find who, Mr. Morelli?"

"Betsy."

She then realized that he was delirious, not entirely outside himself, but adrift, roiled by the fever and floating in disconnected pieces. She was oddly disappointed, that his need for her was incidental. He would probably hate himself if he ever realized the extent of his vulnerability.

"Okay," she said simply.

He let her go and nodded. "I know you will."

Angie knew better than to look. Never look for something you really don't want to find. Yet here she was, curiosity poised and ready to bite. This had begun idly, innocently, as she killed time while letting the brain reboot, the way most people check email or go on Facebook. Log onto the internet and see where it takes you. She rationalized, there isn't a snake under every bush. Even so, don't look under a bush unless prepared for the creepers.

Angie had Googled Morelli before with limited results. Sometimes Google was too literal. Sometimes, not literal enough. There were thousands of Morellis, and more Leonards that she would have guessed. Safety in numbers. Hidden among shared nomenclatures.

Then she remembered he went by his middle name. His full name was Lyle Leonard Morelli. She Googled that. And got an eyeful. Oh, there were still other Lyle Leonard Morellis. But it was all there. She just had to dig. Something unseemly controlled her fingers.

The first expletive, and a minor one, came when she found L. L. Morelli listed as a principal of over a dozen companies, with an estimated net worth of around two hundred-fifty million dollars. This information was available because several of the companies he owned substantial shares in were publicly traded. She already knew this, if not the specifics. This was more a 'boy howdy' than a 'holy shit'.

Still, she dug deeper.

She found an obituary from three years ago for Beverly Marie Morelli, his twice-afflicted wife. Poor man. They had made it through nearly thirty years together, in two shifts, only for her to succumb to heart disease at seventy-six. She knew this, too, but hadn't known for sure they had been together at the end or the gloomy details. Seeing the picture for the first time made it a little more substantial. She had been lovely.

The second expletive was stronger, straight-from-the-gutter-brawny, and multiple- syllabic, even when uttered only once. This was a lulu, a kind of in-your-face slap on the kisser. A, 'well, this makes sense in a warped kind of way, but still sucks' revelation.

A Morelli company owned Morningside, walls, floors, and pharmaceuticals. Everything, including her job, was his. This explained his quarters. This explained Nordgren's insistence. Morelli was his boss, his overseer, his borrowed ride to the promised land.

The third and fourth expletives provided a litany of such volume, Leona heard her through the partially-open door, and peered in. Angie waved her off with an apologetic wag of the head. Tears threatened but was overshadowed and vanquished by the sheer bile coursing through her.

Beverly Morelli's previous married name had been Nordgren. And 'the kid' as he had been referred to, now the 'fat quack', was Dr. Neil Nordgren, graduate of the University of Colorado Medical School of Aurora, Colorado, and current President of Morningside Senior Homes. Morelli's stepson.

Morelli sat outside in a jogging suit, capless, wisps of hair feathering upward in salute. The sun surrounded him in a pale aura, Indian Summer's last homage. Angie stalked outside, her arms crossed. The old man actually smiled a little when he saw her.

"Where's my milkshake?"

"You own Morningside," she said meanly. She was irked and ready to rumble.

His expression morphed into something—defensive, disdain for being caught with the cookie jar, even if they were his cookies. The same look people on the phone give when they hang up suddenly after someone unexpectedly enters a room.

"So?"

"Dr. Nordgren is Beverly's son."

"Who else would give that lump a job?"

"Why didn't you say something?"

"Because it's none of your fucking business."

"You're a jerk."

Then she turned and left.

She sat across the wide desk as still as sculpture. She was seething but kept it in check. She was ready to rip his throat out. Nordgren was contrite, leaning forward as if to cut the distance.

"I've put you in an awkward position and I'm sorry. I should have guessed you would be...curious beyond the normal scope."

What, it's my fault now, you twerp! "Maybe I overstepped—a little—when I decided to look deeper into his history."

He sighed heavily. "The truth is—and you've probably realized this by now—Mr. Morelli and I aren't...close. My mother loved him, but we've never really connected. Our conversation regarding this company lasted all of thirty seconds." He lowered his voice and added an edge in mimicry. "I bought this company. You think you can run it?" Then he smiled, trying to set aside the tension.

Angie nodded in understanding. "What about the evaluation?"

"Legit. *Nobody* goes away that deep and then just wakes up. You know that."

"He did."

Nordgren smiled ruefully. "Yeah. The bastard."

"You could have told *me*," she softly protested.

"Yeah, maybe I should have. I didn't want to influence you. I'm sorry."

She rose to leave but stopped at the door. "It's none of my business, sir..."

He looked up. "Yes?"

"You could make peace while there's still time, if you wanted."

He paused for a long moment, his expression unchanged. "Thank you."

Do people with dementia dream of dementia, or have every thought colored by dementia? No one knows. Angie had come to believe that the subconscious is the last bastion of sanity, a glowing ember of everything once considered *perfect.* The subconscious rights the wrongs, or at least brings them to the fore, where they can be righted. The subconscious elevates the *truth* into the light-of-day, however hushed and vague.

If the lessons of life have been cruel, the subconscious may somehow inform that the worst is over, and that peace is at hand—that no imposition extends beyond the frail elements of being. The subconscious may cleanse the thorny roots of failed endeavors.

When life has been tranquil in uncounted days, and in uncounted ways, the subconscious may whisper that nothing has been left undone, that no additional effort is required to be at rest. The journey is over. There is no need to expend a single mote of energy to be...anything. We are complete. *Whole* by the palliative standards of finality.

More than this, however, the subconscious may also remind us of things that haunt us, and not in any savage face, though perhaps persistently, that should our fears rise to devour us, these may yet be set aside for the sake of the core goodness in every heart, though untended, dormant, unremembered in the passage of time.

The subconscious ultimately binds together all untidy ends and gently closes the door.

The next time Nordgren called her she answered him simply. "He's dying, Sir."

She wondered if she did this job for forty years what kind of vegetable would she become. Not a turnip. Lettuce, maybe. Still green and leafy.

Two weeks went by. She saw her other patients. She filed her reports. She squelched the desire to march into Morelli's room again and light him up. She lived her life. But she wasn't the same. She didn't know why, exactly, but she craved an ending—any ending—more satisfactory than what she had. She had no idea what form it would, or should, take, but she felt she would not reclaim peace in the near time without it.

When Angie finally grasped what had been needling her, she was surprised to find that it was simple arithmetic.

"Four times married," he'd said. Beverly counted as two marriages. Zelda had been one. Someone was missing. And she knew who it was, or at least a name, just as she thought she knew the where and when, a time nearly as old as his life itself, and in a place he would not discuss. Betsy. Florida. Corinth.

It was late and she should've been elsewhere. She found the old man propped up on his bed, watching CNBC. She handed him a large Styrofoam cup absent of logos or markings.

"Try this," she said.

He eyed her warily but took it. He sucked. Hard. His cheeks nearly turned inside-out. Finally, he got a blob on the end of his tongue and sealed his mouth around it. He looked at her. "What is this?"

"You like it?"

He set it aside to thaw. "It's good."

"It's homemade French vanilla ice cream with a little whipping cream mixed in with the milk."

He picked up the cup and got a bigger mouthful. "Yeah. You're onto something." He tilted the cup until the straw pointed at the loveseat. "Sit, if you're staying."

He stuck the straw into his mouth and stubbornly kept his cheeks taut until he met with success, if modest.

She waited for what seemed an age. "Tell me about Betsy."

Suddenly, his expression was empty and lost, as if again struck by the disease that would eventually take him. She expected him to flare, and wasn't disappointed, but now more in annoyance than anger.

"You've been snooping in my fucking business again."

"No, sir, I haven't. You referred to her more than once. When you were sick, you told me to find her."

He looked at her in disbelief. He seemed to struggle, as if fighting to stay angry, his blood up, his muscles tensed and his face flushed. But all this faltered, and again, he was disoriented, as if doom had come for him with beckoning hand, and he was afraid.

She began again. “This is about Florida. About Corinth and shoes and everything else, isn’t it?” Her voice had never been so tender with him.

He cast his eyes away, faintly alight but haunted. “She had such tiny feet,” he whispered. “Fours. A child’s feet.”

“At Corinth.”

He nodded, looking up but not in her direction. “I’m sure you’ve figured some of it. This was the early fifties. Ike. Black-and-white TV. Penny loafers and saddle oxfords.”

“I’m with you.” She paused, taking a turn looking outward, seeing mainly the darkness. The blanched echo of a streetlight at the property’s edge. The glow of car lights near the college. The pinprick of starlight on the lake. The clouded light from the windows in the adjacent rooms. The rest was impenetrable night.

“Betsy,” she repeated, just as tenderly.

“She came from a strict Baptist family. Wanted her in a *Christian* college,” he said, the word still unpleasant upon his tongue. “Make sure she was surrounded by the right kind of people.”

“You said you went there because it was cheap.”

He smiled again, his lips pulled tightly against his teeth, almost a grimace. “I wanted to go there. At one time, I...believed.” That horribly sorrowful smile rose anew. “For a holy roller school, there were quite a few of us who really wanted to figure things out. Do things, you know. We had a little group. Seekers, you might say. Betsy was part of it.”

She noticed a change in him. His face became fuller and brighter, as if the recollection was transforming him somehow, not so much erasing years, but returning to him a kind of serenity long since overcome by toil.

"We were kids who were going to be teachers or doctors or accountants or office workers. We all had to take Bible courses, but most of us just wanted an education. One night I walked Betsy back to the dorm. I must've talked nonstop. She listened. I don't remember exactly what it was, but I'm sure it had to be something like how we could change the world. Blind as a newborn baby. But she encouraged me. Told me I was special. I was bowled over. I'd never been taken seriously before in my whole life."

"But you were only eighteen."

"Well it hit me. Hard. I loved her almost immediately. Believed in a kind of destiny. And it was right in front of me, within my grasp. How we could have a life together. "

"It must have incredible to have those feelings."

Then, his tone grew a slight, jagged edge, perhaps not noticeable unless you were sharply focused, or had listened to him in all weathers. "A guy named Mitch was kind of the leader. He was a senior. I looked up to him. We all did. I think Betsy idolized him."

His hands trembled more than due to age. Angie waited, not moving.

"I had fears. Horrible insecurities. Jealous. Suspicious. Envious. I was falling apart."

"You were so young."

He sighed. "Looking back at it all, it's so stupid now. But then...Anyway, I told Betsy I thought we should take a break. To see if what we had was real. Because I was going nuts and if I couldn't see past that, I couldn't be what I needed to be...for either of us."

"A mature approach."

"Fear, mainly. Of losing her. So I made a preemptive strike. We had a couple of classes together, but I didn't speak to her or even make eye contact. It was killing me, but I had to find some...moment-of-truth. And the strange thing was, I got stronger. I can't say I had a sense of peace about it, but I believed I was doing the right thing."

"How long did this go on?"

"A month or so. But, I began to function better, even though I was hurting. Everybody knew something was going on between us. It was a small group. Mitch even came to me and I told him what I was doing. He said he would reach out to Betsy, too."

A trace of anxiety crawled its way up Angie's neck.

"A few weeks later, Betsy came up to me and poured her heart out. She said she wanted to be my partner and she loved me with all her heart and didn't want anything to ever come between us again. To me, it was the revelation I had been looking for. With that kind of faith in me, I knew I could accomplish everything I wanted to accomplish, and we were going to do it together. I told her we should get married. It was silly. We were too young, but we could just do something between us. A dedication ceremony."

"So you weren't legally married."

He shook his head and his eyes clouded over. "We wrote these vows and pledged ourselves to each other—and God—and promised to build the lives we wanted. We decided we'd wait until we were legally married before sleeping together. We would finish school first. Everything was perfect."

Morelli took a breath and settled back as if bone-weary. Some of the light left his aspect.

"A bit later, she became very quiet. She didn't pull away from me. In fact, she clung to me harder than ever. But she didn't have any energy. I worried that she was sick. 'Tell me' became a kind of mantra, because all I could think of saying was "what's wrong?", and, of course, her answer was always "nothing". "

Angie looked then to see tears streaming down the old man's cheeks. They followed a pattern, welling in both lower lids, then releasing one at a time, the next following as soon as the former cleared, both eyes in near-unison.

"One night the Dean came and woke me up took me back to his office without saying a word. Then he told me Betsy had...died. He wouldn't give me any information so I flew out of there. I made it to this tree near the main entrance. And I let it out. I cried and screamed until my ribs ached. I threw up three or four times, and then began sobbing again. I don't know how long it went on."

Angie's eyes mimicked his. "What happened?"

When he looked at her then he was every shred a decrepit piece of humanity, wasted and useless. His voice barely rose above a whisper, and even the low hum of the vents threatened to overwhelm his words.

He gulped air as if starved for breath. "She had killed herself," he uttered, and in those four words came the awful burden of a lifetime. "She had gotten her father's shotgun and stuck the barrel against her stomach and pulled the trigger. Later, I learned she had gnawed the ends of her fingers as a reflex against the pain before she died."

"Oh God. Why?"

"She was pregnant!" he cried. "She had used the gun to try to disguise it. And everyone thought I had done it."

"Oh Mr. Morelli. I'm so sorry."

His visage suddenly became hard and spiteful, amid all the pain, as if to beat it down with raging fists. "I knew Mitch had raped her when we were apart. I went to the Dean and I told him. I think he already knew. But nothing was done. No proof. And why ruin the future of a decent young man who had already repented."

"Dear God."

"Fuck God!" he spat. "Fuck all those people. I was not allowed to go to the visitation or the funeral. I had to wait until she was in the ground before I could say good-bye. I left school. I was done."

"How awful."

"A few years later, when I had the resources, I hired a lawyer dig up dirt on the school. He found plenty. The school closed." The tears flowed more freely now and he shook his head. "But I still bore the guilt."

"Oh, Mr. Morelli. For what?"

His brokenness was evident in every minute expression. "For believing."

"In God?"

"In—possibility—to let it consume me, give me hope, take my heart and soul and bleed...me... dry..."

Then, he cupped his face in his hands and sobbed. His entire body trembled. Angie stood, unsure of what to do. Finally, she went to him, stood beside him, and awkwardly put an around his shoulder. He sloughed it away at first, but when it returned, he let it be. And she remained there until everything drained away, spent, and he finally curled up, and slept.

That worn, ancient link, so bent and rusty from neglect, somehow held together.

Three weeks later, Morelli's rally ended.

Likewise, Emily Blackfeather did not live long after her arrival at Morningside. Just shy of a year. Liver failure claimed her before her dementia progressed much beyond its original stage. She was only seventy-two

As she lay dying, her dark eyes jaundiced, her tiny body swollen, she asked the nurse to leave her alone with Angie. Angie bent near to listen.

"What can I do for you?"

"A drink."

Angie wasn't startled. Little surprised her any longer. "I can't. It's not allowed. Besides, you've been clean so long."

"I want to go with a taste on my lips."

"Why?"

The woman seized in pain, but it only lasted a few seconds. "So God will know it's me."

Against all common sense, and everything she had ever learned in that morbid school of execration, she sneaked in an ounce of Jack Daniels. She put it on a spoon, as if she was an old country doctor administering a tonic.

The Indian sipped the spoon dry and coughed. Then she nodded and settled back. She closed her eyes. Angie never looked into her eyes again. She died the following night.

Morelli left most of his holdings to charities, none religious. He left Morningside to Dr. Nordgren, or as specified in his will, 'his useless stepson, the fat quack'. He also instructed that Angie keep her position unless 'she does something stupid and goes nuts on somebody'. He was cremated and had his ashes returned to California and buried beside Beverly.

The day after he died, a warm fall day, Angie went to his room with a milkshake. The room had already been cleaned and his personal effects removed. The room seemed much emptier then, all the memories there faded into the ether.

She dragged a chair out onto the patio and sipped he milkshake, feeling its sweetness on the back of her tongue. She gazed out at the lake, seeing as if for the first time how great an empty space it was. Then, she simply closed her eyes and let peace take her.

Morelli left her ten thousand shares of Microsoft stock, with the proviso that it be kept away from any future husbands, and in case she ever decided to write a book about him, she would have something to live on. She smiled at that. She was secure but worked harder than ever.

Perhaps what we recognize as endeavor is nothing more than the means through which we trace the time. We spend our years in a silver fog, relishing the days, if we're lucky, looking to the future for relief when we aren't. But more demonstrable than these are the moments we spend examining our footprints, looking back at faded trails, marking the paths with all our senses, altering our outlook, just as our mood-of-the-day alters our perspective. At times, we are relieved just to have survived them. At other times, we measure ourselves against them. We may look to them for comfort, or for them to illuminate the way ahead, with at least some frame of reference for what is possible, as optimism or caution. Or even dread.

Regardless, we always look back, even when we do not seek, even when the day is filled with contentment, and for whatever reason, because all these things exist, are stored, even if ignored—and are eternal. They may blanch, but do not evaporate. They may be hidden, but do not depart. They may be draped in disguise, but peer through the veil at any given time. Whatever else is true, or how well or poorly we are served, we are to be ever reminded of all we have seen, heard, spoken—all we have been. And the greater our years, the deeper the trove of hoarded things.

Though customary, and in all seasons, it is never enough to say the moment at hand is really all we have, or all there is. What our mind's eye sees looking back is what nudges us forward, even when we collapse and remain unmoved, just as the cells of our bodies continue to change even when we are unaware of anything about us.

No matter our temper of the hour, hope and caution and unspoken misgiving, it is the past that always finds us, and has named us.

Made in the USA
Columbia, SC
11 June 2024